LOVE

WILL

tear

us

APART

a novel

THREE RIVERS PRESS
NEW YORK

LOVE
WILL
tear US
APART

Sarah Rainone

Copyright © 2009 by Sarah Rainone

All rights reserved.
Published in the United States by Three Rivers Press,
an imprint of the Crown Publishing Group,
a division of Random House, Inc., New York.
www.crownpublishing.com

Three Rivers Press and the Tugboat design are registered
trademarks of Random House, Inc.

Library of Congress Cataloging-in-Publication Data
Rainone, Sarah.
Love will tear us apart / Sarah Rainone.—1st ed.
p.   cm.
1. Self-realization—Fiction. I. Title.
PS3618.A397L68   2009
813'.6—dc22   2008050659

ISBN 978-0-307-45066-1

Printed in the United States of America

Design by Maria Elias

1 3 5 7 9 10 8 6 4 2

First Edition

To my mother,
Kathleen Ann O'Connor Rainone
1951-2007

To that dear home beyond the sea
My Kathleen shall again return.
And when thy old friends welcome thee
Thy loving heart will cease to yearn.
Where laughs the little silver stream
Beside your mother's humble cot
And brightest rays of sunshine gleam
There all your grief will be forgot.

—Thomas P. Westendorf

coNtentS

Intro

Love Will Tear Us Apart

Bonus Tracks

There are no darker beings than children . . .
we're so bad when we're children that
when we grow up we choose to forget it.
—Rodrigo Fresán, *Kensington Gardens*

But sometimes, we remember our bedrooms
and our parents' bedrooms
and the bedrooms of our friends.
—The Arcade Fire, "Neighborhood #1 (Tunnels)"

Why is the bedroom so cold?
—Joy Division, "Love Will Tear Us Apart"

to do
~~Beer~~
Cuervo?

Stripper
—Call Raspallo's cousin?

Killer Soundtrack

Mr. and Mrs. Philip DeAngelis

Request the honor of your presence

at the marriage of Mr. DeAngelis's daughter

Lea Dawn DeAngelis

to

Daniel Patrick O'Shaughnessy

Son of Mr. Charles O'Shaughnessy

and Mrs. Kelly Pawlowski

On Saturday, the —th of July, 20—

at four o'clock

Madonna Della Panni Cathedral

Galestown

Reception following ceremony

Windham Mansion

Galestown, Rhode Island

INtro

BEN

I can't believe my boy Dan is getting married. I mean, I can believe it, it's not unbelievable; it's not even unexpected. It's just weird. And the fact that he has chosen me to be his Best Man, well, that's even weirder since, let's face it, I've never been the best *anything* (and of many things I have been the worst).

Since best men are honest men, I should admit that I wonder if his choosing me was his *only* mistake. . . . Now before you go thinking I mean the kind of Speak Now or Forever Hold Your Peace mistake that never even happens outside of movies starring that British dude who for some inexplicable reason has made every one of my ex-girlfriends seriously consider donating their wombs to the Monarchy, let me assure you, Lea is the apple of Dan's eye, the belle of his balls, the fruit of his loom. I'm talking about his *groomsmen* . . .

To put it plainly, we all suck. The way things are looking, his bachelor party is going to start out with some chicken-tipping (there's no cows in Galestown, Rhode Island), and end in milk and cookies at Dan's mom's house.

Now, Dan's already made it clear he doesn't want any sluts around prior to the big day—and I can respect that, truly, I can—but I seem to be the only one who understands that it is our God-given duty to ignore Dan's wishes and give him exactly what he doesn't know he wants. But how can I fulfill these duties with the hacks I've been teamed up with? Contrary to popular belief, sluts do not grow on trees.

To start, there's his cousins. Idiots, all of them. I've known Dan for decades now, and I still don't know how many of them there are—Seven? Three? One, but with so many freckles that we're tricked into thinking him three-fold? What I do know is that the Molloys are a bunch of rock-jawed bulldogs who drive pickups and break hot-wiener-eating records at the New York System joint on Olney Avenue. They played *hockey*, for Chrissakes. If it weren't for the star-spangled crew cuts and the fact that they were all junior officers in ROTC, I'd think they were Canadian.

And then there's Shawn Riley, who's an okay guy if you can get past the fact that he hates my guts. Okay, to be honest, it's sort of my fault that he hates my guts, but it is *not* my fault that he's too much of a pussy to forgive my guts. All I'm saying is, if Mr. I'm So Cool Cause I'm in a Band and Live in New York City doesn't want to return my calls about whether to order a stripper from Dexy's Midnight Runners or Fantassies, well, then I cannot be blamed for leaving his name off the card.

But lest I sound unexcited about the Big Day because of my distaste for my fellow men in arms, allow me to admit that, just this very afternoon when I opened my mailbox and was greeted with, along with my trusted copy of *Ass Magazine*, an invitation to the wedding of Daniel Patrick O'Shaughnessy and Lea Dawn DeAngelis, an actual, honest-to-God tear fell from my eye, splashing sound-lessly onto the steadfast buttocks of one Ms. Jinifer Starr. And luckily, my position as head bartender at one of Rhode Island's premier nighttime hot spots, PJ O'Malley's, gives me a unique window into the world of adult entertainment that should more than make up for the shortcomings of the rest of Team O'Shaughnessy.

Not to mention that the more I think about it, the more I realize that this wedding is going to be dope as fuck. Lea's dad is fucking loaded—loaded by Galestown standards, anyway—so he's putting us all up in the Windham Mansion for the night. I'll be honest with you: The choice of location is more than a little fucked up, given that the place is old-fashioned, drafty, and . . . oh, you know . . . *haunted.*

Daniel-san and I first became acquainted with the Windham on a field trip meant to educate us about religious freedom or the slave trade or some shit (I'm not a reliable source, given that we smoked a fair amount of chronic first). Anyway, possibly because the place is haunted, and probably because Kyle Riley has a habit of dipping his chronic in Drano before selling it to the youth of Galestown, I became totally convinced that I saw some crusty phantasmagoria getting it on in one of those moldy four-poster beds. My point is, I'm not trying to have any flashbacks at my boy's wedding, and you'd have thought he'd have been a little more conscientious about that kind of shit, especially considering that *he* was the motherfucker who picked up the velvet Louis XIV chair and started waving it in the air at some long-dead Windham butler. But I'm willing to let it slide—that's my way. After all, I don't get the feeling that he's had too much say in the whole wedding-planning thing.

Okay, so that's not exactly true. In exchange for allowing

himself to be roped into all that stupid wedding shit (Dan's words, not mine) Lea convinced Big Philly DeAngelis and his juicy little tomato Lucia to grant their Guinness-swilling son-in-law-to-be one last wish: uncontested control over the wedding-reception playlist. And Dan, a true man of the people, decided to let his oldest and dearest friends have a say in the acoustical atmosphere. Stuffed inside that fatty of an envelope filled with invitation, reply card, directions, request for firstborn son and whatnot was a note asking for song suggestions, a note that went out to Shawn, the bridesmaids, and me alone. He'd have asked his cousins, too, if Lea hadn't put the kibosh on any songs featured in movies starring Sylvester Stallone or Tom Cruise (though I myself can think of worse things than encountering the Eye of the Tiger on the Highway to the Danger Zone).

But, in all seriousness, the fact that Sir Daniel has involved us in the decision is most appreciated. We were all there the day he and Lea met, and we've been there, in one way or another, ever since. Which is why I've got no frigging clue what kind of songs I'm supposed to pick to properly mark this momentous occasion. It's not like I'm a Whitney Houston kind of guy, you know? And I hardly think that the bride would appreciate me offering up such modern-day love songs as Tupac's "Me And My Girl- friend" or, seeing as we're from the East Side and 'ery- thing, the more geographically relevant (and potentially offensive) Biggie Smalls's "Me and My Bitch."

Still, if it were up to me, each song I'd choose would have those old folks looking up from their Italian cookies and Irish coffee and being all, like, What the fuck? In fact,

I consider it my duty as best man to get this party started quickly *(right?)*, which is why, with all due respect, you will not be forced to suffer as a mustachioed DJ named Vinny subjects you to the solid-gold disco hits he first heard at fucking Sha-booms back in '77. Children of the '80s, unite! No longer will we subject our wedding guests to the Chris de Burghs, Celine Dions, and Peabo Brysons of the world. This is not your parents' wedding.

Okay, okay, I realize that's exactly what it is . . .

Listen, don't get me wrong. I know this is not about picking the song that will allow me to do my signature belly slide across the dance floor (Meatloaf's magnum opus "Paradise by the Dashboard Light") or the jam that was playing in the background when Tammy Paglinaro and I lost our respective virginities in the backseat of my CRX ("Here Comes the Hotstepper" by Ini Kamoze). But that doesn't mean it's going to be easy.

See, the toughest part of being Dan O'Shaughnessy's best man is understanding that it's not about me (or my belly slide, awesome as it may be). It's not about me at all.

Which, when you get right down to it, is also the toughest part of being Dan O'Shaughnessy's best friend.

CORT

I have to call my mother. We agreed upon this time, so I have to do it and I know that and okay, well, the fact that I took some shrooms a half hour ago was maybe not the best idea in the world but I said I'd call and if I don't she'll worry but if I do she's gonna know I'm gone, but then again, I'd rather have her think I'm gone, than, like, have her think I'm *gone*. So I tell Kyrie that I've got to get to a phone and she looks at me like I'm crazy because Medeski Martin and Wood are on and there's a storm brewing and so the sky is all gray and spooky and if I leave the bandshell now, right when the shrooms are kicking in, I know full well I'm going to miss the whole set and get lost and never be able to find my way back, but I have to call my mother because that's what we do: talk each Saturday at five on the dot, and really, I gotta admit, ever since she got sick, she's been a lot cooler with the way I live my life, but then, it's my life and my money, so it's not like she has a choice. I tell Kyrie I've seen this band, like, a thousand times and I'll find my way back just fine; there's a phone right outside the music tents, and I'll grab us some beer, too, while I'm there, and just be cool; I'll be back, okay, but now I have to call my mother, and if for some reason I don't make it back, we'll meet at the Candyland playground area at seven, dig?

And Kyrie looks at me with her big blank eyes and says, Cool, right, and then she smiles and goes back to her hippie-girl boogie and I wonder if I should tell her that her right boob is about to pop out of her tank top and I think, Nah, that's the point.

People have been saying that it's going to rain for days and that it's going to rain hard and I'm glad I'm wearing my Rainbow Brite rain boots. The shrooms are kicking in a little, I think, because one second I'm nervous and nauseous and the next I'm not, and everything around me starts looking crisp and clear and perfect like it's another planet or something but, you know, a cool one, like Saturn, and I laugh and let myself ease into the way Medeski's organ is blending in with Guster's drums at the next tent over, and I forget all about counting out the different rhythms in my head, I just let it happen and trust that everything's gonna be fine, and I realize that sometimes the best place to be is in between the songs.

There's no line for the phone, which is nice, but also not so nice, because it reminds me that there are a lot of good bands on right now, and no one wants to miss them. But I have to call my mother so I walk up to the phone slowly, watching my boots take each step forward and liking the way they look with my skirt that Kyrie says makes me look like Princess Zelda and I take my rupee which is really a credit card and swipe it into the phone and call my mother.

–Cortina, she says, before I say anything.

–Mommy, I say, and then I start crying a little because I wish I was with her right now because she is so beautiful, even after her black hair fell out and grew back white and fluffy as the clouds that were rolling overhead before this storm blew in and she would maybe even like this and I could really talk to her, like, *really* talk to her, and she would totally understand me, and we wouldn't fight and Dad wouldn't scream and I wouldn't have to leave and everything could be perfect and . . .

–Tina, honey, how are you? Where are you?

–I'm great, Mom, great, just great. And um, I'm, um, at this concert in, um . . .

I look at the sign above the phone.

–Tennessee.

–Tennessee, she says, slowly. How do you like it?

–It's going to rain, I think, I say. How's Daddy?

–He's at work.

–Oh.

–He misses you.

–I miss you, too, Mom, but Uncle John and me'll be heading back up soon, I think . . .

–Well, it looks like you'll have to, she says. Then she says something else, but I miss it because my ears have just now decided to hear nothing but a kind of waaaaaaa aaaaaaaaaaaaaaaaaaaaaaaaaaaaaaaaaaaaaaaaaaaaaaaaaaaaaa aaaaaaaaaaaaaaaaaaaaaaaaaaaaaaaaaaaaaaaaaaaaaaaaaaaaaaa aaaaaaaaaaaaaaaaaaaaaaaaaaaaaaaaaaaaaaaaaaaaaaaaaaaaaaa aaaaaaaaaaaaaaaaaaaaaaaaaaaaaaaaaaaaaaaaaaaaaaaaaaaaaaa aaaaaaaaaaaaaaaaaaaaaaaaaaaaaaaaaaaaaaaa and this goes on for what feels like an hour but is probably only a minute since the phone isn't demanding more change, and then, like that, my hearing comes back and my mom is talking about something but I'm not getting what she's saying at all and I start to freak out until I remember to do the deep breathing Kyrie taught me to do when trips take a wrong turn and as soon as I do, my mom's words turn back into English, but I've missed too much so I say, Huh? I'm losing (myhearing mymother mymind) . . . reception. I'm losing reception.

My mom keeps on talking and I wonder if she heard me or if I even made a sound, and it gets me thinking, What if my mom *can* read my mind? Because that would explain why she was always so mad at me even when I didn't do anything wrong, because she knows how evil I am on the inside despite what everyone else sees and thinks and then she interrupts me and asks if I've heard anything she's said, proving that she is indeed psychic, and when I don't say anything, she says, About the wedding, and I say, A wedding? Whose wedding?

She answers.

–Danny Lee? Who's he?

She says the name again.

–Who?

My mom says what I think is, Your best friend, but there's the waaaaaaaaaaaaaaaaaaaaaaaaaaaaaaaaaaaaaaaaaa aaaaaaaaaaaaaaaaaaaaaaaaaaaaaaaaaaaaaaaaaaaaaaaaaaa aaaaaaaaaaaaaaaaaaaaaaaaaaaaaaaaaaaaaaaaaaaaaaaaaaa aaaaaaaaaaaaaaaaaaaaaaaaaaaaaaaaaaaaaaaaaaaaaaaaaaa aaaaaaaaaaaaaaaaaaaaaaaaaaaaaaaaaaaaaaaaaaaa again and I'm thinking maybe I'm going deaf and I say the name aloud again, Danny Lee, Danny Lee, and I still don't have a clue who she's talking about.

Until . . .

I do.

ALEX

Danny and Lea are getting married.

And I want to die.

SHAWN

–No.

  [. . .]

–No way, Alex.

  [. . .]

–I said no!

  [. . .]

–I don't care what you say, I'm not going.

  [. . .]

–Well, you don't have to go either.

  [. . .]

–No, you *don't*. You're just torturing yourself. Besides, I have a gig that night.

  [. . .]

–I didn't tell you because I didn't know about it until today.

  [. . .]

–Fine. Don't believe me. But you *should* be happy for me.

  [. . .]

–Thank you.

  [. . .]

–Yeah, but can you come to Brooklyn?

  [. . .]

–Pretty please?

  [. . .]

–*Yes*, I promise we won't go anywhere "gross."

  [. . .]

–Are we back on that? I thought we'd switched subjects.

[. . .]

–You can say whatever you want. Say you're in love with the groom and don't see how you could hold your peace forever or whatever.

[. . .]

–Okay, okay, that was a low blow. I'm sorry.

[. . .]

–Yes, I *am* sorry. Look, I love Dan too. He's a great guy. He was, like, the only person in Galestown besides you who didn't treat me like a total freak. Well . . . besides you and Jason.

[. . .]

–Alex, quit acting like Jay never existed. *Jesus.* Look, if you could just chill out for long enough to cut through the six-foot fog of lust you've breathed up for Danny, you'd remember that Lea is a total sweetheart and *supposedly* your friend. But Ben Reardon is a fucking worthless piece of shit and I refuse to be in the same room with him, let alone the same wedding party.

[. . .]

–Don't give me that "He's just insecure" bullshit. Who isn't fucking insecure? It doesn't mean you have to shit all over everyone else to make yourself look good. Alex, trust me. He's fucking worthless.

[. . .]

–Listen, I'm not preventing you from going. Have a blast!

[. . .]

–Yes, Alex, you have to pick songs that other people will

like. There's no need to inflict your depression on a reception hall full of people.

[. . .]

–I don't know. Happy songs, fun songs, love songs. No Cure. You've been to a wedding before, haven't you?

[. . .]

–Yeah, they asked everyone in the wedding party, I think. Of course, I'm the only one they asked to sing.

[. . .]

–Don't "Oh God" me. Actually, I think that was kind of . . . I don't know . . . sweet.

[. . .]

–No, that doesn't mean that I want to go.

[. . .]

–Really, Alex, I soooo do not want to go.

[. . .]

–Oh, come on. You know that sexual bribery does not impress me. You know you'd fuck me for free if I'd have you.

[. . .]

–Oh, Alex. It's been *that* long? That's just . . . so . . . *sad*.

[. . .]

–Look, if you can get the groom to make the same promise, I'll buy your wedding gift. But I don't suppose you'd be up for sharing him.

[. . .]

–I know, I know. Another low blow. I'm sorry. Really, I am. You're just so easy . . . I mean, you're such an easy target. It's that dirty mind of yours.

[. . .]
–Oh, I love you too.
[..
....
....
....
....
....
........]
–No, of course I don't have a gig.

BEN

–Today is the last day of the best of your life, man, I say to Dan, real solemn-like, as I crack open a cold one.

–Dude, that's not how it goes, says Moron Cousin One.

–Yeah. You said it wrong, assface, says Moron Cousin Three.

–Assface. You called him assface! says Moron Cousin Two.

Dan and I look at each other. I meant what I said, exactly what I said, and he knows it. I'm losing my best friend and he knows that too. Fuck, man, I want to cry. But I won't. Dan needs me to stay strong, so stay strong I will. For Dan, for me—Christ!—for all the Dans and Bens the world over, because you are not immune to this, oh no, you are most definitely not immune. No matter how many battles you've waged together, how many beers you've pounded, how many times you've proclaimed "Bros before hos," this day will come for you all.

Dan looks at me as if he wants to say, Nothing's gonna change, but Dan is not a lying man so instead he simply lifts his beer to his lips.

I motion for him to hold his fire. Hold on, I say, If we're gonna do this thing, we might as well do it up right. Waitress! Bring on the Patrón!

I say this with sincerity, though I know that Dan and Lea's living room harbors neither barmaid nor tequila—not even Cuervo. We are drinking the Silver Bullet because the Bullet had been on sale. I crack another for Dan, even though he's only had a sip of his first.

–Look, Benny, I told you, I don't want to get too wasted tonight. I've got shit to do tomorrow. You know? Like, get married?

–Are you kidding me? You've got shit to do for the rest of your life! Tonight's the last night in your entire life that you don't got shit to do. Waitress! Make it a double shot.

As if in response, Moron Cousin Two proceeds to poke two holes simultaneously in two Bullets. He shotguns the bullets (like a champ—I'll give him that) foam ricocheting down his chin.

Moron Cousin One burps his approval.

–All we need now is sluts, muses Moron Cousin Three.

He is a moron, but a moron with a point. You are absolutely correct, Moron Cousin Three, I cry. Bring on the sluts!

–Did he just call you Moron Cousin Three?

–Dude, he just called you a *moron*.

–He just called you *all* morons, says Shawn Riley, over his shoulder. Good man. Glued to his game of Mario Kart, he's hardly joining in the festivities, but Shawn's quick, and I respect nothing if not speed (both in Kart and in life). I'm about to smile at him in a way that says, We might not like each other, bro, but at least we've got opposable thumbs, when he *ruins* any goodwill between us by saying,

–And, believe me, he knows one when he sees one.

Assface! I stand up because I can't let him utter such blasphemy and think he can get away with it. But Dan's a step ahead of me, maybe because he's a drink behind me—always has been, half-Irish lightweight—and holds me back.

Shawn, cowering in fear and knowing full well that Dan's arms will not contain my wrath for long, sputters out a pathetic excuse to save his skinny ass. All right, Danny, he says, trembling, I'm out. My voice is gonna be shit tomorrow if I don't get to sleep soon . . .

Dan's not going to argue, not when he can feel my sinews ready to burst through their epidermal cloak. Word, he says, letting Guitar Guy slink away with his tail between his legs. Bastard doesn't know how lucky he is. Good riddance, song boy. Go . . . pluck your strings.

Only after the door slams shut do I drop my fists of fury and let my rage subside. That's right, I think triumphantly. Of course, now that it's just me, Dan, and the three stooges, I'm almost sad to see Shawn go.

Almost.

But no matter. The night is young. I check my watch and see that it's 8:57, which means the sluts will be here any minute. And their arrival will mark the moment when I single-handedly salvage this sorry excuse for a party and make Dan's last night as a free man one for the books.

The doorbell rings at nine on the nose. No one can say that sluts aren't punctual. My, I say, who could that be at this late hour?

Dan gives me a look and gets up to answer the door. If this is what I think it is, he says to me, you're an assface.

Me? An assface? Obviously Dan hasn't seen the Fantassies ad in the back of the *Galestown Herald*, which promised Super-SeXXXy Entertainment for Any Occasion, The Hotttttest Ladies in Town, All Your Bachelor Party Needs Met!

–Well, would you look at this? The cops are here, says Dan.

–No way. We weren't being loud *at all*, says MC3.

–Hide the cheeba, says MC2.

–That won't be necessary. She's not that kind of cop, says Dan.

–What kind of cop likes cheeba? says MC1, dumbfounded.

–The stripping kind. Clearly Ben wasn't listening to me . . .

–Wasn't listening to you *when*? I demand.

–Um, when I said "Ben, under no circumstances are you to order strippers."

–I don't know what you're talking about. (This is so awesome.) I didn't order strippers, I swear. Come to think of it, I think I double-parked.

–Oh, you're so full of shit, Dan says, looking at me. Lea is going to kick my ass if she finds out.

–S&M is sexy, I say.

He throws his Red Sox hat at me—narrowly missing my jugular—and opens the door.

–May I help you?

I can't see who's at the door, but I do hear a kittenish voice say, We're looking for Danny O. We've got a warrant for his arrest.

–Oh, yeah? says Dan, What's the charge?

I wait for the punch line.

-Well, we've heard you've been a very bad boy, and need a spanking.

Yesssss! Not very original, but still . . . Yessssss! At that, two women wearing little blue uniforms and big black boots step in the front door. They're a little . . . let's just say . . . *longer in the teeth* than I expected . . . but their implants are novel enough to give us a good focal point. The one with handcuffs and a bottle of pink champagne takes off her cap and lets down her mane of bleached-blond hair. The one carrying a billy club and a boom box bends over, sticking her ass in our faces as she starts playing the music I requested.

-Dude, you are so awesome, says MC1 when he hears the jam.

TAKE THE BO . . . TTLE. SHAAAKE IT U-U-UP.

-Fucking sweet, says MC3.

BREAK THE BU . . . BB . . . LE. BREAK IT U-UP.

-Yeah, you're the fucking best, dude, says MC2.

-Not the best *dude*, I say, patting my lap and inviting one of the cop sluts to pour an ample amount of sugar on me. The best *man*.

After the sluts pulled back on the shorts that barely covered their asses and the shirts that didn't button up far enough to keep their tits from popping out . . .

After the one who'd been sitting on my cock all night tried to pretend like she didn't really want a piece of Benny B with her lame "But it's against the rules" line—I mean, it was clear I was only asking for her digits *in jest*; we both knew I wasn't going to hit that *for real* . . .

After we all discreetly slipped to various rooms in the O'Shaughnessy/DeAngelis household and finished off what the sluts had started . . .

After we downed the Bullets and the bubbly and the morons passed out, one by dopey, drooly one . . .

Well, then it's just me and Dan.

–Dude. *Where* did you find those girls? The Rhode Island Mall? he says, then shoots a Bullet across the room and into the green plastic garbage pail (nothing but net . . . and the crowd goes wild).

–I don't want to talk about it.

–I mean, cause they were . . . um . . . pretty . . . what's the word I'm looking for? . . . *Elderly?*

–Look, it's over, okay? I say. Now I just want a shower.

He laughs. Oh, reeeeeally, he says. You didn't seem to think that when the one with the cunt ring had your eyes rolled back in your head.

–Oh, would you shut up already? I pick up a can that's resting on MC2's inhaling and exhaling beer belly. I aim for the pail, but end up knocking over a pile of porn instead. Fuck. And anyway, I say, you should be happy you actually *found* a woman and aren't doomed to a life of getting dry-humped by cop sluts from West Warwick.

–Ben, you know that you have more to look forward to than that. I'm sure there are some nurse sluts from . . .

Johnston or . . . North Providence who are way more your speed.

–Ha ha, Mrs. DeAngelis. Real fucking funny.

Dan starts walking around the room, picking up whatever telltale signs of squalor are not stuck to the ground, carelessly tossing my beloved film collection into my backpack as if limited-edition copies of *Footballin' Rearleaders* are easy to come by, looking worried about what Lea's going to do when she sees that the place has regressed into a medieval manhovel. Hey bro, I say, you've got a big day tomorrow. I'll clean the rest of this up.

–No way. We're in this together, he says, before sinking another can. We're partners, Benny. Same as always.

And here's the thing about Dan: He actually believes that. As if we've been mano a mano all these years and not Numero Pizzeria Uno and Numero Dos Equis, with yours truly coming in a Mexican-piss-fueled step behind, every fucking time.

But you've got to hand it to Dan. Not only does he not rub it in your face, it's like he never even noticed the ever-deepening chasm between us. Like how he graduated Magnum Cum Louder from Providence College and I . . . let's just say I found the whole secondary-education atmosphere uninspiring . . . or how he's working at a Boston marketing firm while I spend my nights pouring pussy shots for Ivy League assholes from Brown . . . or how when we were the only kids from our elementary school to get picked for the gifted program, everybody said we were going to do great things someday, only somewhere along the line, they stopped saying that about me.

But, man, would you listen to me? I mean, it's Dan's day and all, not mine. I should be talking about his triumphs, his glory, his sparkling future, his storied past. Like, did you know he was the Little League World Series Player of the Year? I shit you not. Champion pitcher, that kid. The whole town was so fucking proud of him—but nobody more so than me. I almost blew out a lung cheering for him back home in Rhody, watching the game on my shitty TV with the coat-hanger antenna, trying not to listen to my dad screaming at my mom that it should have been me out there, if she hadn't been so hell-bent on turning me into a pussy. And my mom yelling back that I was Gifted, did he hear that, Gifted, and if he thought she was going to allow me to miss the Future Storytellers of America Convention for some baseball game, then he was dumber than he looked.

No, I didn't hear any of that because I was too busy watching good ol' Dan do our country proud.

–Benny, I got something for you. A little gift for the best man.

–Not necessary, dude.

–I know, it's no big deal, really, I just thought you'd like it.

He hands me a small square package that I rip open with utter fucking abandon. It's a blank CD.

–You got a CD burner, I say, realizing this was just another in the long list of things that divided us.

–Yeah. Lea got it for me. Engagement gift or whatever.

–Engagement gift?

–I know. How the fuck was I supposed to know about engagement gifts? I just acted like hers hadn't been delivered
yet, then got my ass to Zales first thing the next morning.

–So what's on here?

–No way, dude. You gotta play it to hear the songs. I
want it to be a surprise.

I can feel some eye condensation coming on—fucking
ice-brewed Bullets—so I turn my back to Dan and walk
over to his CD player. I pop in the CD and press play.

Track One: the Boss. Fuck yeah! I give Dan a quick
(manly) hug, then jump up on the couch and launch into
my signature slow-motion E-Street air drumming. Dan
shakes his head, laughing. You're crazy, he says.

Born down in a dead man's town

–Great fucking song, man, Dan says. I still can't believe
we saw the Boss live. Remember the way he . . .

He stops abruptly, as soon as it hits him that we don't
exactly share a collective memory of the Boss's appearance
at the Little League World Series. But I'm not gonna let
that bring us down, so I say, Fuck, yeah, Dan. Of course I
remember. You were like fucking Clemens, man . . . Dan
glares at me . . . I mean, Clemens before he went to the
dark side.

–How could you even mention that name here? You
know the rule. He points to the dart board he'd created
out of a Derek Jeter jersey.

–Sorry, dude. But who he is today doesn't take away
from who he was yesterday. That's, like, hating on little
Anakin Skywalker before he even *meets* Palpatine.

–I disagree. He's dead to me now.

–At least he's not a fucking Canuck anymore. I mean, I'd rather be demon spawn than be Canadian.

I was boooorn in the USA-ay-ay!

–Fucking Canadians, Dan says.

–Oh, please. Look at your cousins, dude. They're, like, total Canadians.

–What the fuck is that supposed to mean? Dan says, but then he looks around at the passed-out trio. And, maybe for the first time, I think he sees what I see when I look at the gene cesspool that is the Molloys—the tight pants, the hockey jerseys, the party-in-the-back hairstyles dancing ever so slightly toward mulletdom—because as soon as he looks back at me, my boy just about busts a nut, he starts laughing so hard.

–Fucking Canadians, he says, shaking his head, before joining me on the final chorus.

ALEX

I hadn't planned on this. Running late, I mean. Everyone can think what they want, whatever, but it was not some kind of subconscious rebellion on my part to passive-aggressively protest a marriage that in no way, shape, or form should be happening.

In fact, if you ask me, I'd say the fault lies not at all with me but rather with the Universe herself. I mean, it's not like I *made* it rain, which is the main reason why my train was so late getting into Providence. And it's not like I had any control over the utterly ridiculous amount of traffic clogging up the highway, which is why at this very moment I'm stuck on 95 instead of standing at the altar, even though the wedding *technically* started ten minutes ago . . . okay, make that eleven. I know what everyone's thinking—it's easy to know what everyone's thinking in a situation like this: that I stayed up all night doing blow or whatever rather than packing for the wedding or otherwise preparing for my bridesmaidly duties. And they're *totally* wrong. One hundred percent wrong.

Okay, to be totally fair, they're maybe only 73 percent wrong, because I did stay up all night doing blow, but that's totally beside the point. That's, like, a personal life choice. And I'm working on it, you know?

And anyway, who's to say that the Universe wasn't equally responsible for Caitlin asking me to go in on an 8-ball yesterday? I mean, I told her all about the wedding—Caitlin, not the Universe—and she got it anyway and, look, I don't know about you, but I was *not* going to let my roommate do that much coke alone. That's just, like, utterly selfish and completely irresponsible. You know, cause you don't save friends from their drug abuse by letting them overdose on an 8-ball. You save them by diving in, spreading things out, making it clear while she's in that place (and you're right there with her) that there's nothing *wrong* with that place per se but that the other place is so much better, so much sunnier, so much more *real*, really, and then you make a solemn vow in the name of sisterhood as the sun comes up that you are never, ever going to chase the moon again.

Except sometimes you don't make the vow when the sun comes up because you don't even *know* the sun came up because how *could* you know when you live in a basement apartment that, despite being in the East Village, faces west and is also inhabited by a third roommate who took it upon herself to throw out your alarm clock last week cause it had been going off for an hour . . . but you had taken two sleeping pills so, like, how on earth were you supposed to hear it?

Bitch.

So you ask Caitlin what time it is as she slices up six more fat lines because your cell phone died and you can't find the charger (and don't really *want* to find it because what is time, anyway, but a constant reminder of a patriarchal system set up around the planting of crops and the revolution of the sun without the faintest regard for the cycles of the moon or the ocean tides, and what is telecommunication, anyway, other than a method to enslave people in a system of perpetual labor when the nine-to-five model is hellish enough and sexist besides, having been created with the understanding that the women would bear the children and the men would work all day and be home in time for supper?) and when Caitlin said, Ten eighteen, you said, Whatever, Cait, It was two o'clock, like, an hour ago, and she said, Try eight, and that's when you realized once again that two, three, four, five, six, seven, eight, and nine are the eight trickiest hours known to mankind . . . I mean, humankind. They're, like, the moon getting her revenge on the sun for always being the goddamn center of attention and the sun acquiescing because no one's up anyway.

Except you and Caitlin.

–My train was at ten! And the wedding's at four. What the fuck am I supposed to do now?

Caitlin just sat there and stared, her right leg bouncing up and down so fast I could see it in three places at once. After what seemed like an eternity, a minute at least, she said, Well, you don't want to go anyway, right? Here's your out.

–I don't think "outs" count on the day of the wedding when you're a BRIDESMAID, I said. I hopped up off my bed (the fold-out couch), ran to my closet (a small coat-rack and a pile of clothes behind the TV), and started raiding it. Cait, I said, you gotta get out of here, cause I gotta get to Penn Station, like, immediately.

–Alex, I *live* here.

–Oh. Well. Well, can you go into another room or something so I can concentrate?

–I still don't understand why you couldn't have taken a train last night . . .

–That is *not* helping me, okay? Besides, have you ever *been* to Rhode Island?

–Yeeeesss, you know I have. I almost went to RISD, re-member?

–RISD is *not* Rhode Island. RISD is, like, another fuck-ing universe. Try being one of the townies that the college kids look down on.

–Oh, she said, you mean like how you look down on people from New Jersey?

–*Exactly.* Hey, can I get a line?

–Girl, take the rest of it. You're going to need it more than I do.

–Thanks, Cait.

And thank you, Universe, for bestowing Caitlin with a generosity that rivals the size of her trust fund.

–Hey, Alex?

–Yeah?

–You gotta get over that guy.

–Yeah, I know.

–I mean it. This isn't junior high we're talking about. He's getting *married.*

And the moment she says that is the moment the good part of the coke high so brilliantly decides to wear off, hurtling me back into a reality marked by no profundity of language, no realization of connections previously hid-den, no superhuman coolness. Nothing but stark awake-ness and a nagging feeling that everything is soooo not going to be okay.

I bent over, picked up the credit card, and did all six lines, one after another, for dramatic effect; five in the left, one in the right because I'd been favoring the right all night. Caitlin patted my back, stood up, and shuffled soundlessly to her room.

 -Are you sure you don't want any?

-Nah. Greg's getting some E tonight and I'd rather keep things simple, she said. I laughed out loud—a short head-shaking snort—at the thought of ecstasy being simple. We haven't gotten pure MDMA in months, and now the stuff is so cut with speed, dope, Anthrax, chalk, dandruff, and Pez that I can brag about how I've done every substance known to man—chemical, mineral, vegetable, metaphysical—without even trying. Still, I felt a twinge of jealousy that they were getting E and all I had was some coke, which did nothing to disguise the terribleness of an evening, only blurred the edges in between bathroom breaks. Cocaine is like adulthood, like giving up, like resigning yourself to the fact that this is as good as it gets. Then again, I thought, as the drug began to work its lack of magic, at least with coke you know exactly what you're getting yourself into.

I threw my makeup bag into the suitcase and poured the contents of my laundry bag in next so I could do a few loads at my parents' house and avoid having to spend money when I got back to New York. The clothes spilled out in a colorful wrinkled heap and I prayed there was at least one decent dress in there since I'd forgotten to drop my work clothes off at the cleaners. Whatever. They were probably going to fire me anyway for missing three Fridays in a row but, really, that just might be exactly what I need to jumpstart my *real* career. Let's face it; I need a job that allows me waaaay more freedom than temping. A nine-to-five just isn't my style, and temping was, like, killing my ability to keep up with the trends, which is totally necessary for launching a line as politically relevant as mine is, one inspired equally by the death of electroclash in post–September 11 New York, the reemergence of Valley Girl chic, and the Riot grrl movement. I'm calling it Kunt.

I packed my sole pair of Louboutins and two clean pairs of underwear—Agent Provocateur, because you never know: Maybe Shawn would be feeling straight today, maybe Danny would be feeling . . . No. Stop. Bad. Shaking away the thought by closing my eyes and literally shaking my head, I draped the plastic bag that contained the Badgley Mischka dress Lea had bought for me over my shoulder. Leave it to Lea to pick bridesmaids dresses so tasteful and understated that you couldn't even be pissed at her for that. But I was pissed for so many other reasons that I decided, Fuck delicacy, and I folded the bag in two and shoved it into my suitcase, only later realizing that the only one affected by this lame act of rebellion was the bridesmaid stuck wearing the stupid wrinkly dress. Me.

And a very pissed me, at that. I'd been back to Rhode Island exactly three times since my college-graduation party—once for Lea's mom's funeral and again for her bridal shower and bachelorette party—and that's three more times than I'll ever go back after this dreadful wedding is over. Thankfully, my parents were in Sedona, so I wasn't obligated to spend time with them, just had to pick up the Jeep that they'd left for me in a Providence garage, make my cheerful presence known at the wedding, and stop home to do laundry and snag a few of my mom's Valium before taking a late Sunday train back to the city.

If I could catch an 11:00 train, I could definitely be in Galestown by 3:00. It was tight, but not impossible—assuming there even *was* an 11:00 train. I had no idea what time it was when I finished packing but I knew the trains ran pretty regularly and it wasn't, like, a holiday or anything, so I wasn't *that* worried, especially because those who regularly go to Newport or the Vineyard *don't* take Amtrak. The fact that I was out of my skull also helped. I threw on my sunglasses, trying not to think about how many times I'd found myself on the wrong side of sunrise, how many times I'd needed these shades, not to shield myself from UV rays or a future so bright but to protect the world from my burned-up eyes. I popped out the handle to my suitcase, wishing that my own ankles had little wheels that I could fall back on in times of extreme fatigue. For someone with at least a gram of coke running through her bloodstream, I was not walking as rapidly as you'd think. I was mentally buzzed, but physically exhausted—when had I last slept, like, for real? If only my toes had nostrils.

As I stepped out of my apartment and onto the sticky carpet of the hallway (whatever you do, don't think about *why* it's sticky), walking took on the sensation of maneuvering my way through a huge vat of those brightly colored balls at Chuck E. Cheese, which always seemed like they'd be so much fun to jump around in, or at least they did until Andrea Vitalli accidentally on purpose kicked me in the eye at her stupid Chuck E. Cheese birthday party and I had to wear an eye patch for a week, which meant my mom got to be all, "I told you so" about how dangerous and pointless the ball vat really was.

After shuffling down the hallway and stairs, I opened my front door and that's when I heard it. Rain. Gushing, crashing rain that no girl in Miu Miu platforms should ever have to endure. The kind of dirty gritty city rain that could only be battled with a pair of galoshes except I don't wear galoshes because contrary to what every other woman in New York seems to think, they look fucking ridiculous. Oh, whatever, fuck fuck fuck fuck fuck.

I stepped outside, where there were actually a bunch of people stupid enough to be out in this monsoon. (It's Saturday morning, people! In a city where you can get ice-cream sundaes, cigarettes, and psilocybin delivered to your door in less than an hour. And you're outside in the rain . . . why?)

I had no choice but to face it head-on. It was hot, this being July and all, and there are, I suppose, worse things than warm rain. Like the burnt-metal chemical-garbage scent of warm rain, this being New York and all. I started to run but after a few steps slowed down to my normal pace—partly because running in platforms is suicide, but mostly because I didn't want to be like the rest of these people, running with their newspapers over their heads like the rain was some kind of terrorist attack. It wasn't. It wasn't that, at all. And so I walked through it, knowing full well that people around me were looking at the girl with the formerly nice clothes now soaked and ruined and slept-in-looking (though not *actually* slept in since that would have required sleep) and thinking I was a crazy person. I walked in spite of it, sneering at the people around me who weren't half as brave as I was, who wouldn't dream of facing the elements like this.

By the time I got to Second Avenue, I was drenched. My hair, or what was left of it after I let Shawn convince me to get it cut in fucking Williamsburg, was a disaster and I could barely keep my eyes open even with my now-irrelevant sunglasses taking the brunt of the deluge. Cabs were whizzing by me, full, and I almost cackled at how much of a sign this was that the marriage was totally doomed. Or that I was doomed. Whatever. I didn't care. For the first time since the month or two when every asshole in the country considered themselves an honorary New Yorker, I didn't hate my city. But maybe that was only because leaving it was such a pain in the ass.

I saw a cab at the other end of the street, the light on top mercifully signaling its emptiness, but before the yellow streak came crashing through the 8,000-thread-count sheets of rain, I looked out at the puddle that had spilled over from sidewalk to street. The water had long ago washed away all the plastic cup/broken glass/dog shit that usually lined the streets and sidewalks and now it was moving, rippling with ornately patterned puddles: a diamond, a tapestry, star-crossed lovers, a wrinkle in time. It was beautiful. So beautiful that I almost considered giving Caitlin back all her coke because if something so simple could be so beautiful then maybe you didn't need drugs—

until I remembered that these kinds of observations don't count if made while *on* drugs.

And it was only when I was out of the rain and splashing through the streets in a cab that was never going to make it to Penn by 11:00 that it hit me: Caitlin was right. I needed to get over this guy. And I needed to do it fast. Like, five hours fast. Because he was never going to be mine again, and if I was really honest with myself, he had never been mine anyway. But Lea used to be mine. She was my first friend, which is ultimately more important than your first love because at least your first friend is a choice.

Oh, whatever, I'm so full of shit sometimes. Lea wasn't my first friend and I know it. That illustrious title goes to Brianna Russo, who gained it as most childhood friends do: by being the first person to speak to me in kindergarten. But, God, if I'd known what a total Jesus freak she'd turn out to be you can bet I'd have been a little more discerning. You can't tell that kind of stuff when you're five, though; all you care about is that your friend doesn't smell like chicken soup, have lice, or eat paste (though the paste rule is not hard and fast). And before Brianna started dating the Mormon or whatever, she was pretty cool. Okay, so part of me liked hanging out with her because she did everything I told her to—and who wouldn't like that? Besides, I would have done everything she told me to do if she'd asked. But she never asked.

Or if she did, I wasn't listening.

CORT

–And what exactly am I supposed to do with *this*? Lucia, Lea's dragon lady of a stepmother, is holding my dreads up in the air, away from her, looking at them like they're a pile of squirming snakes.

–Um, I don't . . . *know*? I scrunch up my shoulders in an attempt to free my hair from her red-tipped talons. I'm breathing a deep yogic ujjayi breath in an attempt to filter out the toxicity of all the chemicals buzzing around the room right now but I know resistance is futile, what with Lucia wielding Aqua Net like a machine gun and the manicurist from her salon insisting that the ingredients in her polish are "all-natural," although I guess in today's day and age dibutyl phthalate is considered all-natural, and I want to cry.

Lucia snaps her gum and says, Yuh such a *pretty* girl. Why on earth would you do this to yuh hay-uh?

Like many Rhode Islanders, Lucia lacks the ability to pronounce the letter *r* in places where its presence is traditionally required.

–Oh, Lucia. Will you . . . please? Cort's hair is beautiful, says Lea. Of course, she adds, I do miss your curls. No one had curls like yours.

I suck in a breath, close my eyes, and repeat the mantra the girl had taught me at that festival in the Berkshires. Or was it that shaman at Burning Man? Whatever its origin, it seemed to work because all of a sudden Lucia turns her wrath from me to the other bad bridesmaid.

−Shouldn't she be hee-yuh by now, Lea? she asks. It's gonna take me long enough just getting *this one* fixed up. If the othuh one doesn't get huh little New York ass hee-yuh soon, yuh gonna be late for yuh own wedding.

Lea looks at me. Have you heard from her?

−No, sweetie, I say. I don't really know her that well, you know, anymore.

−Okay. Lea looks at me, her sister, and her Guido cousins. Am I allowed to start freaking out yet? Because I think I'm going to start freaking out. Cort, will you or *somebody* call Shawn and ask if he's heard from her?

No one moves. Um, Lea, I say. I don't really know Shawn all that well anymore either, and I'm not sure who does.

Lea stands up. Fine, she says. *I'll* do it. Just like I've done everything else.

Once again I feel terribly guilty for having skipped out on her bridal shower. It's just, I had the Coachella ticket long before I ever knew about the shower. Or, at least I had *planned* on getting the ticket long before. And anyway, how was I supposed to know that Alex was going to fuck things up as cosmically as she did, waiting so long to book a restaurant that the only place that would take them was The Elms, except no one informed Alex that they'd be keeping the bar open because the Sox were on so Lea was stuck opening kitchen goods and negligees while a bunch of drunken retired mafiosi screamed at Nomar?

Lucia gives me a look before retreating to the bathroom and I smile politely in spite of myself because what I'd really like to do is tell her what a sorry replacement she is for Lea's real mother, who was one of the only people in the world who never made me feel guilty for being the way I am, who actually seemed to be proud of me, in fact, but instead I just smile and watch her go. I walk over to the window, where Lea is furiously pounding in numbers on her cell phone, and I put my hand on her shoulder, relieved that she doesn't shake it away. Touching people does not come easy to me, probably because my mom was so weird about me being such an affectionate kid. Like this one time I hugged the old man who took care of the ponies at Roger Williams Park because I knew he loved animals as much as I did and my mom yelled at me the whole way home. Now I'm never sure what to do when people touch me and when it's okay to touch people myself and if I do whether I'm doing it right and if I don't whether they'll think I'm angry at them and I'm always amazed that some people seem to do it without even thinking.

–Machine. Lea groans, gives my arm a little squeeze, then pulls away and starts pacing around the room and I decide the Vicodins I've been saving for the reception will be just the thing to chill her out.

–Hey, Lea, I say. When she turns around, I open my stupid little bedazzled-looking purse and take out two tiny pills.

–What are those?

–Painkillers. They'll help you relax.

–No way. Danny and I made the decision to do this sober.

–Look, Lea, it's not like we're talking natural childbirth here. It's your wedding day. It's supposed to be fun.

–And I'd like to remember my wedding day, thanks.

–Lea, says her cousin Carmela, who's pretty in a big-haired Bon Jovi–fan kind of way, Do you want to remember a wedding day where you're totally freaking out?

Lea looks at us and then says, Okay, fine. Hand them over. Jesus, you are such a bad influence. And Alex isn't even here yet . . . God knows what she'll be on.

If she ever gets here, I think.

–What time is it, anyway? Lea walks over to the window and looks outside, as if that will get Alex here any faster, and says, How long does it take for these things to kick in? I'm seriously on the verge of freaking out here.

I'm feeling guilty again. But then, I've felt guilty around Lea ever since her mom died. It was weird, because Mrs. DeAngelis got cancer when we were teenagers and I'd just started fighting with my parents all the time. I'd tell Lea what a bitch my mom was being and then Lea would get all quiet and I'd feel terrible, but the truth was, my mom was a bitch.

And now my mom's the one who's sick and I feel guilty all over again because unlike Lea, who took a semester off from Villanova so she could take care of her mother, I didn't come home when my mom got cancer and I have no intention of staying here now. And it doesn't matter that my mom has Dad, and Lea's mom had nobody since Mr. DeAngelis left her for Lucia. What matters is that Lea's a good daughter, and I'm not.

It's not the only area where we differ.

I look in the mirror and try swirling my pathetic excuse for dreads into a kind of loose bun. God, sometimes even I think they look really stupid. I drop them, then begin to count them, one by one. Lea was right—I would kill to have my old hair now, so I could just fit in, blend in, hide, get into costume as the good bridesmaid, the good friend. Why couldn't I just be more normal for once? More lady-like . . . More graceful . . .

More like Lea.

BEN

Whoever suckered the middle class into thinking limos are luxurious, well, I'd like to lay myself down at his feet and say, Teach me Your Ways, O King of Illusion and Deception. Because there is nothing remotely cool about being ass cheek to ass cheek in a car full of dudes, our pants soaked with beer foam, our shirts damp from donning tuxes in this ridiculous humidity. Gimme a Bentley over this bus any day. Christ, gimme a bike. To make matters worse, Shawn is playing some gay-ass song on his guitar and the Moron Cousins keep interrupting him by flipping their lighters and screaming, Freebird!

–For Chrissakes, I say, and pull *Illmatic* out of the CD case in my backpack and hand it to the driver. Can you play this, bro?

The limo driver looks at Danny, who shrugs and says, Whatever, man, if it will get my best man to stop acting like a *bitch*.

I open my mouth to let loose on his ass, until I remember that Danny has a Get Out of Jail Free card today. And anyway, how mad could I get with my boy about to get hitched?

No, today was a day for love, not war. A time for getting bent, not throwing 'bows. I reach over the stocky legs of the Moron Cousins and grab a St. Pauli Girl from the cooler I'd stuffed with cold brews and hot grinders and look out the window. We've just passed the Reservoir and the limo's cruising up Main Street to the highest point of town, the hill where the town's two oldest churches stand, my own small wooden church, St. Malachy's, and the ornate Madonna Della Panni Cathedral, where all the Italians went. It had been pouring all morning, but now the clouds are breaking and the sun's even peeking out a bit, which is definitely a good thing for my boy 'cause no girl wants it to rain all up in her nuptials and you *know* that would not bode well for Dan tonight. If I close my eyes, I can imagine all of the good city of Galestown, flattened and laid out before me, suburban strip-mall ugly and beers-with-old-friends beautiful. Mostly, though, I see the people. There are good people here, the kind of people who stop by with a lasagna when someone dies, the kind who go to church and mean it, the kind who have book clubs and coach Little League and drink Bud, Coors Light, and Beast. Sure, it's a town like any other, but it's one I know I'll never leave.

SHAWN

As we pull into the church parking lot, I tell myself I'm nervous because I've never played a church before—but that's something of an understatement. Technically, I've never played an *anything* before, though not for lack of trying.

But hold on, you might ask, what about my steady gig as singing waiter/mad scientist at the Halloween-themed restaurant Frank and Vlad's, a charming establishment complete with electronic bats with bad Slavic accents and vampiric waitresses who'd rather be getting safety pins sewed into their legs on St. Marks Place than slinging I Vant to Suck Your Bloody Marys to tourists who came to the West Village because they were told it was kind of like Disney World, only with fewer rides and more fetish shops? Well . . . despite the fact that at least five times a day I catch myself humming some bit of the *Monster Mash/ Thriller/Ghostbusters* medley that plays approximately seventeen times a night at F&V's, it's not exactly the kind of work that inspired me to move to New York.

Okay, fair enough, but how bout back at college, when my band Seasonal Affectedness Disorder was a fixture in the basement of Beta Omega Iota, bastion of socially accepted brotherly love, secret society of trust funders who grew increasingly more bi-curious with each passing semester? Well, I might answer, despite BOI's penchant for late-night blow jobs, boy lips be damned, playing in front of three E-heads and sorority girls too drunk to notice the true nature of stares passed between brothers, I decide, is not rock 'n' roll. And it most definitely is not in the same ballpark as a church filled with about three hundred or so total strangers, none of whom looks very happy, what with the wedding on hold because one of the bridesmaids is no doubt selling her nubile young body for some high-grade Colombian.

And I don't even want to get into what a pointless waste of time this is. What I should be doing is practicing with SAD since, let's face it, we are an atrocious band. Even the frat boys would get bored by our original material and wander upstairs to listen to techno or have an orgy or whatever—and if you can't turn on people whose brains are being temporarily hijacked by thousands of bursts of serotonin a second, you're probably not going to impress industry executives who are already going to be deducting points for the bassist's unfortunate decision to wear fucking gym shorts to the gig.

–How about those nice Diesel jeans you wore to Harry's the other night?

–Dude, it's Syracuse.

–Don't "dude" me. You do not entice A&R representatives with fucking gym shorts!

–Shawn, he said, flicking a pick at my skinny tie, dressing fancy might be your style, but it's not mine. And do you really think an A&R rep would come to Syracuse?

–Derek, I said slowly, as if talking to a child (albeit an oafishly large and poorly dressed one), that is not the point. We play Joy Division covers, we are called Seasonal Affectedness Disorder, and we will not always live in Syracuse. *Make* it your style.

Of course, we've had even bigger problems ever since fucking Interpol came along and absolutely *ruined everything* and while I might have been able to make a convincing case that it was time to revive, I don't know, The Kinks or the Silver Apples or something, Derek started hanging out at some dirty little jazz dive, where he met some "cats" who "turned him on" to Jaco Pastorius.

Fucking bassists.

But instead of practicing, or at least helping Derek understand that if God wanted bassists to play melodies, he wouldn't have invented Gibsons, I'm here at the Corleone-McCoy wedding. That's the thing about these shitty medium-size towns (which are even worse than shitty little towns because you don't even have to know everyone to know exactly what everyone is like). You think you've escaped because you got a scholarship to a school seven hours north by bus, four and a half by a car you don't have, also located in another shitty medium-size town which is better than yours only because it's *not* yours. You think you've made it because after four closeted years at a Big East school whose orange mascot didn't exactly mean the place was rainbow-friendly, you finally moved to a place where even the straights want to be gay, but the joke's on you—you never escape and you just might never make it. There's your brother's bail hearing and your mom's house that needs roofing, there's your high-school lab partner's wedding or the death of a grandmother who never gave a shit about you when she was alive because you were "funny"/"artistic"/fill in the blank with another euphemism for sucking cock but still, you gotta do the right thing, you always do the right thing, and so you come home and kneel down in front of the jury of your brother's peers, or the shingles, or the bride and groom, or the carcass, whatever. You think, This is why I left in the first place, these banalities, and someone thinks back at you, Well, you should have thought about it before you went and got yourself born here.

When the town calls you back it doesn't give a fuck about what it's pulling you from. Stuff that, like, involves your, you know, *career*, not that anyone would understand. But you understand. You understand that your being here is just a foreshadowing of your eventual defeat. What's making you nervous isn't the fact that you're playing a wedding, it's the fact that you're going to be playing weddings *for the rest of your life*.

If only Alex were here. But as usual, when it really counts, she's nowhere to be found. Truth be told, I'm not sure I ever expected her to be. When I couldn't find her at Penn Station, I wasn't exactly asking the Amtrak clerks if they happened to have noticed a little ray of sunshine with a bright smile on her face and her trusted copy of *Wedding Blessings* tucked underneath her arm. I mean, it's not as if this is the first time the Mistress of the Dark has failed to insinuate herself into the land of the living before nightfall, even when her presence is at least somewhat required. So why do I even bother, you ask?

Well, it's not like she has the ability to calm me down or anything, that's for sure. Usually it's the other way around, with me coaxing her out of whatever K-hole, literal or figurative, she might have fallen into that particular day. But—and I think this somewhat guiltily—having that kind of human barometer of fucked-upness is reassuring. It's like, she's such a mess that I can't help but feel like a success in comparison.

But who am I kidding? I'm every bit as underqualified for my role as musical director as Alex is for her role of bridesmaid. At any moment Dan and Lea are about to realize that they should have hired an octogenarian harp-and-flute duo instead of some loser who hasn't picked up an acoustic guitar in, I don't know, eight years or something. I should have given them a Thanks, guys, awfully nice of you, but I'm no good unplugged; I need feedback to hum out the wrong notes, electricity to fuzz up the sound of my broken voice. But they insisted, and I didn't even have the energy to come up with a lie. Why did I have to pick this song? Why did I always have to make everything about me?

When I tossed out my idea for a song at their engagement dinner—Wouldn't it be funny if we played "Here Comes Your Man" instead of "Here Comes the Bride"?—they looked at me blankly and I said, You know, the Pixies song? and Danny said, Is that what you want to play, Shawn? and I said, Maybe . . . I don't know . . . I just know you guys said you wanted to do some stuff different, so what if instead of having your dad walk you up the aisle, Lea, you were already there, and Dan's mom could walk him up instead? It would be ironic, you know . . . like rain on your wedding day . . . and Lea looked nervous and I said, No, no, that was just a joke . . . you know, Alanis? and Danny said to Lea, It's not going to rain, baby. It's going to be the most beautiful day ever, almost as beautiful as you, and then he said to me, If that's what you want to play, then that's what you're going to play, and Lea asked me to sing it, so I did, and she could hear right then and there that the song was really about hobos riding to Nowhere Plains and still she said, Weeellll, you know I hate the idea of my dad giving me away after what he did to my mom. Lea frowned for a moment, then shook it off and smiled. Without missing a beat, she continued, plus the song is utterly absurd and inappropriate, which means Lucia will hate it. Perfect! And then Danny asked if that was the song I played at the junior prom, and Lea gave me a curious look, and I realized, My God, they don't remember. They don't even realize that the real reason I'm playing this has nothing to do with being clever or pissing off Lea's hag of a stepmother; it's because I'm pretty convinced that this was their song. I saw the whole thing from the stage, the way they looked at each other after Danny asked Lea to dance because Alex had ditched him for Ethan Garrity—it's what made me want to play music for the rest of my life.

But how could I have expected them to remember that? They weren't like me, marking every occasion not with the words spoken, but with the music that drowned them out. And how was I supposed to tell them that? Who am I to say when they fell in love? They have their own idea about that—Or worse, I think in horror, maybe when you marry someone you've known forever, things like the moment you fell in love cease to matter. After all, it's not as if that was the difficult part.

The difficult part is now. The old ladies whispering that

the missing bridesmaid used to date the groom, Lea waiting at the back of the church, probably freaking the fuck out. I know all those stupid people in the pews are thinking, That's what happens when you let a queer in the wedding party; don't *think* He doesn't notice. I'd shoot a look of death at all of Lea's doofy-looking cousins, they of the bellies padded by years of eggplant parm, if I hadn't seen *The Godfather* enough times to know that nothing good could come of that.

Do something, I scream at myself, and just as I realize that "something" would probably entail nudging Cort, the maid of honor, and suggesting we walk the aisle anyway, seeing as Alex, not being the most, *ahem*, punctual of women, might be otherwise entangled, when out of God knows where, certainly not from one of his goodly servants in the pews before me, a loud banging echoes to the grand heights of the cathedral ceilings, bouncing off Peter and Paul and all the other misguided fools judging the poor souls below. I pause, look to the priest for direction. He slowly lifts up a hand to hold me back, as if this kind of thing happens all the time. I glance at the bride and groom, expecting to see Danny all cool grins and Lea ready to unleash some bridal fury.

But it turns out I know them as little as I'd originally assumed, for Danny is the one nervously shuffling from foot to foot and Lea is smiling beatifically, quite possibly stoned. Cort is wearing the same glazed look and I wonder why no one offered me any of whatever it is they're all on. Ben, who I've managed to avoid all day save for a few mutual grunts (and grunting comes easier to him than to me), seems utterly uninterested by what could only be Alex on the other side of the heavy wooden doors, staring, as he is, at the mother of the groom's remarkably preserved and unnaturally tanned legs, without seeming to care how gauche it is to perv on the groom's mom in a goddamn house of worship.

Why are we all just standing here?

I drop my guitar, push my way past Ben and Dan's drunk cousins, and yank the door open, revealing one very late and very, *very* coked-out bridesmaid.

–Shit, says Alex as she stumbles in, shit shit shit shit shit shit shit shit shit shit shit shit shit shit shit, she says, her word echoing to the metaphorical heavens and back again, causing everyone who wasn't already looking back at us to whip their heads around. Alex is shaking and very likely on the verge of weeping, as she is wont to do. The priest's hand is still locked in the pause gesture and his mouth is pursed in a judgmental pucker. Well, fuck him. I'm not waiting around to watch my friend fall face-first into an apology at a moment we all can agree would be most inappropriate. I pick up my guitar and start walking down the aisle, not fucking waiting for the priest to lead us. As I launch into the opening lick, all heads turn to me, as if I were the one fucking up. Well, fuck them.

We march forward, past paintings of the deadly sins, or maybe it's the apostles, like there's a fucking difference, and slip into our rightful places at the altar. Once Lea steps up to the altar she dopily reaches out her hand and sort of pets Alex on the shoulder and Alex smiles sheepishly in return and am I completely mistaken or is that look that's passing between them actually an acknowledgment—however brief—of the existence of their bizarre love triangle?

Whatever it means or doesn't mean—forgiveness, an admission of defeat, an "I deserved it"—I'll never know, for just as soon as it appears, it flutters away, as the bride beckons her groom to come forward with a smile, and the bridesmaid's eyes cloud over, glassy and lost, too gone for me to tell her that a pair of sunglasses are resting atop her head. As I strum the last bars of the song, I can't take my eyes off poor Alex, and it occurs to me that people never cry at weddings for the reason you think. As my best friend weeps the tears that can only come from discovering that your man was only ever your man in your mind, the ceremony begins.

After I finish, the priest flashes me a look signaling that my job is done, and I join the rest of the groomsmen. I step away from the sacristy, my eyes glued to the velvet rug to avoid further eye contact with Alex. But before I take my place, I look up just long enough to see that the worried impatient faces of a moment ago are all smiles now. Amazed that I've been so well received, I take a deep breath and smile back; only after making the effort do I realize that the smiles have nothing to do with the song, which in all likelihood was hated by 98 percent of the attendees, and a lot more to do with the lovely couple standing before them. Oh, well, what had I expected? A record contract?

LOVE
WILL
tear US
APART

sunglasses
at night

ALEX

Cort is whispering something to me but she's trying to be all respectful or whatever so I can't make out what she's saying.

–What? *What?*

–Your sunglasses, she says, loud enough this time that I can hear her. They're, um . . . She raises her eyes and tilts her chin ever so slightly upward, and I realize that my elegant Chanels are sitting on top of my head in a most inelegant way. I slip them off and let them fall from my fingers onto my bag though, of course, they slide off and land on the floor with a clack that can be heard throughout the church.

Will someone please kill me? Like, now?

I mean, seriously . . . *what* am I doing here? I shouldn't even be at the wedding, let alone in the wedding party. And Lea knows it. I mean, God, look at her smiling and staring into Danny's eyes and acting all perfect just like she always does, when anyone who's taken the time to get to know her as well as I have knows what a total bitch she really is. Oh, sure, she'll be nice to your face, but the second you walk away she'll tell whoever will listen your deepest darkest secrets—just ask Shawn how it felt when Lea told the whole school that he was gay just cause he wasn't interested in her dirty hippie friend. I mean, sure, anyone with half a brain could have figured out Shawn was gay, but back then he was trying to, you know, like, *survive* high school without being murdered by someone on the hockey team and why Lea had to go blabbing it to everyone when I *told* her she couldn't tell *anyone*, I'll never know. He wouldn't talk to me for, like, a month after that—and all because Lea couldn't keep her big fat mouth shut.

She must know how I really feel about her, right? I mean, it's not like I've been discreet. And she must have other people she could have asked to be in her wedding party. I mean, she surely has other cousins, college friends—fucking manicurists—a hell of a lot nicer and more responsible than me, so I don't really buy her line that she wanted everyone in the wedding party who wasn't family to be old friends, dear friends. The only reason I'm up here is because she couldn't resist showing me that she won or teaching me a lesson or whatever. And you know what? Fine. I give up. She, like, totally beat me, once again. She got the perfect boyfriend, I mean, *husband*, and they're going to have the perfect life together, and not only that, but she gets to parade me, the loser, up in front of the whole world to see, just in case anyone had any doubt about whether or not she was the victor.

Luckily, I know better. When she's stuck in Rhode Island for the rest of her life, popping out a million babies or whatever, I'll be somewhere far, far away, which is where I should be right now, in fact. I mean, Danny might look like David Beckham, but let's face it, he's boring, Lea's boring, the life they've chosen for themselves is boring, and if there's anything I hate, it's boring.

I've so totally outgrown these people, this place, although it's quite possible I outgrew it all a long time ago, that instead of settling for the public-school gifted program, I should have persuaded my parents to send me to a Swiss boarding school, where I could have studied French and met all kinds of interesting people who do not consider shrimp cocktail a delicacy.

Now I have to worry about slipping back into the accent I've spent years trying to hide, about gaining, like, a gazillion pounds from all the revolting peasant food they'll no doubt be serving at the reception.

The last time I've seen most of these people was at high-school graduation, when Danny gave his ridiculous valedictorian speech that quoted Ghostface Killah, some nonsense about how if you forget where you come from, you're never gonna make it where you're going and everyone was cheering and acting like what he said was so profound and true. The way I see it, the only way to make it where you're going if you come from a place like Galestown is to forget it—and while you're at it, forget whatever persona has been imposed upon you by your parents and your social class (not to mention patriarchal oppression) and become someone else entirely.

I'm usually good at forgetting, but for whatever reason—the lack of sleep, the insanity of the day's events—today it's, like, impossible. And it's not only my days at Peterson that are rushing back at me with the force of the rain I'd escaped this morning but, like, my entire childhood—before I found out I was "gifted," before I realized that being "gifted" was social suicide, before I met Danny and Lea and the rest of them.

Like, I'd completely forgotten that for the first four years of school, Brianna Russo and I were inseparable—

perhaps because of fate, perhaps because our last names were next to each other on all the class rosters—and it seemed nothing would tear us apart. Not gymnastics, which took away most of my weekends—or piano practice, which sucked up her weeknights.

Nothing could get us, we bravely and foolishly thought.

Or at least that's what we bravely and foolishly thought until we learned about the disappearances of the fourth-graders.

They didn't disappear for good. We're not talking about what happened to Kenny Castalucci and that other kid whose name no one remembers down by the Reservoir. I'm talking about the fourth-graders who let themselves be taken away. The fourth-graders who left Dewey behind.

The Gifted Ones. The Chosen Ones.

The Lost Ones.

At first kids only whispered about them. About how they went away and came back Changed. Your older sister gets Lost and though she's still physically there in the house, something's different; she stays up in her room reading all the time and only comes downstairs to play the violin or ask your parents about current events. Your next-door neighbor doesn't join the pack walking to the bus stop like always; you watch in horror as a small bus comes directly to his front door and he steps on, looking confident and . . . different. The next time you see him playing outside, it's with some other kid wearing glasses and he doesn't even bother to introduce the two of you. Or worst of all, your best friend calls you tearfully to break the news that she's leaving; she tells you she doesn't want to go and you want to tell her she doesn't have to, but both of you know that she does and she does.

Each year before the start of fourth grade, one student was plucked from the safe, sturdy halls of Dewey Elementary and whisked away via the small buses we thought were reserved solely for the handicapped and retarded, and transported to some school on the other side of Galestown, a school a lot like Dewey, we were told, only with a program for the "gifted and talented." We were all terrified at the prospect of getting Lost—and yet fascinated by the thought of a way out of Dewey that had nothing to do with sixth-grade graduation or a move to a nicer neighborhood or different military base. By March of our third-grade year, we could contain ourselves no longer and the whispers rose from throats as yelps of full-on paranoia and glee.

–I heard Peterson looks like *Willy Wonka & the Chocolate Factory.*

–For real?

–No way. You're lying, doofus.

–I'm glad he's lying. That movie is scaaaary. Did you see the part where they go through the tunnel and that monster's mouth starts chomping open and shut like it's gonna eat everyone?

–You are such a baby. That was just a chicken.

–I heard that all the gifted and talented kids have to work for NASA. Some kids even blew up one time but NASA covered it up, just pretended like it was only that teacher who died.

–You're soooo lying.

–Well, I heard the gifted kids get pizza every day. And not the cardboard stuff we get here. *Real* pizza. Like, from Pizza Hut.

And so forth.

Both Brianna and I could do long division while jumping rope, so it didn't surprise either one of us when we were chosen to take the test that would decide if our future would involve Pizza Hut or community college.

I suggested to her that we both fail on purpose, but she gave me a look that said she knew I couldn't fail anything, not even if I tried, and I nodded in agreement and said, Let's just do our best and see what happens. I don't remember much about the test other than the fact that the man giving it was wearing a most unfortunate sweater, black with purple and turquoise lines. It looked a little like the "laser" option you could have as a background for your school photos.

I hated his sweater even though I coveted the laser option as I did jelly shoes and white lace leggings, but my mom would have none of it. That's what the poor kids chose, she explained, the ones whose less enlightened parents didn't care about ankle sprains resulting from inadequate footwear, who didn't understand that sensible clothing was the first line of defense against pedophilia, who didn't plan on ordering the deluxe packet of school photos—one large for the living room, four medium for offices and piano tops, plus forty wallet-size for nondenominational holiday cards—an assortment whose myriad uses left open only one option: the tasteful choice of basic blue—not the profile silhouette, not autumn leaves, and certainly not laser.

It's not what you want to hear as a kid when all the laser kids get grouped together, which meant all the cute boys and the cool girls were sharing plastic combs, while I was lined up with the same high-level readers I always got stuck with. Of course, as soon as I was old enough to realize the inverse correlation between coolness and socioeconomic status that existed in suburban public schools in the late '80s and early '90s, I realized my mom was right.

As soon as I got home, I called Bri so we could compare our answers to the questions. Do you remember the picture of the guy standing next to the tree? she asked me.

–Yeah, I said. What did you think was wrong with it?

–Well, the sun wasn't out, but he cast a shadow.

–Oh, I answered. Crap! My answer was that it was nighttime but he was wearing sunglasses, which was weird and reminded me of that Corey Hart song—and so I told the man in the unfortunate sweater that the problem with the picture was that Corey Hart wasn't African American like the guy in the picture. The man asked me who Corey Hart was and I explained that he also wore sunglasses at night, and the man laughed, and I hated his sweater even more.

I knew in that instant that I had failed and Brianna was a super-genius who would leave me behind. I'd have no best friend, no one to dress up in my mom's clothes and entertain me, and I'd be stupid on top of it.

So you can imagine my surprise when my mom and dad called me into the living room a week later to tell me I passed the test, was one of a select few in the west side of the city who passed, the only one in my school. It was the first time I remember feeling several emotions at once: terror, that I was to become one of the Lost Ones—did this mean I was going to have to wear glasses and care about current events?; excitement: I liked Pizza Hut as much as the next kid; but, most of all, sadness: If I was the only kid from my school who passed, that meant Brianna had failed.

When I told them I didn't want to leave Brianna behind, my parents said that if that was my decision they would support it, even if it did mean missing out on an excellent opportunity. But the thing is, that *wasn't* my decision. I felt bad about it, maybe even cried a little (I cry a lot; sunglasses help), but as I looked into my parents' eyes I knew I couldn't let them down. At my new school, they said, there'd be other kids like me, kids who were really bored with the work at school, kids who were so far ahead of the others. But I didn't really want to think about being ahead of Bri. We always had done everything together, or at the very least, I'd always let her do everything with me.

I called her because I couldn't wait until the next day to tell her (I might change my mind, and I knew that would be a mistake) and she said she was happy for me and we both cried and said we'd always be best friends—just like the song we learned in Brownies—

Make new friends, but keep the old.
One is silver and the other gold.
A circle's round, it has no end.
That's how long I want to be your friend.

I crossed my heart when I told her that things would be just like always, that I'd call her every day, that we'd see each other every week, that things would never change— but my mind was already racing forward to my new life.

Months passed. I never called Brianna every day like I said I would, never saw her once a week. When we met up again in high school, we were strangers. She'd traded in her pigtails for a crucifix, and we were way past the years when Madonna made that ironic. We had spoken less than six words to each other in those four years.

But who cares about all that, right? I've forgotten all that.

Or maybe I haven't. Nor have I forgotten what a terrible friend I always have been and always will be. Because I wasn't thinking about keeping old friends that first day at Peterson; I was only thinking about making new ones who would worship me the same way Brianna had. But who? I thought, as our fourth-grade teacher Mr. Donovan called me and three other students to the board to solve a long-division problem. Through a haze of chalk dust, I watched as a girl with light brown hair finished her equation seconds before me, the first time I'd ever been beaten. Her hair was long and shiny, not a snarl in sight, and when I looked at her wiping the dust off her jeans, expecting to see a smug gloat, I was shocked to see a shy smile instead. Realizing that this Lea DeAngelis girl could be my true north in this sea of strangers, I returned her smile and accepted defeat gracefully.

For now.

like a
prayer

CORT

A friend of mine who calls himself Uncle John but who made me swear on Jerry's soul that I'd tell no one that his real name is Blaine once told me that certain indigenous peoples won't have their pictures taken because they believe that a camera has the power to steal the soul. I know by now to take most of what Uncle John says with a grain of salt—he's a fabulist of the highest order, the kind of guy I could imagine stealing away on boxcars and howling at the moon if I wasn't pretty certain that he was really a rich boy from Greenwich, Connecticut, with a trust fund fueling his freewheeling ways.

But I like that bit about the camera. I see the truth in that. Lea's face is so caked up with makeup that it's like she's someone else, she's this bride-creature imprisoned in a cage of white lace and flowers and something borrowed, something blue, and I know they do the makeup for the album, not for the day, like she's an actress playing a bride, and maybe that's all she is, I think, as the photographer snaps another one of her red-mouth grins and then is all, Now, let's have one with the maid of honor and I put on a big grin too and tell myself I'm happy for Lea, and I am, but I'm sorry for her too, that she feels like she's gotta put on this big show as if she has to prove her love, or prove Danny's love, to any of us, when she doesn't have to do anything of the kind.

I think I'll get married someday, but when I do it will all be different, it will be in a field or on the beach and there'll be a drum circle and maybe even some of those

cool firebreathers, and I'll be barefoot with scarlet bego-
nias in my hair and Uncle John will preside over the ceremony and there'll be no talk of possession or ownership,
no need for blood or sacrifice or sin.

–And now how about one with all the girls? the photographer says and Alex mutters, *Women*, under her breath,
because apparently she's a *feminist* now, and she and
Lea's sister and cousin join me in an awkward embrace of
the bride. Lea smiles and I smile back for real now because even though she's a victim of capitalist oppression
Lea is my friend and I love her and I want her to be happy
even if she needs a whole bunch of artificial means to get
there.

We're standing in the front foyer of the Windham, and
in the ballroom the dance floor is full of people, young
and old, which is funny when you consider that not too
long ago probably half of them had wanted to ban the
song playing, the one by the young woman who'd taken
the Virgin's name in vain.

Lea squeals, Let's go dance, and after grabbing my hand
and pulling me toward the ballroom, stops abruptly. Oh,
shit, Cort, I am . . . I totally forgot to ask . . . but how's
your mom?

–Oh, I say, knowing this is not the last time I'll have to
answer this question today. I mean, it's nice that people
ask and all, I guess, but don't they realize that means I
have to talk about it all the time, when I don't want to
talk about it all the time, when talking about it is the last
thing I want to do, and Lea of all people should know
that. I mean, Kyrie and Uncle John understand—that life

should be about the reality that you're experiencing right now, because when you think about it, nothing else truly exists. It's all just talk, just a story you tell about the past and future, not what's real.

–Oh, I say again. She's doing pretty well, you know . . . considering.

Considering that she's, you know, dying. But I couldn't get into all that with Lea now, not today, not when everything's already reminding her of her own mother not being here. So I smile and give her a little hug.

–Let's catch up tomorrow, like, really catch up, she says. Are you coming to the brunch?

–There's a brunch?

–Yeah, at my dad's place.

I start feeling something I haven't in years, the anxiety that had often overwhelmed me as a kid, one that arose whenever I was needed in three places at once: the first dreaded and obligatory, the second social but predictable, and a third, an unknown that brought with it risk and guilt at leaving family and old friends behind, but also excitement and novelty, a choice all my own.

Most of my life, I picked door one or door two and learned to ignore the feeling in the pit of my stomach that my real life was waiting for me behind door three. Though it might surprise people I meet these days, I wasn't always a rebel, wasn't always interested in challenging authority or living outside of society the way kids like Jason Lane seemed to do so naturally. Not that it got Jason much of anywhere, but still.

Which is why it shocked them all when I decided I

didn't want the life my parents had mapped out for me, didn't want another four years of school followed by a good job, a handsome husband, a happy life. I wanted something else. I mean, I always wanted something else, but it took me eighteen years to act on it, and I haven't looked back since, haven't wanted anything but this, this life of sunshine and music in the summer, of roughing out the cold winter months at Uncle John's place in the mountains.

Except being back here now, back in the place I used to call home—it's shaking my foundation just like Uncle John said it would; it's making me look back at the two doors I closed long ago and wonder if it's time to open them back up.

–But I don't want to go back, I'd told him. There's nothing for me there. My home is here.

And he'd just shrugged in that way that I used to find Zenlike but now just annoys me, because what I wanted him to do was say he knows that his home is my home and the caravan's my way and he didn't want me to go anywhere, but instead he was acting as if he didn't care whether I came or went, lived or died, because a million other girls with flowers in their hair were already lining up to take my place.

And now part of me's thinking about coming back to Galestown, about using what I've learned over the years to heal my mom. Hadn't my yoga classes and chants helped so many of my friends come down from bad trips? Didn't the special tea that I brewed from the herbs in our garden keep us all from getting sick after a particularly muddy festival? The oracle on the Haight had told me I had the gift of healing, after all—who better to use my talents on than my mother? What better way to heal the wounds we'd built up after all those years of fighting?

When Uncle John dropped me off on Friday, never saying where he was going so I knew it was probably his parents' country house for boating and tennis, he didn't come inside, said he was too susceptible to bad vibes what with Mercury in retrograde and everything for him to think he could handle my mom's illness. I understood, right? He had a responsibility to the whole group, you know, and it was bad enough that my constitution had been compromised by my proximity to illness, the evils of Western medicine and overconsumption at the wedding but for us both to be exposed would have epic consequences. I'd said I'd understood, even though I thought he was full of shit, threw my pack over my shoulder, and walked up the front porch.

–Don't forget to read to her from the *Tibetan Book of the Dead*, he called after me.

I knocked on the door and when no one answered opened it gently and walked in. My dad was stretched out in a recliner in the living room, half-asleep in front of a baseball game, skinnier and with hair that looked a lot more gray than I remembered.

–Don't get up, I said, but he did and we met halfway in an awkward embrace.

–Where's Mom? I said.

–Sleeping. It was a bad night, he said, but didn't elaborate when I asked him. Instead, he asked about me.

I told him a little about my friends, our plans for a community garden, and my ayurvedic and macrobiotic studies, though I called them "cooking classes."

–Hey, maybe I could go grocery shopping tonight and make dinner. Maybe a summer squash and quinoa casserole with a beet gratin. Foods can be really healing, you know . . .

–Cortina, he said, cutting me off, Dr. Veltri said she should eat whatever foods she likes best.

–Oh, you mean the foods that got her sick in the first place, I said, the self-righteousness tumbling out of my mouth before I could pause and think about nonviolence of thought and word.

–Cortina, she has cancer, my dad said, raising his voice but not loud enough so as to wake my mother. Not food poisoning.

I had to count to ten to keep myself from telling him that their whole way of living was poison—the food they ate, the TV they watched, the medicine they took, the consumerism that consumed them—but instead I just put on a smile and said I was happy to help him make supper, whatever it was.

–Tina, a voice called and attached to that voice was a ghost in a pastel nightgown and shock of white hair. I almost stopped breathing, for here was the woman who for so many years could bring me to tears with one word, one look, one small sign of disappointment that I'd turned out so awful . . .

Only it wasn't her. She was half the size she once was, seemingly twice as old, the treatment—Western voodoo,

Uncle John called it—sucking the life out of her just as quick as the illness. I don't know why I was so surprised. I guess I'd got it into my head that she'd look like one of those fierce cancer ladies you always see in TV shows and ads for breast-cancer awareness, the ones who look like wood nymphs with their pixie hair, slim bodies, and general aura of wisdom. Instead, she looked . . . sick.

What we said then I don't remember, it was a blur of hellos and how are yous and how are you feelings and is there anything I can dos?

–You could come to church on Sunday, my dad said. And then maybe we could get breakfast afterward if Mom . . . if we're all feeling up to it.

–Would you like me to go to church?

–Yes, said my dad. It's . . . it would be nice for us all to go together, which was his way of saying, Please let me have a family for just a little while longer.

–No, said my mom, It's . . . you don't have to, which was her way of saying she knew it didn't matter, life was too short to go places you didn't want to go to.

And now as I try to remember the choreography that Lea and I created so long ago, sometimes on roller skates in driveways, other times in basements while boom boxes blasted Tiffany, Cyndi, Debbie, and Madonna, I know I'll spend the entirety of Lea's wedding night obsessing about what I would do on Sunday and every day after that, torn between obligation to the woman my mother was now and unresolved anger at the person she used to be, at the people we both used to be, a desire to atone and an equally strong urge to run away. But why was I thinking of it as running? It was simply returning to my real life after a brief pause in a place where nothing counted.

Jason Lane used to say that nothing that happened in Galestown *ever* meant anything, which I didn't really understand then, but do now. But Jason always got it, probably because he had lived so many other places, places no more real than Galestown but that collectively had provided him with the perspective that people who'd only been one place lacked.

Lea once said she thought it was the settling down that killed him. And maybe it's true. Because now that I've been free I think settling down in a place like this would kill *me*, too. I think suburban life would start eating me from the inside out the same way it ate the fierceness out of my mom, the same way it swallowed Jason whole, beautiful, beautiful Jason.

Not that Jason always acted beautiful. But who could blame him with everyone always whispering about him? Whispering about his crazy dad and his deadbeat mom, whispering about how Jason came to fifth-grade graduation drunk and how he replaced the communion wafers with Flying Saucers, whispering about how he got thrown out of CCD for telling off Father O'Malley during a lecture on the sanctity of life.

–I'm not justifying it, Father. I'm just saying the decision has nothing to do with you. I mean, why do you care so much? Why do you want women you know nothing about to have babies they clearly don't want?

The class was silent. Jason sat back in his chair with his arms folded. And then Father O'Malley did the unthinkable. He picked up an empty desk in the front row where Alaina Santucci would have been sitting were she not out sick with mono and threw it, not at anyone but seemingly at everyone, at the entire world. Then he walked out of the classroom never to return. The next time he wanted to pass along a message to the children from Jesus or the pope or whatever, on not drinking Pepsi on account of Madonna being in their ads, on the evils of homosexuality, birth control, and Sinéad O'Connor, he let the devout young men and women who taught us all the word of God serve as his mouthpiece.

It wasn't long after that incident that I told myself reaching out to Jason was the Christian thing to do, like Jesus touching the lepers, the whores, the thieves, told myself it had nothing to do with how much he looked like Johnny Depp, had nothing to do with the fact that I wasn't exactly rolling in friends myself. And so one day after our gifted teacher Dr. Falcone told us to pick a partner for Scenario Planning, one of the many strange rituals of days spent in gifted class, where we weren't just presented with reading and math problems like the normal kids but rather tasked with solving real-world problems like how to save the polluted Narragansett Bay, contain the spread of possible global pandemics, and peacefully negotiate future trade deals with potentially hostile nations, I didn't sit back and hope that this would be one of those days Lea would be feeling charitable enough to pick me, or Alex would be feeling political enough to not pick Lea. I went ahead and asked Jason Lane to be my Scenario Planning partner.

This small act of boldness started a chain reaction of chaos as the girls scrambled to be Shawn's partner and their usual partners looked dejected at discovering their unimportance. Jason just gave me a shrug and a bit of a scowl and started walking to the back of the room toward the gerbil cage.

After we sat down, I waited for Jason to say something but he didn't, so even though it's not in my nature to talk first I started reading out the story about the growing threat of AIDS in Africa that Dr. Falcone had given us, a scenario that was intended to inspire twenty questions, the best of which were intended to inspire twenty solutions, the best of which would hopefully inspire a plan.

–Cortina, stop, stop, Jason said. I can read too, you know.

–Sorry, I just . . . I thought one of us should . . .

–If you don't *need* to say something, why say anything at all? Jason looked at me, generally puzzled as to why I would want to read the story out loud when reading the story out loud was what we always did in Scenario Planning.

–I don't . . .

–Cortina, don't you ever wonder if this is all just a big experiment?

–Scenario Planning? I'd asked.

Jason sighed, clearly disappointed. Not *just* Scenario Planning. The entire gifted program, all of it.

–I . . . I never thought of that before.

–My dad told me the government does experiments on people all the time, we just don't know about it. Like, they give people drugs that haven't been tested yet or unleash diseases on them or shoot radio waves into their head with, like, subliminal advertising, or even just tell them things that aren't true. Like, maybe we're not gifted at all. Maybe we're really retarded but some professor had this theory or whatever that if you tell retards that they're gifted they, I don't know, figure out how to prevent acid rain or stop the spread of AIDS.

–You think we're . . . retarded?

–Not retarded, but maybe, I don't know, crazy. I mean, look at Alex, she's completely twisted and evil, and Shawn, he's probably messed up because Father O'Malley's always extra nice to him, too nice, and Dr. Falcone could be some kind of psychiatrist or something. She's always making us play these *games*! About AIDS! When do any of our other teachers make us play games about AIDS?

–I don't . . . know, Jason. I think it was just an IQ test that got us here. I think we just have high IQs. And I think Dr. Falcone thinks games are a good way to teach us stuff that's, I don't know, harder than stuff kids our age are supposed to be learning.

When I think back to that day, I realize Jason was what Uncle John would call an old soul, a mad genius in the body of a beautiful eleven-year-old kid with a psycho for a dad and a mom who had disappeared on him when he needed her most.

Disappeared. That's how Shawn put it at Jason's funeral

years later, his voice flat and devoid of emotion. How could someone do that, he'd asked me. How can someone just disappear, Cort? But I didn't have the answer because I didn't know if Shawn was talking about Jason's mother, Jason, or his own father, who'd recently taken off for Florida with his secretary.

–How can people just . . . disappear, Cort? Where do they go?

–I don't know, Shawn. Life is a . . .

I stopped myself before I said something untrue, before I spoke the clichéd words that are the stuff of pop songs and funerals. Shawn wasn't looking for an answer because he knew the answer didn't exist.

And if you don't *need* to say something, why say anything at all?

born in
the u.s.a.

BEN

–Dude, I say to Dan as I slide up to him at the raw bar. I can't help but notice the DJ hasn't played any of my tunes yet. I mean, look, I know I gave you, like, more than three songs . . .

–Thirty-two, he says, sucking down an oyster.

–Thirty-two?

–You gave me thirty-two songs.

–That many, huh? Couldn't have been. The card wasn't very big.

–You wrote very small.

–Well, I'll be damned. I didn't realize, I say, then wait for Dan to hoover another bivalve before continuing. Here's the thing, Dan. I know you only asked for three, but every last one of those songs had special meaning, you know?

–I'm sure they did, Dan says, then puts his arm around my shoulder as someone snaps a picture from across the room. He grins like a movie star and the flash lights up his teeth and it kind of ticks me off, because, I mean, let's put things in perspective, you know? They'll give anyone a marriage license these days, even former members of Mötley Crüe and stars of *Melrose Place*. It's not like it's an accomplishment or anything.

–Whatever, man, I say, and toss off Danny's embrace. I just wanted this day to be special, okay?

Dan laughs. I know you did, man. I know. It's just . . . look . . . we couldn't play all of them. You understand that, right?

–Dan, c'mon, give me a little credit. I am nothing if not understanding, I say and chomp on a shrimp. So what made the cut?

–I . . . I can't remember all of them, Ben, he says.

–Definitely "Scenario," right?

–You know, I . . . I don't think that one did.

–Whaaa? You're trippin', dude. So you must have gone with a lot of the De La instead, then?

–Um, you know, I'm not . . . no . . . no De La Soul songs.

–But Three is the Magic Number!

–I'm sorry, bro. Not today it isn't.

–Well fuck me figuratively, I say. So . . . well . . . "Feelin' It" made it, for sure, right? That was, like, the unofficial anthem of ninety-six.

–Uh, I . . . I don't think the DJ had any Jay-Z.

I frown. This wasn't looking good. O . . . *kay*, I guess. "Passin' Me By"?

–Uh . . . no.

–"The Bridge Is Over"?

–No, not that one, either.

–"Mass Appeal"?

When Danny shakes his head no, I take a deep breath. Well I know you couldn't have left out *"Sometimes I rhyme slow"*?

–No . . . he says and before I can open my mouth, he goes on. No "Nice and Smooth," at all.

–Okay, what gives, Dan. You love those songs. Those are *great* songs.

–I know. But . . . look, when it came to the music, Lea and I had to . . . there was a negotiation.

–A negotiation?

–Yes.

–With *whom*?

–You know the answer to that, he says.

He was right. I did. There across the room, dancing with the bride to fucking "Butterfly Kisses" or some shit, was the Tipper Gore to my N.W.A.: Phil DeAngelis.

–So what was the negotiation?

–You've got to put things into context. Lea's dad wanted us to hire a Sinatra tribute band.

–Oh God, no.

–And naturally we protested.

–As you damn well should have.

–And we got the DJ.

–Because God is a DJ.

–But the DJ came at a cost.

I bite my knuckles. Give it to me, I say.

–No rap.

–No rap?

–No rap.

–No rap *at all*?

–No.

–No "Cock the Hammer"?

–No.

–No "Nuthin' but a 'G' Thang"?

–No.

–No "Wu-Tang Clan Ain't Nuthin ta Fuck Wit"?

–Geez, Ben. No.

–That's so . . . *racist*! I told you all those old Italians are fucking racist. Are you sure you want to marry that girl, Dan?

–It's not . . . *Keep your voice down*. It's not . . . *racist*. He wouldn't let me have any Beastie Boys or House of Pain, either.

–What does he have against rap?

–I don't know.

–No, really, what does he have against rap? I want an answer!

At this, Dan takes me by the shoulders and says quietly, Ben, today is not about you, okay? Do you understand that?

I nod, but Dan keeps going. It's not about you. And you know what? It's not about me, either. It's about Lea. And I can't let you ruin this for her like you . . . like . . . Oh, just shut the fuck up, okay?

–Fine, I say, but not until you give me an answer.

Dan sighs and throws his shrimp down without even taking a bite.

–Because he's fucking racist, okay?

–Thank you. That's all I needed to hear.

Dan and I stood there for a few seconds, silently, our arms locked in furious b-boy stances.

I was about to walk away in disgust when all of a sudden I heard it. A song by a man so pure and true that I'd dub him a bodhisattva were I a lama, a song that broke a smile on the faces of myself and my pussy-whipped compadre and pulled us out onto the dance floor where our air-guitar performance put paid to all of those brave men and women who've windmilled and duck-walked before us, a song that had been in the air that summer, the best summer of my life, the summer the Galestown Gators represented the good old U S of A in the Little League World Series.

—Pack your bags, Benny. We're going to Pennsylvania! were the first words I heard after my teammates did the proverbial "We Are the Champions" jog around the Worcester Wildcats' outfield, basking in the screams of our adoring fans who'd just watched us fucking smoke the home team, 4–0, in the New England Regionals.

It was my dad, looking as if he was the one who'd just pitched a no-hitter against the Massholes. But I guess the old man had done as much work getting me into shape as I had, dragging me out of bed to field grounders at the crack of dawn (when all the slackers were sleeping, he said), buying me my first Louisville Slugger and my silver Wilson A2000 glove, teaching me the difference between pitching from a full windup and pitching from the stretch. After I put my arm around his waist as we walked to the dugout he just kept saying over and over again, I'm so proud of you, Benny. I'm so proud.

But pride goeth before the fall or, in my case, before the First Annual Future Storytellers of America Competition, most inconveniently scheduled for the same weekend as the championship game. To add insult to injury, I'd allowed myself to be signed up for the contest solely because my gifted teacher Dr. Falcone wore see-through blouses, for I am, was, and always will be a slave to white lace brassieres and the nipples they cannot conceal.

And so, even though I played my heart out in the semis and quarter finals, I secretly hoped for defeat. Only, in a form of irony so supremely wicked that I understood it even then, the Gators didn't lose. Of course, it goes without saying that our wins had every bit as much to do with me and my curveball as they did with any of the other guys on the team. For though my mind prayed for elimination, my arm refused to comply, caring not that there was no way I was going to convince my mom that baseball was more important than some bullshit story contest.

Not that I could completely blame her. It's not like *she* noticed that the entire team turned their backs on me after we killed the Natchez Knights in the semis—or that Len Respallo threw his glove at my head after we walked off the field (that shit hurt!); it's not like *she* heard everyone except Dan calling me a pussy as I packed up my stuff, leaving Dan my bat since he hit better with it anyway. (My dad and I didn't talk about it, but Ken Ling's Easton was much better suited to my lightning-quick swing.)

–Hey, gifted geek . . . afraid you won't cut it against Taipei?

–Go write your fucking story, Rear-entry.

–Fucking nerds, man.

It's not like *she* cared that my dad was right; all I wanted to do was play ball. All *she* cared about was that her pride and joy was some kind of prodigy, even though I knew I was nothing like any genius I'd ever met. Besides Dan, I couldn't stand any of the other gifted kids, with their grandma glasses, their zombie-flesh breath, their clammy packs of Dungeons & Dragons cards. And they hated me even more—when Dr. F. recommended me for the Competition, Erik Manzelli (a Lawful Fighting Gnome) threatened to use his newly acquired Firestrike spell on me and I was like, BRING IT!!

I didn't say much on the ride back up from Pennsylvania, just listened to the Boss on my Walkman as my parents argued in the front about whateverthefuck—me, Dad's drinking, Mom's being all uppity about her book club. I wished they would just go and get divorced already, so that I could live with whichever one of them was being cool that day and then peace out when things got too confining. That's what Dan said he did, anyway.

Being in the car with Ralph and Alice was bad enough, but the Storytellers Competition was going to suck even harder. I knew all the other kids had been practicing for weeks, with their pointless piles of books and sample essays. Some dork from North Kingstown even called me up to see if I wanted to join his study club; all I needed to bring, his mom told mine, was a few sample essays, some opening paragraphs for group story preparation, and a "desire to win!"

Riiiight.

My parents were still going for each other's figurative jugulars when we pulled into Rhode Island College's parking lot the next day. Whatever dumbass had dreamed the whole thing up decided to further torture those such as myself who had about as much interest in being future storytellers as we did in being bodyslammed by Hacksaw Jim Duggan by holding the competition in the college athletic compound. I could see the baseball team practicing on the field—lucky sons of bitches. I bet none of their mothers trotted them around like storytelling monkeys when they were kids.

I didn't wait for my parents to get their Donna Reed and Ward Cleaver on, just bolted out of the car like the proverbial Bat Out of Hell and followed the signs pointing to the huge concrete building sucking the life out of the sunny day. I kicked a sign over, then readied myself for the satisfying thud, only to watch it float soundlessly into the grass.

I looked over my shoulder to make sure nobody saw me then ran toward the building, up the stairs, skipping two at a time, and pushed open the door of the gymnasium so hard I could practically see the doorjamb wither from the force of the blow. I walked up to the front desk covered with crepe and construction paper fashioned in the shape of books, fountain pens, and typewriters and stepped into the line for kids with last names from N–Z.

–Hey there, storyteller, the woman at the front desk said cheerily, holding out her hand to make my acquaintance.

I gave her a look that caused her to lower first her hand and then her eyes in cowering fear. She began shuffling her pile of name tags. So what's your name?

–Ben Reardon.

–Ben Reardon, Ben Reardon, she said, then, to my horror, did that gross thing that teachers and librarians always do—licked her filthy finger before flipping through a stack of paper, as if dousing pages with saliva were the only way to keep them from sticking together.

—Ben Reardon . . . Ben Reardon, she repeated. Here you are, kiddo. So where are your parents today?

I shrugged. Dunno.

She gave me a puppy-dog look to match her droopy face, then handed me a name tag that said BENJAMIN REARDON.

—This isn't me.

—You're not Benjamin Reardon? She looked puzzled. You just said you were.

—No, I said I was *Ben* Reardon. Just Ben. (Actually, my real name is Beagan, which means "small" in Irish and "Please kick my ass" in English, but I wasn't about to tell her that.)

—I'm so sorry, Mr. Reardon, but these cards were made months ago. I'm afraid it will have to do.

—Thanks for nothing, I mumbled under my breath.

The gymnasium was a hive of nerdosity. Everywhere around me kids were zipping around like dweebmachines fueled by little else but overzealous parenting and precocious vocabularies—Ritalin had yet to reach the popularity of Flintstones vitamins in the late '80s, remember. With no figure of authority to steer me in the right direction, I wasn't sure where I was supposed to go, so I scanned the room until I saw a kid who looked normal enough. He was the only one who wasn't rehearsing monologues to an audience of two or moving his lips as he read Shakespeare for Young Readers, and he was even holding a pretty gory-looking comic book. I walked up to him and tapped him on the shoulder.

–Hey, what you reading?

–*Blood-sucking Bots.*

–Oh, cool. I'm Ben.

–Zeldor Zinkbot.

–Your name is Zeldor Zinkbot?

–Affirmative.

–Okaaay . . . Zeldor. Do you hate this shit as much as I do?

–Dirty word alert. Dirty word alert. Dirty word alert. Abort mission. Abort mission, he said, then made a few beeping noises and scuttled away, like C-3PO with a bad case of the runs.

Oh, Christ. This was worse than I'd imagined. But still, I could deal with dweebs like Zinkbot, I could deal with their belief in extraterrestrial life and delusions about the import of *Star Trek*, I could even deal with their twitches, weird smells, and speech impediments. I could not, however, deal with the fact that I'd let my team down for this, or for anything for that matter. As my dad always said, when you signed up for a season, that meant you showed up for every game—sprained ankles, slumps, and storytelling competitions be damned. Anything less was giving up.

Just as I'd begun to conjure up a picture of the battle about to be waged on Pennsylvanian soil, a voice came over the loudspeaker, welcoming the future storytellers and their families to the First Annual Future Storytellers of America

Competition, and directing us to the bleachers where some big-deal writer was going to share his thoughts on the importance of stories in American life or the fate of the novelist in a capitalist society or the thrill of revision and the agony of, oh, whothefuckcares . . .

I scanned the crowd for my parents and found them, unfortunately for me (and anyone else within viewing distance, but especially me), groping each other's habeas corpuses behind a giant fern near the bathrooms, as if that really offered any cover. Duuuuuude. No. I . . . no.

Now, I wasn't exactly thrilled about listening to some writer dude spout off about life and adverbs and whatnot, but I didn't want to watch my parents hump, either, so I walked over to the bleachers, climbed the stairs, and sat in the back row, which gave me an unparalleled view of the last-minute cramming of my opponents.

After a boring introductory speech from a white woman in a dashiki about how we all had the power to "write our own futures," the writer dude stepped onstage. To my utter shock he wasn't at all what I expected him to be, as in, he didn't look like a grown-up version of all the kids in the stands with me. He looked more like, I don't know, like he'd seen stuff. His shirt was wrinkled, he was wearing a leather jacket, and it looked like his nose had seen a fight or two. He cleared his throat and took a sip of the water at the podium, then started talking.

–Am I the only one who thinks it's a little absurd—me being here? Talking to a bunch of kids about writing, as if any of you are going to remember what I've said when you're old enough to decide whether or not you actually want to be writers? So I'm not really going to waste your time. It's nice outside. You should be out playing baseball or something. I mean, how old are you kids? Eleven? Twelve? What the hell do you have to write about? What have you seen? What have you experienced?

The writer dude took another sip of water, then just stood there, staring at us, then went on, Look, are you the future storytellers of America? Maybe. But some contest sure as hell isn't going to determine who is or isn't.

Whoa. Mark Twain up there just totally *dissed* the contest. Bad *ass*. I looked at the teachers and contest organizers in the front row and saw that most of them looked pissed. But as I scanned the faces of the nerds and their parents, I was amazed to see that none of them looked fazed. It was as if they hadn't even heard what the dude had said, so mesmerized were they by their stupid study guides. But I heard him loud and clear and started clapping when everyone else seemed too stunned, pissed, or preoccupied to do anything.

The writer dude put down his glass, then walked off the stage. A few seconds later, the woman who'd given me my name tag shuffled by him, as if whatever had caused his badassosity was contagious and she *so* did not want to be infected. As she took the mic in her hand, causing a big feedback *sccccrreeeeeeeeeech*, her fake smile didn't disguise the fact that he'd gotten her granny panties all up in a bunch.

–What a profoundly . . . succinct . . . and *original* . . . speech, she said, from our PEN Faulkner Award–winning writer. How about a round of applause for this, mmmm, literary giant?

The crowd started clapping and I couldn't help but laugh at all those lameoids. Dude was right. What the hell did young Ben Reardon have to write about? I might have had a Little League World Series to weave a good yarn about if it weren't for this bullshit contest . . . and you know what? Fuck it. I didn't have to be here, and the game was starting in an hour. I could still catch it on TV if I came up with a brilliant enough plan to get my ass out of here.

And, like that, I had it.

–At this point, we'd like to ask all our Future Story-tellers to join us in room 328 for the first portion of the competition, "To Be Brief: The Short Story!"

As the bots rolled toward the classrooms, I walked in the other direction to the bathroom where my perform-ance would begin. I kicked open the door and was re-lieved to discover that it was blissfully free of my fucking parents and, even better, free of my parents fucking. I walked into the farthest stall, leaned against the wall, and turned on my Walkman and listened, really listened, to Bruce singing about being born in the USA.

It was the first time I really heard the words, and my face got hot and red when the Boss said something about killing the yellow man, because that was racist and I didn't want the Boss to be racist, but after I listened to the whole thing through, I realized that they weren't his own words; he was just telling a story, he was telling an-other man's story in another man's voice, and I thought that took real balls to talk in the voice of someone who wasn't you, and I knew that none of the other pussies in the contest with their expensive study guides and their loaded parents would ever have the cojones to do that.

I waited a few minutes until I was sure the contest was already under way, then stepped out of the stall, walked over to the sink, and stuck my head under the faucet. I squinted my eyes and clenched my teeth as the water came out fast and freezing, but it was worth it. Once my hair was wet enough to mimic real-life clamminess, I splashed some water on my shirt, my face, and my hands.

I was so goddamn smooth—too bad I couldn't have faked *dumb* to get out of this thing sooner. I walked over to the hand dryer and turned it on, then stuck my fore-head directly under the blast of hot air until my head got good and hot, sending a small film of sweat to the surface, despite the fact that the rest of me was still feeling the effects of the cold water soaking my shirt. I caught my mug in the mirror and decided my face still looked too normal, so I thought of the most terrifying thing I could—the creepy dude with the chattering teeth from Clive Barker's *Hellraiser* . . . Holy mother of Christ! Why had Danny and I insisted on watching that? As my face took on a distinctly paler pallor at the thought of the S&M monster, I decided I could pass for puke-worthy.

Now all I needed to do was find the man with the mini-van. I stepped out into the foyer and—lo and behold—noticed a sign for the parents lounge. Jackpot! I followed it, careful to walk slowly enough to pass for sick in case anyone spied me before I reached the lounge. I took a deep breath and thought of *Hellraiser* once more—Jesus, Mary, and Saint Joseph!—shivered, then walked in.

As I'd suspected, the free wine was too good an offer for my old man to pass up. There he was, sipping from a plastic cup, and there was my mom, staring off into some husband-free space as she took unconscious nibbles of crackers and cheese. Obviously the second honeymoon had come to an end because my mom was looking less than pleased.

And then she saw me.

–Beagan Caleb Reardon! What are you *doing* here? Aren't you supposed to be writing—she consulted the booklet in her lap—a short story . . . right now?

–Sick, I croaked. I feel real sick. I've been throwing up, and I feel . . . I feel like I'm going to fall down, I said, and then I collapsed into her arms in tears.

–Oh, Ben. She put her hand on my forehead. You're burning up. You must have caught something from one of those . . . foreigners . . . at the baseball tournament. Oh, it's okay, hon. We'll get you home.

I wailed even harder. But Mo-om, I cried, I want to *stay-ay*! I don't want to miss out on the Com-pe-*ti*-tion!

–Well, I'm afraid you'll have to. The first contest is almost over.

I threw in a dry heave for good measure.

–What's going on here? Why is *he* here? my dad asked. I could tell by the tone of his voice that he wasn't drunk yet—his voice got real high when he was—but I also knew by the way that his left eyelid was drooping that he was well on his way.

–He's sick.

My dad opened his right eye wider and lowered his eyebrows, which was his way of saying "I'm onto you."

–Oh yeah, he said, what's wrong with him?

–Feel his forehead. He's burning up.

–Cooling down, more likely. What did you just stick your head up against? The radiator? You fall for his shit every time, Irene. Can't you see the boy doesn't want to be here and that he's doing whatever it takes to get out of this?

At this point I retched in a way that I'll admit bordered on the melodramatic, but it did the trick, because my dad jumped back. No sane man, however tipsy, wants to play Regurgitation Russian Roulette, especially not when his wife forced him into his best shoes.

–All right, all right, he said, if the boy's so sick, then Christ, let's get him outta here. Lord knows he's not the only one who thinks this whole thing is a waste of time.

We walked out of the gymnasium to the sounds of the moderator calling contestants back to the bleachers for round two: "All Together Now—The Group Story!" and I sighed with relief at the success of my ploy.

As we drove home in silence (I didn't dare ask them to turn on the radio) I leaned my head against the window and felt the spring breeze wash over me. There was baseball out there, damnit, I could smell it as sure as I could smell the cut grass flying from lawnmowers and stabbing pasty legs all over town, as sure as I could smell the sticky sweetness of Del's famous lemonade and the stink of the infamous pig farm the next town over. My own field of dreams was calling, but I could not follow its siren song.

After the shitty-van came to a stop with its signature

shaky rumble, I waited for my mom to open the door. I took her hand and let her lead me to the front door of our house, which was actually kinda nice, and made me think I should play sick more often. As soon as we stepped inside, I checked my watch: 4:56. I nearly ran to my room, till I remembered how sick I was and slowed my pace accordingly, grabbing onto the walls for dear life and slinking around the corridor and into my bedroom. I shut the door and turned on the TV.

Immediately, I heard my father let out a wail worthy of that sick banshee from that movie *Darby O'Gill and the Little People*.

–Turn that set down, Ben. What are you, deaf?

Stupid thin walls.

–Oh, let the boy be, Michael. He's sick!

–Sick, my ass. I know a faker when I see it and that boy's fakin'. If he's so sick, then how'd he pitch a perfect game just last night?

I ignored him and focused on the commercial for the newest volume from *Life's Mysteries of the Unknown* series, the one that promised to explain the mysterious connection between the pyramids in Egypt and the canals on Mars. Holy shit!

–I don't care what you say, Irene. You should have let Ben play in that game.

–Michael, enough already. His education is more important than some game.

Welcome back, folks. You're joining Chris Smith and Ron Carmine of ESPN, here at the Little League World Series in Williamsport, Pennsylvania. And for those of you just joining us, you couldn't have made it here at a better moment. We've got a very special guest performing the National Anthem here tonight . . .

That's right, Ron. Let's have a big round of applause for the Boss himself, Mr. Bruce Springsteen!

–Some game? The Little League World Series is a . . . character-building event.

–Don't make me the Mean Mommy here. He just spent a week in Pennsylvania building his character, thank you very much.

The Boss saluted our great nation with song, then spoke the words that send shivers down my spine every time.

–Play ball!

Ron, tell me a little about the team taking the field right now, these Galestown Gators, hailing from the state that is neither island nor road, the biggest smallest state in the Union, Rhode Island.

Well, the state might be small, Chris, but one thing sure isn't and that's the size of this team's determination.

–What I don't get is why you think some story contest is more important than the Little League World Series.

–Because of the academic scholarships, Michael! Do you ever think of that? I mean, how else do you expect to pay for his college education?

–For Chrissakes, Irene, he's in fifth grade.

–Oh . . . and you think colleges don't look at fifth grade?

–I think colleges look at the Little League World Championships, too. It's . . . extra . . . curricular.

Chris, taking the field now is one of the young men who's been instrumental in Galestown's previous matches, starting pitcher Daniel O'Shaughnessy.

What? *Starting pitcher* Daniel O'Shaughnessy? Surely they'd made a mistake. I'd pitched all three playoff games and Coach had only taken me out when wins were imminent. Dan was our second baseman. A mighty fielder, no doubt about that, but he was *a closer, for Chrissakes.*

–Michael, don't give me that horseshit. You're just trying to make Ben live out your own pathetic fantasies. You're like . . . Al Bundy or something.

–That's a really nice thing to say about the father of your child, Irene. That I'm an effing failure. Real nice.

–I didn't mean . . .

Look at that fastball, Ron! I'm told they call O'Shaughnessy the "Blarney Stone Thrower" on account of his sinkers.

His sinkers? *His* sinkers? They were *my effing* sinkers! And that was *my* nickname! Dan wasn't even 100 percent Irish! And possibly even . . . Protestant!

–I am not having this conversation with you. You're drunk.

–So what if I've had a few? Does that give you the right to come down on me?

Hold on a moment, Chris. Ted here is telling me that this is O'Shaughnessy's first night starting out on the mound. It seems another Gator pitched in the semis and the quarters.

Damn straight. Finally, a little recognition where it was due.

–Will you keep your durned voice down? He's going to hear you.

–He's not going to hear me. Do you hear how loud he's got the goddamn TV on?

That's right, Ron. It seems the other pitcher had to leave the tourney early. Something about a math contest. But we don't have yesterday's roster here, so we're not sure of his name.

Well, Chris, I am sure of one thing and that's that I bet he wishes he was here right now.

–Beagan Caleb Reardon, turn that goddamn television down now! You hear me?

Ya never know, Ron. Kids these days, they just don't seem to know what's important in life. Whatever happened to that good old-fashioned love for the game?

It's a different time, Chris. A different time.

blasphemous
rumours

ALEX

–So how long was everyone waiting, I ask Shawn, who is trying to flag down a waiter with a tray full of satay skewers. Was it really bad?

–Weeell, he says, settling instead on a waitress hawking some rather vomitous looking mushroom puffs. No, it was . . . fine, and I know he's lying because otherwise he would have said something bitchy about (a) Lea's stepmother (b) 97 percent of the wedding guests (c) all of Galestown or (d) life in general, but Shawn is utterly incapable of bitchiness in times of gravity, a most inconvenient trait in a gay best friend, if you ask me.

–Should I, like, say something to her?

–You haven't talked to her yet?

–*Of course* I did. Everyone was talking in the limo.

–I mean, have you *apologized*?

–No! I mean, how could I? She's kind of, you know, tied up? And, anyway, I just think sometimes it's better to let these kinds of situations, um, resolve themselves.

Shawn shook his head. Jesus, Alex, go say something to her. Like, now.

–Hey, you know I'm not the type to say I told you so or anything, but you're the one who didn't even want to come today, and now all of a sudden you're Mr. Matrimony.

–I'm not even gracing that with a response. And I am not talking to you until you go fix things. Seriously.

–Shawn, can you at least try to hold your plate still? Unless you, like, think prosciutto is a fashion statement.

Shawn sighs and gives me a look. Alex, I love you but Lea's entire family is giving us the evil eye and—Shawn lowers his voice—they're frightening people.

–Shawn, Lea's family is not in the mob. Well, not, like . . . officially or whatever.

–Oh, sweet Christ. Will you please go talk to her so I can sleep in peace tonight?

–Okay, fine.

–And can I get a little bump?

I reach in my purse and pull out a bag for Shawn and, really, it's about time. The coke will take his focus off me and put it squarely on himself which, if you ask me, is where everyone's attention should be. If we all stopped worrying so much about everyone else and started thinking about ourselves the world would be, like, a lot better off.

God, this is boring. Why on earth anyone would willingly bring together people from the different parts of their lives is a mystery to me. I've done a fairly good job of keeping my worlds from colliding and the few times I've failed to do so have been disastrous. Shawn is the only one who I allow to move freely between borders and even with him I've had to be careful because coke has a tendency to make him weepy and dim, which in certain circles can be a dead giveaway to his lower-middle-class roots. But then, he's skinny and slutty and hot and we live in New York where those little details go a long way.

I take a small bite of the least offensive looking thing on Shawn's plate, a cherry tomato, and nearly choke on it when someone taps my shoulder. I swallow the tomato

nearly whole, the bit of juice that my bite released sting-
ing my sore gums, and turn around.

–Lea, I say, suddenly feeling a lot less sure of myself
than I had a second before.

–Alex, she says, smiling, and yet with a bitterness in her
voice that I hadn't noticed in the limo ride from the
church to the Windham.

She's shaming me with silence and after a few seconds
of it I give in. Hey, thanks so much for understanding . . .
about me being late and everything.

–Who said I understand? She's still smiling but only, I
realize, with her teeth.

–I . . . well . . .

–The only thing I *understand*, Alex, is how fucking selfish you are. You don't even care that you were late. You
don't even feel bad about it.

–I do . . .

She laughs. Actually, you probably do. You probably care
that you made an ass out of yourself and that everyone
here is pissed at you. You probably feel bad that you even
had to be here today instead of doing whatever it is you do
with yourself these days . . . a lot of coke, I would guess.
But you don't care about how any of this affected me.

–I do . . .

–No, I don't think so. You only care about yourself.
And the worst part about it is, it's *destroying* you. Look at
yourself, she says sharply, shaking now. You know what, I
don't even care that you were late; you're the one who
looked ridiculous, not me. But I do care that you're . . .

–Hey, what's going on here, says Danny. He's trying to

look all nonchalant and in control and Dannylike but I see from the look in his eye that he's terrified of what we might be talking about.

–Nothing, Lea says.

Danny closes his eyes slightly and exhales inaudibly in a way that only I notice.

–Hey, you two aren't fighting, are you? Because . . . that's no good. You love each other too much to do that. Lea, you can be pissed at Alex tomorrow for oversleeping.

Lea snorts. Oversleeping! Look at her; she hasn't slept in days.

And then she starts to cry which would seem like the most terrible possible thing she could do to me . . . until she does something even worse.

–Alex, do you know how much it sucks for me that my mom's not here today? Do you know how hard that is for me? How a few years ago I had a *mother* and now I've got some trashy manicurist from Johnston and . . . oh God . . . do you even care? I can't even . . . You're throwing your life away—do you know how hard it is for me to understand why?

I don't say a word through all of this because, really, what can I say? And now people are starting to look at us because wedding tears are supposed to be happy tears and these are most definitely not happy tears and, I mean, where is Shawn when you need him? I just want to run away, just get the hell out of Galestown and never come back and then Danny, because this is just what he does, puts his arms around us both and says, Would you two kiss and make up already? You're, like, *ruining* my wedding day, and he's so fucking charming that Lea laughs and I might have, too, if Danny's arm around my shoulder wasn't sending a searing pain of longing down my side. I slide out from his grasp and give Lea a quick kiss on her cheek. I can't do the same to Danny and he knows it, but with Lea, I can.

–I'm sorry, I say. I fucked up.

And not just today, but pretty much throughout our entire friendship. It's just . . . do you know how difficult it is to be friends with someone as perfect as Lea? She was exactly like me, smart, wealthy, pretty . . . only, when I'm really honest with myself . . . nice. And not nice like how Cort pretends to be with her fucking save-the-whales bullshit or whatever but, like, *really* nice.

Which makes things complicated.

As soon as we started Peterson, the normal kids automatically lumped Lea and me together with the rest of the Falcone freaks, as they called us, never thinking that we might need or want other friends. In time Cort would worm her way into our twosome and eventually push me out completely, but for the first few years of our friendship, the normal kids assumed that because I was gifted I wasn't interested in a social life, even though I already recognized that popularity was a much more challenging and thrilling skill to master than advanced geometry. They assumed I still played with dolls like Cort, or that I liked Tiffany, Debbie Gibson, and New Kids on the Block, whose buttons all but obliterated Lea's stonewashed jean jacket, but thanks to my cousin Sabrina, I already had an impressive collection of new wave and post-punk mix tapes. In short, they thought I was a nice little gifted girl.

But they were wrong.

By sixth grade, I'd already made a few attempts to sully my image: I called Jessica Calveccio a bitch after she spent an entire lunch period shrieking that there was a spider in her HoHo even though it was her own damn fault for eating HoHos, which everyone knew were vastly inferior to Yodels. People were so shocked that a gifted kid would be bold enough to swear that it didn't even matter that Jessica was technically not a bitch but rather a drama queen with an overactive imagination. I used my knowledge of probability to become the master of MASH, and though the other girls were clearly impressed with the way I always seemed to end up living in mansions with the cutest boys in the class, somehow no teacher ever caught me running marathon sessions of the game during our free reading periods and so I was unable to shed the nerd label. I even convinced my mom to let me get trashy white-blonde highlights at her salon, which might have turned some heads had Erika Andrade not worn an ill-fitted white silk blouse that very week that revealed a purple lace bra underneath.

It soon became obvious that these actions had been totally half-assed. If I was going to win the hearts and minds of the popular, nongifted girls at Peterson, I needed to do something major. Because I was a nerd at heart, I knew that the best way to get good at something was to study. And the only way I was going to become the kind of girl I wanted to be was to study the literature on popularity and cool.

Luckily, it was 1990, so the literature was vast.

I pored over issues of teen magazines—*YM* for tips on beauty and boys, *Sassy* to help me keep my edge. I traded in Nancy Drew for the Sweet Valley twins once I realized the only mystery I needed to solve was how to hide my intellect. I listened to Depeche Mode, the Cure, INXS, and New Order for insights into the cruelty of the world. I rented every movie about the teenage dilemma I could find:

The Last American Virgin, Fast Times at Ridgemont High
Ferris Bueller's Day Off, The Breakfast Club
Porky's, Goonies, Gremlins
War Games, Lucas, Heathers
The Lost Boys
Valley Girl
Can't Buy Me Love.

Teen Witch, Teen Wolf
Risky Business, Dirty Dancing
License to Drive, Dream Machine
Girls Just Want to Have Fun
Some Kind of Wonderful
Dream a Little Dream.

Sixteen Candles, Less Than Zero
Pretty in Pink, Rad
Say Anything . . . , Weird Science
Better Off Dead.

The worlds in these movies were nothing like my own—the '80s were over and slumming it had begun to replace social climbing as the posture of the day, though all that would change again a mere decade later—but that didn't mean that I couldn't learn from them.

I knew right off the bat that I didn't want to be like the heroines in these films—they were honest, trustworthy, virginal, good . . . and boring. And anyway, how could I be that girl when Lea DeAngelis already fit the role to a T? She was the kind of girl that John Cusack would serenade with a boom box, the kind of chick who was truly dazzling, the kind of girl who never was and never would be nada. I realized that no matter how hard I tried I would never be the good girl, but I could be the next best thing: the bitch who in real life would have beaten her every time, stealing her boyfriend with a smile on her face, consoling her with backhanded compliments in bad times while plotting her demise in good. And so I studied those wispy things with perfect hair and cruel intentions: the Kellys, the Lisas, the Heathers, the Blairs who could cut you with their words, their eyes, their nails. I didn't mind if people hated me or feared me, as long as they noticed me.

And after a month of study, I had a plan.

It was simple, but that was the beauty of it. I basically let Jenna Tessitore, the biggest gossip in school, think that Lea had her period. I didn't actually *say* that Lea had her period, nor did I lie when Jenna pressed for information. I just let it slip that Lea had complained of cramps the day before, neglecting to mention that the cramps in question were shin splints spurred on by a failure to stretch after track practice. I knew this rumor would not endear Lea to the normal girls, who'd be jealous that she was developing so rapidly, especially since so many of them were Catholics and would be totally freaked by the sinful implications of such an early onset of womanhood. And the boys would just find it gross—which would mean that I would become the most likely candidate of all the gifted kids for inclusion into normal society.

Before I knew it, the entire class was coming to me, Lea's best friend, for details about Lea's precocious uterus. Once again, I didn't lie, just didn't do anything to make them believe that her menstruation was anything other than a rumor started by me.

The next day at recess, I didn't meet Lea by the water fountain like I usually did—or rather, I couldn't, because the popular girls had swarmed around me.

–It figures. Lea always finishes her assignments first. Why wouldn't she get her period before the rest of us, said Jenna.

–I know. All those gifted kids think they're so much better than us, said Alaina Santucci. Then she looked at me and said, Except you, Alex. You're not like the rest of them.

–Yeah, you wear nail polish and everything.

It was true. I was more like these girls than the other gifted kids. I mean, I didn't even wear glasses. And I'd convinced my aunt to buy me three contraband pairs of lace leggings my mom said "obscured the goodness within me" and I had already proved I totally wasn't afraid of swearing. My plan had worked perfectly; now all I had to do was damage control with Lea.

I might have been able to avoid Lea at recess, but I knew it would be way more difficult once we got back to class, since it was one of our "gifted days" with Dr. Falcone. I walked to the gifted classroom slowly, mentally preparing a little speech as to why I didn't meet her as usual on the playground.

But when I got to class, Lea wasn't sitting in her normal seat, at the orange table no one else dared claim because they knew it was ours. Instead, she was in the back of the classroom, watching Cort water Dr. F's dumb Venus flytrap as if it were the most fascinating thing she'd ever seen.

Did she know what I'd done? Was this her countermove? Was I going to have to find my own replacement friend from among the other dorks? I looked around the room at my classmates whom I'd already begun viewing with the eyes of a normal kid. I suddenly understood why they found us so repulsive: We were loud and sure of ourselves, we got jokes that should have only been understood by adults, we snorted when we laughed, we had squeaky voices, we liked wizards and dragons and robots and elves, we had ideas for plays to direct and thoughts on how to make the world a better place. We were weird, awkward, self-conscious, and strange. We were total freaks.

And I was one of them.

As I was thinking of what a terrible mistake I'd made coming to Peterson, thinking of how alone I felt, how lost, the worst possible thing happened: Lea looked up at me and smiled. I knew at once that I'd made a terrible mistake.

I smiled back weakly, then stumbled backward out of the room and into the hallway. I stood there for a few seconds, then ran to the bathroom, locked myself in a stall, and threw up my Salisbury steak, mashed potatoes, and peas. All of a sudden, I wished that my parents were religious the way crazy Cort's were instead of "spiritual" like my mom and an asshole like my father. But because my father always said he'd believe in God when Democrats stopped bleeding him dry and my mother learned to cook, I didn't know what to do in this kind of situation. I just sat there in the stall with my arms around my knees and whispered the lines to my favorite songs slowly and softly enough that they began to sound like prayers.

Overcome for the first time in my life with anything remotely resembling guilt, I picked myself up off the floor, pulled myself together, and stumbled back to class. Luckily for me and for Lea, the Depeche Mode song was right about God and his sick sense of humor. Of course, the thing about a sick sense of humor is that even though most of the time the joke is on you, every once in a while he lets you in on it. Because while the rumors about Lea might have haunted her (and me) for the rest of elementary school, fate stepped in and chose another victim.

Later that afternoon, in gym class, Craig Carbone broke his leg. No one knew exactly how it happened, but things with him and Justin Capirchio were never quite the same after that, so some of us suspected foul play.

As he lay on the cement, writhing in pain, we knew he

was dying. We'd never seen a boy who wasn't our brothers cry like that, so we knew it was serious. The Catholic and therefore guilt-ridden among us wondered if they'd somehow played a role and the rest of us were just happy it hadn't happened to us so soon before summer vacation.

When he came back the next week, a bright red cast on his foot and a scowling attitude which was clearly affected to overcompensate for his tears, no one admitted that they'd secretly hoped for his death. See, as much as we all liked Craig, the breaking of his leg was the most exciting thing that had ever happened to us; his death would have given us something to talk about for the rest of our lives.

Instead, our talk was short-lived and revolved around where we were when Craig broke his leg, what we did afterward, how we coped as we waited for the prognosis. It was, however, the kind of monumental event that trumped all other news of the day, a kind of foreshadowing of the O.J. Simpson car chase that created the twenty-four-hour news cycle a few years later.

Summer came and went, and by the start of sixth grade Craig's leg had completely healed and Lea had gotten her period for real, as had half the girls in our class.

And so we waited patiently for someone else to bleed.

nothing else matters

SHAWN

About an hour into the reception, the strange thought occurs to me that thanks to Alex's little baggie and the halfway decent music I'm actually having a good time. As I walk back from the bathroom, the DJ is playing some techno remix of The Cure's "Lovesong" which would no doubt sound terrible in real life but sounds *amazing* now. I'm seriously debating joining Dan and Lea and their college friends on the dance floor, when the DJ inexplicably decides to slow things down. Before the lyrics to "Nothing Else Matters" even begin, I start to feel my eyes tear up.

I would so never admit this to anyone, but rock ballads make me cry. And not just the moderately cool ones like "Unforgiven," "November Rain," and "Patience"; I'm talking "Faithfully" or "Heaven" or, if I'm feeling particularly lame, "The Wind of Change."

I immediately turn around and head straight for the bathroom, wiping my eyes with my shirtsleeve and shaking my head at what a wuss I am. It's not even like this song means anything to me. All that hair-band crap, all the crescendos and tacky makeup and tight pants that went with it, that was my brother Kyle's music, that was what was blasting up from his subterranean bedroom that he prohibited me from entering as soon as he hit puberty.

Before he got to high school, he never seemed to mind when I was around, but then one day he moved all his stuff out of the room we'd shared for years and into the basement, just like when Greg Brady got the attic or Mike Seaver set up his bachelor pad above the garage. But what bothered me wasn't the move per se—the bunk bed's replacement with a twin, the newfound closet space—it was that as his stuff vanished from my room, so too did he from my life, which might not have been so bad if our dad hadn't just pulled the same disappearing act on our entire family a few months before.

I figured it was because Kyle hated me or was embarrassed of me or blamed me for my father taking off for Florida with his new girlfriend, all of which I could understand since I felt the same way about myself. I'd eventually find out that I was wrong, that Kyle's disappearance from my life had nothing to do with me—nothing at all.

But not until it was too late.

The day everything became clear, or at least a little less cloudy, all the gifted kids had been pulled out of the stock-market game with Dr. Falcone for our weekly DARE class, where we'd learn all about our brains on drugs—Any questions?—from a city police officer whose portly stature did nothing to dispel the rumors of his kind's addiction to Dunkin' Donuts.

As we filed into our regular classroom, the one where we spent most of our time yet still felt like outsiders, the normal kids groaned at our arrival, not because they disliked us outright but because our teachers had a terrible habit of making a big deal out of us, of holding us up as exemplary, of singling us out. And so the normals took their frustration, spurred on by large class size, burnt-out and underpaid teachers, and undiagnosed learning disabilities out on us, though it affected some of us more than others. It was bad enough for Erik Manzelli and Jessica Patterson who embraced their geekiness, playing Dungeons & Dragons on the bus, at lunch, and during recess—either lacking a full understanding of the consequences of rolling the twenty-sided die or possessing a brave and foolish disregard for them.

It was bad enough for Steve Wood and Tina Ngyuen, whose ethnicities gave the kids who'd been raised racist by their parents double ammunition—but then, not only did most of us recognize the stupidity of racism, we also saw how frequently the racist kids suffered from head lice and ringworm so we were, needless to say, not only wary of such beliefs but also of the holders of them. When asked how she dealt with assholes like Lou DaSilva, Tina would calmly explain that her parents' stories of life under the Khmer Rouge were, you know, worse. And we would have asked Steve the same question but we already knew the coping mechanism he'd been forced to adopt since his Waterloo, the premiere of *Family Matters* on TGIF and with it the arrival of the quintessential black nerd Steve Urkel: silence.

It was bad enough for me, who'd just had the word *faggot* added to my vocabulary after classmates had applied it to my manner of walking, my decision to avoid Hypercolor T-shirts and Z. Cavariccis, and my refusal to taint my crisp enunciation with misuse of the letter *r*—I'd gotten my ass kicked so many times that my brother wouldn't even look at me anymore—but even then, I knew I was smarter than every last one of them, so it didn't bother me much.

I won't say that it was worse for Danny and Ben, who were the only ones who'd been enrolled at Peterson since kindergarten, who'd gone there for four years before its population was split into gifted and non-, who knew there was nothing particularly special or mysterious about Peterson or the gifted program, just that the school was the only one in the western district that harbored an extra classroom and a teacher with a PhD, particularly suited for meeting the needs of smart children. But I will say that the taunts from our classmates, the Fruit Wrinkles, kickballs, and sucked-on Jolly Ranchers being hurled at us from the Four Square courts, surprised the two in a way that didn't surprise the rest of us.

See, they'd been just like all the other kids at Peterson— until they weren't. The rest of us were aliens, and as soon as we'd landed, the normal kids would defend their territory and do whatever was in their power to destroy us. But Ben and Danny must have seemed like weak-livered hosts who'd allowed their bodies to be invaded, who'd allowed their minds to be snatched and replaced with bigger, better models, but most important, who'd figured out a way to teleport themselves out of regular class every third day and into a classroom with brightly colored tables instead of desks, two gerbils, and a Venus flytrap.

The ones who took it hardest, though, were Lea and Alex. Their low self-esteem and need for socialization was both cultural (they were Italian) and biological (they were girls), which meant their desire for social acceptance was much stronger than the rest of ours. It was painful to watch them pass note after note to the popular girls on the days that we joined the normal kids in their classroom lessons, knowing full well that they'd never be invited to any of the roller-skating or rock 'n' bowl parties.

The only one who wandered through it all unscathed was Cort, who seemed so oblivious to the hierarchy that was already establishing itself in the lunchroom, at recess, in class, that we all secretly wondered whether she shouldn't have been shipped to a school that had a special-ed program instead.

And, oh yes, there was Jason, but he, as always, was in a category all his own.

Mrs. Kennedy told the class to calm down, which they did immediately because Mrs. Kennedy looked like Bruce Willis in a curly gray wig, and we all streamed in. Lea began walking toward an open seat next to Jenna Tessitore, but she was no match for Alex, who had crossed diagonally across desks to get there first. As Alex took her seat, Jenna smiled politely, but a second later turned her back to Alex and passed a triangle-shaped note to Megan Brown.

Erik and Jessica slinked to the back and I wondered if they cast D&D spells on all of us or just the normal kids, Tina smiled upon noticing a spot next to Emily Dunn, who was either too nice or too dull to treat any of us cruelly, Cort floated in quietly, Steve held his head almost high enough to make us think he didn't hear the Urkel snorts, and Jason found a chair up front and dropped his bookbag so purposely and loudly that everyone in the room jumped. Jason gave them all a look that said, Don't think I won't fucking cut you, and even the toughest of the normal kids, Dylan Iacobucci, averted his eyes. Feeling less nervous now that Jason had established his superiority or, perhaps more accurately, his volatility, I found an empty seat and smiled weakly at him. He gave me a silent nod then turned around to face the chalkboard.

I did the same, and saw that this time, our friendly neighborhood policeman was not alone. There were three teenagers standing next to him, my brother's best friend, Wayne, among them. Wayne had long greasy hair like my brother's, but unlike Kyle he was ugly and fat and maybe even a little retarded. As usual, Wayne looked bored and mildly confused, at least he did until he saw me. When he did, his eyes widened, then he blinked and I wondered what my brother had told him about me.

—So today, class, DARE's going to be a little different. We're going to break you up into groups so you can ask some teenagers firsthand how they successfully deal with drug-related peer pressure.

Mrs. Kennedy told us to split up into our reading groups, which we did more successfully than usual, not surprising considering that there was a cop in the room.

Wayne began walking to the direct opposite side of the room from where my reading group, the Sharks, had gathered, but Officer Ruggieri pulled him back and said something to the three teenagers that we couldn't hear. He then pointed the girls toward the Eels and the Stingrays and guided the shoulders of a reluctant-looking Wayne toward my group.

When Wayne joined us, he looked unsure of whether to sit like us or stay standing; he looked to his fellow DARE counselors for guidance, one girl fat and sluggish, the other petite and loud. The loud girl was standing, the fat girl was sitting, and Wayne ultimately decided on a hybrid of the two actions, pulling a desk toward him with an eardrum-shattering screech and leaning up against it in a cross-armed pose.

–So what do you want to know?

–How'd you get stuck doing this? Jason asked, and everyone laughed.

–I . . . I didn't get stuck . . . Wayne said. I, like, wanna be here, okay?

–*Okay*, Jason said, mimicking Wayne's voice perfectly and laughing. I laughed too, in spite of myself, amazed that someone from my world could one-up someone from my brother's.

Then Wayne leaned over conspiratorially and admitted, Plus, if you do this, you get an extra study hall.

–Have you ever done drugs? Jessica asked, clearly annoyed that Jason was trying to take things off track.

–No way, said Wayne, a little too quickly. Drugs are . . . they're not my thing.

–Has anyone ever offered you drugs? Like . . . a *pusher*? Jessica said.

–Nooo, Wayne said slowly. But look, guys, um, it's not like when you get to junior high all of a sudden there are going to be . . . uh, *pushers*, like, lurking around every corner. That's not really how it works.

–How *does* it work? said Ben.

–I don't know. I guess people get drugs from their friends or whatever.

–What kind of drugs? said Jessica, furiously taking notes. Uppers? *Ludes*?

Wayne laughed. I don't think people do ludes anymore.

–Oh, said Jessica, clearly disappointed.

–What *do* they do, said Ben.

–Oh. Um . . . well . . . Wayne looked uncomfortable. I don't think that's, like, what I'm supposed to be talking about today. I'm here to talk about peer pressure.

–Well, I don't see how you're an authority on peer pressure when you just said you've never been offered drugs, said Jason.

–Yeah, said Ben. That's right! You suck at this.

Jessica raised her hand and started waving it in order to catch Officer Ruggieri's attention. When he didn't seem to notice, she called out, We want another peer counselor. Ours is no good.

At that the class went wild. Craig Carbone chimed in on behalf of the Eels, Ours isn't any good either. She told us she *never* experienced peer pressure.

The loud girl looked ready to cry.

–Same with ours, said Ben.

A bunch of kids started talking at once until Mrs. Kennedy spoke up. Class! All of you! I am Embarrassed, no . . . she said, I am Disgusted, and as soon as she spoke these words we were amazed to find ourselves equally Embarrassed and Disgusted.

–These young adults have taken time from their busy

high-school schedules, she continued, to help you understand how to better prepare yourself for junior high and all you can do is—

–That's not why he's here, Mrs. Kennedy, said Jason quietly. He even told us so. He said he's just here to get an extra study hall.

A few kids started to laugh, but most of us knew better, leaving those who lacked self-control red-faced and bashful. Officer Ruggieri frowned, but Mrs. Kennedy went on, I don't care why he's here, Mr. Lane. While he's here, you'll listen to him. *Now*, she added, and went back to talking to Officer Ruggieri.

–Thanks a lot, Wayne said to Jason.

–My pleasure, he said.

After about ten more minutes of torturing our peer counselors, Mrs. Kennedy informed us that our time was up but that, as a result of our disrespectful and immature behavior, we were all to write a two-page essay about a time when we'd experienced peer pressure. Everyone groaned, and Craig punched Ben in the shoulder because he was too scared to do the same thing to Jason, who was already out the door anyway.

I began collecting my stuff when Wayne walked over to me.

–Hey, Shawn.

–Hey, Wayne. Sorry about . . . all that.

–Oh, we're, you know, used to that. Whatever. He stood there for a moment without saying anything.

–Wayne?

–Yeah?

–Do you, like, want something?

–Oh, right. No. I mean, yeah. I mean, I don't, but I'm, I don't know, hanging out with your brother after school today. You need a ride home?

I didn't want to spend any more time than I had to with Wayne, but I wasn't going to pass up an opportunity to hang with the brother who'd become nothing more than a ghost these last few months.

–Uh, yeah, but I have my bike.

–That's cool, he said. I can fit it in my trunk.

–Okay, I said, unsure of why someone who'd once submitted me to a form of torture he'd dubbed "fag-tying," which involved wrapping me up in a blanket, tying up the ends with a bungee cord, and tossing me over his shoulder all the while shrieking "Seeew-eeeee, little faggie, seeew-eeeee," was now being so nice to me.

After I unlocked my bike and wheeled it over to Wayne's Pontiac, he lifted it up and put it into the trunk. It stuck out a little, so he used a bungee cord (likely the same one that had once held me captive) to secure the hatch shut.

Wayne didn't say much on the first few minutes of the drive, so I started fiddling with the radio knob. I stopped on WBRU because "Every Day Is Like Sunday" was playing, but as soon as I did Wayne lifted his hand from the wheel and slammed his hand down on the radio in a move intended to shut it off, but which only switched it to AM. I turned it off for him.

–All right, Shawn, let's not dick around here, he said. You're not gonna rat me out, are you?

–Huh? I said. What are you talking about? Rat you out for what?

He snorted. Don't play stupid, Shawn. You know that I work for your brother. He stared at me.

–The baseball-card business? I said. I thought he gave up on that.

–Not baseball cards, fuckface, I'm talking about his *other* business. Don't act like you don't know what I'm talking about.

–But I don't!

–Whatever. But if you rat on me, you're going to get your brother busted too, you know? And what would your poor mom think about that?

–Whatever, Wayne, I said. I'm not going to rat on you, okay?

Mainly because I still had no idea what he was talking about.

–Good. I'm glad we understand each other.

We pulled up to my house, but instead of parking in the drive, Wayne just stopped the car and kept it running.

–Aren't you coming in?

Wayne laughed. No, I'm not coming in, he said, slowly and deliberately, I supposed, in an attempt to mimic my speech the way Jason had mimicked his earlier. That was my cover, dumbass. See? He said, tapping his head. Smarter than you think.

–Yeah, sure, whatever, Wayne, I said. I stepped out of the car and slammed the door.

I started walking toward the house when I realized my

bike was still in his trunk. Fuck! I turned around, but Wayne had already screeched around the corner and there was no way I was running after him like a little bitch. After all, I knew he was too scared of my brother to fuck with it, and I also knew that no matter how shady my brother had been acting lately, he would never side with a loser like Wayne over me. No one was home, so I pulled the spare key from the fake rock on the side of the house and let my-self in. I thought about everything Wayne had said that af-ternoon. What were he and my brother involved in? I tried to imagine in what capacity my brother could be employ-ing Wayne. I knew about Kyle's failed entrepreneurial ef-forts: the landscaping business that folded when he nicked the tail of Mrs. Mederios's cat with a lawn mower, the time he stocked up on about fifty complete sets of Topps base-ball cards so he could sell off the MVPs at a profit (he only later discovered that for every Keith Hernandez, there were about fifty players as desirable as Rey Quiñones).

I walked over to the basement door and knocked quietly but received no reply. My brother had padlocked the door, a gesture my mother expressed displeasure with, but only halfheartedly—she was so scared that we'd ask to go and live with our father which would mean she'd have to pass along the devastating news that he didn't exactly . . . technically . . . *want us*, that those days all disapproval was halfhearted.

Luckily, I knew of another way in. There was a small window in the basement which didn't lock. I knew this because back when my dad still lived with us, he'd made a sorry attempt to transform the basement into a rec room by hauling an old couch and TV down there. Every weekend I'd wake up at six and race downstairs to watch TV, the seizure-inducing Japanese cartoons, the weird live-action shows from the '70s like *H.R. Pufnstuf* with the shaggy monsters and the talking flute, even the stupid religious ones like *Davey and Goliath*; I can still see the light from that window reflecting on the TV as my brother and I watched *The Smurfs*.

I walked outside and around to the side of the house where Kyle's room was. Sure enough, the window opened with a slight push. I knew I was skinny enough to get in so I looked over my shoulder to make sure no one was watching, then slid in.

The room had deteriorated since the last time I'd seen it. There was a funny smell I couldn't place and no real furniture, just piles of clothes that seemed to take the place of chairs, love seats, couches. On the table, there was a pack of cigarettes, shredded tobacco, a soda can with a blackened lid. There were cigarette butts too, some with filters, some without. A wire hanger with some black tar on the end of it sat on the table. It all looked familiar and I tried to figure out why, when I realized that what I was seeing was the same drug paraphernalia we'd learned about in DARE.

Was my brother a . . . *pusher*? It would explain a lot—the red eyes, the padlock, the long-haired guys with their slutty-looking girlfriends coming in whenever my mom was working the late shift.

I had to find out for sure, though, so I started looking around. On the floor, there were broken cassette tapes with their insides unraveled, like they'd been gutted and disembowled; on the walls, posters, one of a sweaty Lars Ulrich, another of two girls in bikinis flanking Tommy Lee and Nikki Sixx, and an endless assortment of Day-Glo skulls, bloody crosses, thorny roses. Kyle's bed was unmade, dirty boxer shorts and moldy looking towels crumpled up under the sheets. But no signs of any actual drugs, none that I could detect.

I walked over to the closet in the corner and opened the door, fearing what would be inside. I saw more of Kyle's clothes and piles of our forgotten toys: Transformers and GoBots, He-Men and G.I. Joes, Matchbox cars and Tonka trucks. And something else—a safe. Was that where he kept his . . . *narcotics*?

I sat there staring at the safe for a long time, and it might have been longer if I wasn't interrupted by the sounds of sirens and breaking glass, by someone—a cop!— commanding, Don't move, and another pointing a gun at me—a gun!

–But it's my house, I said.

–Then why were you breaking in? the first cop shouted. We got a call from your next-door neighbor.

Mrs. Mederios—I should have known. She was old, mean, and half-blind, and both her husband and the last of her cats had recently died, leaving her bored and restless. The second her soaps go off air, she probably whips out the binoculars.

–Because my brother wouldn't . . . I started to explain. But they weren't listening. The cop with the gun had found something, something that looked a lot like one of the pipes we'd learned about in DARE.

–Check this out, Ed, he said to the cop standing next to me. Looks like we have reasonable cause to search this place.

–Is this what you were looking for, son? Ed the cop asked.

–No, I . . . No! I swear. I just . . . my brother . . . he didn't do anything wrong, officers.

The policemen looked at the safe in front of me and then at each other.

–I think we're going to take this down to the station for evidence, the cop who was not Ed said.

–No, please . . . really. It's not what you think, I said.

–If I were you, son, I wouldn't say anything until we get ahold of your parents.

–But . . .

–It's for the best, trust me.

I let Ed handcuff me and lead me up the stairs of my own house while the other cop hoisted the safe above his left shoulder and patted it with his right hand. They'd already bashed in the door to Kyle's basement and the front door of our house. My mom was going to kill me, if Kyle didn't do so first. I imagined I heard helicopters flying overhead, like in that show *Cops*. I'm ashamed to say that it felt kind of cool.

Before Ed could lead me head-first into the car like I knew they did to criminals on *COPS*, I heard the rumbling that could only be my brother's Pinto. I looked up as he pulled into the driveway, Metallica blasting from his crappy speakers.

–What the fuck, he said, after opening the door and slamming it.

–Do you live here, young man?

–Yes, I live here. Kyle pulled his wallet out of his back pocket and showed his license. What the hell's going on?

–We found this kid breaking in.

Kyle started laughing. Breaking in? He's my fuck . . . He's my brother.

Then Kyle saw the safe and stopped laughing. Officer, I'm not going to press charges on my brother for breaking into my room.

–About that room . . . said Ed, holding in the hand that wasn't gripping mine the pipe they'd found downstairs.

Kyle turned away from the cops and to the safe and then back to me. It's for tobacco, he said, glaring at me.

–Then I suppose you won't mind us checking this safe, would you?

–No, Kyle said, I wouldn't. The officers put the safe down on the ground and one of them pulled out a key-chain when Kyle said, Don't bother, and handed them a key off the chain hanging from one of his belt loops.

The officers bent down and unlocked the safe and I took in a deep breath, expecting it to be full of crack vials and angel dust and PCP and amyl nitrate and ethyl alcohol and all the other things we'd learned about in DARE.

But when they opened the safe, the only thing inside was a stack of *Penthouse* and a small worn teddy bear that I knew my father had given Kyle years before because he'd given the same one to me. The cops started laughing and then patted my brother on the back.

–I believe you have to be eighteen to buy those kinds of magazines, son, Ed said.

–And at least twenty-one for the teddy bear, said the other.

–Jay, let's get out of here. They're just kids.

Ed looked at us and shook his head. We'll be keeping our eyes on you from here on in. As he said this he pointed two fingers at his two eyes, then pointed them back at us. We nodded and watched as they climbed into their car.

–We're keeping this, said Jay, palming the pipe.

After they'd driven away, we just stood there. Kyle didn't say anything for a long time, so I broke the silence.

–Boy, Kyle, that was a close one, huh?

–*Don't* . . . don't fucking talk to me, okay? he said, turning his back on me and walking to the house. And don't you ever touch my stuff again . . . ever, he said.

I nodded, even though he couldn't see me do so, and I followed him back to the house, even though I shouldn't have. I should have kept my distance because if I had then I might not have heard what he mumbled under his breath before stepping inside the house and slamming the door in my face.

–Fucking Christ, he said . . . fucking little *faggot*.

send me
an angel

ALEX

I'm about to break into the last of my bags when it hits me.

The second boy I ever kissed is married and the first one is dead.

But the thing is, I'm not even sure which is worse. I mean, it's terrible about Jason and all, but it was, like, years ago, and really, I've had some time to make peace with it. We all have. And anyway, you never feel anything the first time. At least I didn't.

It wasn't love.

It was just, like, experimentation. The first time is practice, prelude. It's the second time that counts, the second time that matters, the second time you'll never forget.

The second one, the married one, would have been my first kiss, if I hadn't been such a chicken, if I hadn't been worried about my Dorito breath, if I hadn't been searching deep into his eyes for confirmation that he didn't want to kiss me, until eventually I found it, or imagined it, as if any of that matters now that he's out there dancing with Lea to their song—except, the thing is, they don't even remember that it's their song. Only I know because it should have been our song.

There's someone knocking on the bathroom door, at first politely, but louder now and I'm starting to think that if I don't open the door soon she's going to break the fucking thing in. How long have I been in here anyway? I don't know. Don't care, really.

I spend a lot of time in bathrooms and, no, not just for

the reason you think; it doesn't matter whether you're in here to powder your nose or adjust your push-up bra, the bathroom is escape, an escape from everything, an escape from anything—the song you don't like, the conversation that isn't going anywhere, the loser who doesn't seem to get it that he is *way* uglier than you and has no business even talking to you, let alone getting your number.

But mostly, I guess, it *is* for the reason you think, even though I hate that stupid cliché, despise the girls slinking into stalls in twos and threes, no fucking concept of discretion. I, like, rarely do drugs in clubs or bars anymore, tell myself it's because I don't need to, but really it's just because I like to have something to look forward to after escaping from yet another lame night.

For some reason I'm thinking of that sad girl at the Dark Room the other night, standing just outside the stall I was trying to step into because, unlike everyone else in the room, I actually had to pee. I asked her if she was in line when another girl stepped out, sniffing and snuffling and talking gibberish—do I sound like that? No way do I sound like that. That's not drug-stupid, that's stupid-stupid—and the sad girl, like, didn't even notice how revolting and weak the girl coming out of the bathroom was, clearly she didn't because otherwise she wouldn't have asked me if I knew where she could find a little *fun*. I mean, who *does* that? Um, helllooo, that's what dealers are for. Like someone's going to just give you blow out of the goodness of her heart. Like even if she *did*, it would be any good. And anyway, you stupid sad bitch, this is not *fun*, I think, my legs shaking as I try to steady the credit card in my lap before I lean down and do three more lines.

There's the knock again. Hold on a second! I scream, as if whoever's out there is going to hear me through the mostly soundproof door. I stand up and flush the toilet for effect, forgetting that I don't need to, seeing as my movement over the last few moments has caused the fucking sensor to go off four fucking times and as I just fucking mentioned, the fucking door is fucking soundproof. I feel momentarily guilty for this—that on top of all my other asshole moves tonight, I have also wasted an obscene amount of water. But that's what I do; I waste things: water, friendships, the lives of innocent victims destroyed by narcotraffic. I grab my bag and push open the door, nearly knocking over a little old lady in a brocade dress.

—Sorry I took so long, I say sheepishly, trying to hold in my sniff until she's shut the door.

—Oh, don't worry about it, sweetie. I take it you had the mussels too, she says, holding her stomach, scooting in the stall, slamming the door behind her.

I plop my bag down on the marble countertop, squinting my eyes so I don't have to take in a full view of my crackhead self in the terrible lighting. But, slowly, I open them all the way and am surprised to see that I actually look pretty good despite the fact that my hair is a bit more reminiscent of Ally Sheedy circa *The Breakfast Club* than I'd like. It's the drugs looking, I know, but I'll take what I can get. I blow my nose, make sure there's no powder underneath it, put on some lip gloss, and step away from the mirror, just in time to escape from getting stuck.

Anyway, the worst is over, I tell myself. The bachelorette party and the penis paraphernalia galore that nobody except me seemed to realize were symbols of female oppression. The vows that I just know came straight out of overpriced books with puke pink covers and titles like *Forever Feelings* and *Her Special Day*. The endless rounds of pictures to memorialize the latest installment of the timeless surrender to patriarchal law—like, let's have one of the bridesmaids admiring the ring! Awesome! And then Lea going totally postal on me for ruining her day or whatever, like it's my fault her mom's dead.

The worst is over, I tell myself, because I don't have to see them anymore after this. I can just fade out of their lives, just like I'd been trying to do before they yanked me back in. I can just slink out the back door, just like I've been doing my entire life. I can just leave the two of them to each other and disappear forever.

Because *that's* love.

I loved Danny O'Shaughnessy so much that when the bottle he spun landed pointing at my purple double-tongued Reeboks that hot June day at Erika Andrade's birthday party, I let him off the hook. I wrinkled up my nose and said I didn't want to kiss him. And he wrinkled up his nose and said that's good because he didn't want to kiss me either. We both sighed and looked relieved, although I felt anything but.

I did want to kiss him, like, so bad. But not here, not now. Not after all those Doritos. Not with my hair still wet from the pool, not when my mom was coming to pick me up at 8:00. Not in skanky Erika Andrade's rec room, on her birthday, with her watching me like a hawk because everyone knew she liked Danny and that he was off-limits. Danny knew it too, knew it was time for him to be Erika's boyfriend. It was his turn. It was understood. It was part of a system that you simply didn't question.

He had just broken up with Alaina Santucci and it was understood that after a boy broke up with Alaina Santucci, the next in succession was Erika Andrade. The same thing had happened with Billy O'Shea, Dylan Iacobucci, and Mike Dean. Erika wasn't pretty like Alaina, but she was popular due to her big boobs and pool, especially now that summer was here. It was only right.

By sixth grade a lot of these kinds of rules had started popping up, rules that I understood were not to be questioned without fully understanding why. Like the way you were suddenly supposed to start hating boys unless one of them happened to be your boyfriend that week. Or the way you were supposed to know who it was okay to gossip about—like Gina San Pietro, who had hairy arms, or Doug Paolucci, who still sucked his thumb. Or the way you knew who was popular: girls who wore makeup and didn't wear glasses, guys with dimples or green eyes, anyone who wasn't too good at school or too bad at sports. Or the way us gifted kids existed outside the system; no matter how hard we tried, what intricate schemes we plotted, we generally weren't considered for popularity, and we certainly didn't have a chance to be boyfriends or girlfriends with anyone else—all of us, that is, except for Danny, who had been accepted as popular for three reasons: his dimples, his green eyes, and because by the end of the sixth grade Erika and Alaina had run out of boyfriends.

–Well, I guess since it's my birthday, that means it's my turn, said Erika, her eyes on Danny, who was shifting uncomfortably on a purple beanbag that was losing some of its stuffing.

Erika grabbed the root beer bottle from me and placed it on the ground. She closed her eyes and took a deep breath and then spun. The bottle twirled around four or five times before landing in front of Lea. As Lea's tanned face turned bright red, Erika pouted and began to pick up the bottle to spin again. Then Craig Carbone spoke up.

–No do-overs. You gotta kiss Lea.

–I'm not kissing a girl; that's the rules.

–Actually, the rule is, you gotta kiss whoever it lands on. Boy or girl, said Danny, smirking. You could tell he was enjoying his final moments of pre-Erika freedom.

–I didn't see you kissing Alex.

–That's different. Alex and me have been friends since we were babies; it would be too weird.

–Yeah, I said, pleased that Danny considered me his lifelong friend. It was true, though. Our mothers went to the same hair salon, Destinies, so every Friday when we were kids, Danny and I were forced to sit in the corner of the salon, where whichever hairdresser was taking a break would give us free shampoos and let us make castles out of the Velcro curlers.

–Fine, whatever. I'll kiss a gifted geek. It's not like I wanted to invite you anyway, Lea. My mom made me.

Lea ignored the comment, holding her head high as she leaned in to kiss Erika's piggy face. She closed her eyes, offered up a quick peck on the lips, and then pulled away, wiping her lips on the back of her hand. Erika did the same and everyone giggled.

Then Lea took the bottle and spun. Not only was Lea the prettiest and smartest girl at Peterson, she was also the most graceful, so simply by flicking the bottle lightly with her index finger, it spun around so fast that the bottle became a circle. As the spinning slowed down and the bottle began to resemble a bottle again, it passed Alaina, then me, then Craig Carbone, then Erika, until it came to a halt in front of Danny O'Shaughnessy.

No.

No. No. No. No. No.

I bit my bottom lip, my tongue registering that it was not as chapped as I had previously believed; still, it lacked that Lip Smacker sweetness that I knew Lea's possessed, since she was an obsessive lip-gloss collector. My own lips were plain pink lips, a little thin, lips that might as well have belonged to a boy.

Contrary to what Craig and Danny had said, it was perfectly acceptable to walk away from the bottle. Kids did it all the time; it was understood. Some of us weren't ready for the things that happened at parties that went past

7:00. Sure, it was summer, but even though 7:00 wasn't as late in June as it was in February, the things that went on at 7:00 parties were simply not the same things that happened at 4:00 parties.

To some of us, parties still meant swimming in the backyard, wiffleball in the street, pretzels and greasy potato chips in little baskets protected by paper napkins with pictures of flowers or apples or American flags printed on them, bottles of Coke and Sprite and Fanta—and cream soda if you were lucky—all of it set down on checkered plastic tablecloths, a plate full of brownies with a crinkly layer on top, and if the household was Italian, which it usually was, or if there was an Italian kid invited, which there always was, there'd be Calvito's pizza strips and maybe a Crock-Pot of sausage and peppers and some wine biscuits and wandies for dessert.

To others, it meant this. Spin the Bottle, Truth or Dare, Seven Minutes in Heaven, and a whole host of other games invented purely for the purpose of sharing saliva with our fellow classmates. But surely Lea and Danny knew things were moving too fast. It was one thing to kiss Erika on the side of the mouth just to shut her up, but a boy-girl kiss was way too much for two gifted kids who already knew basic trigonometry and whose parents made them wear plaid and . . .

And then it happened. Their shocked looks slowly gave way to smiles, and I realized they were going to do it. I couldn't watch. I stood up silently so that no one would notice me leaving, but then again, I doubt anyone really noticed I was there in the first place. I grabbed my sweat-shirt and walked outside, careful not to let the adults smoking on the back patio see me. The yard looked like a festive jungle; it was easy to hide behind the grapevine trellises adorned with little plastic lanterns in primary and secondary colors. As I stepped outside, I heard the last few strains of the dance song "Send Me an Angel." I couldn't believe it was on; you never heard songs like that anymore, now that everyone was into MC Hammer and Vanilla Ice.

The first time I heard it was with my brother. He'd come into my room because he'd seen strange lights outside and was afraid ET had landed, like, for real this time. I grabbed his hand and walked him to the window and saw that it was just faraway spotlights from one of those Italian festivals I was prohibited from attending as a child because my mother's crackpot psychic, Ramona, told her I had a dark green aura and was therefore not strong enough to resist the temptations of the night.

I told Stephen there was nothing to be worried about, but just as I did the song came on with its ghostly vocals and Stephen asked if I believed in ghosts and I hesitated for a moment, listened to the lyrics, and said, Stephen, it's not a song about ghosts, it's about angels, and then he asked me if I believed in angels and, this time, I didn't hesitate.

–No, I said.

But look at me now, I thought, as I crouched down next to Erika's house. Here I am at a party facing Ramona's "temptations of the night" head on and *I'm* the ghost, peeking through the basement window and noticing that

Lea and Danny are holding hands and I have no idea how I let that happen because maybe Danny would have been holding my hand now if I hadn't been such a chicken.

I stayed there for a while, until the adults cleared the soda bottles and paper plates off the white plastic table. I was about to sneak back inside when I heard something. It was coming from the Andrades' pool house and it sounded like laughter. When the adults left the patio, I made my move and walked over to the small cabin decorated with more of the colored lanterns, the way so many Italian and Portuguese houses in this neighborhood were, as if every summer day were Christmas. Even though a lot of us were Italian too, people in my neighborhood, which was farther west, thought this kind of thing was really tacky. I opened the screen door, and ran inside without even checking what was in there first.

Even though it was dark, I knew I was standing in a kitchen. I could hear the buzz of a refrigerator and just make out the outline of a sink and small oven.

–Who is it, a voice whispered.

–Alex, I said. Alex Rossi.

–Oh, cool. Cool, it's only Alex. We're in the bathroom. Straight ahead.

The voice sounded familiar, but I couldn't place it. Who's we? I said as I traced the countertop with my fingers so that I wouldn't fall flat on my face. As I opened the door to what could only be the bathroom and peered inside, a cigarette lighter illuminated two faces: Shawn Riley and Jason Lane.

–What are you guys doing here?

−This. Shawn said and raised up a dark red bottle and added, Mr. Andrade's home-brewed port.

−Like, I didn't even know you guys were invited.

−*Like*, we weren't, Jason said. Then he laughed. Which is the only reason we decided to come.

−You want some of this? Shawn held up the bottle. I didn't say yes, but I didn't say no either, so he held the bottle out for me. I was skeptical about becoming too friendly with Shawn and Jason since they were definitely weird. The good girls in '80s movies I tried so hard not to emulate *always* had weird best friends, but then I decided that Shawn and Jason weren't Dungeons & Dragons weird but troublemaking weird, which was a lot more appealing. I accepted the bottle and took a tentative sip. I'd never had wine before, but I always figured that since it was made from grapes it would taste a little like Fanta without the fizz. But it tasted more like the rubbing alcohol that I put on my earrings to keep my ears from getting infected.

−Gross, I said.

−It's better with a cigarette, said Shawn, and then he took a Virginia Slim from a crumpled-up pack, lit it, inhaled, coughed, and handed it to me. I took them from my mom, he said. She buys them by the carton so she'll never notice that one's missing.

−You guys are gonna get soooo busted. Have you been in here the whole time?

−Oh, don't be such a baby. Nobody knows we're here.

−I'm not being a baby, I just . . . oh whatever, give it here. I took it from him and put it in the corner of my mouth the way I'd seen my mom do when my dad wasn't home and Shawn told me I had to suck it real hard and I said, I know that, asshole, and then I took a puff and held it in and almost immediately felt totally lightheaded and sick to my stomach. I crawled over closer to the boys and put my head in Shawn's lap.

–Do you have any breath mints? My mom's gonna be here soon, I said, and Shawn said, You know it, and gave me a Tic Tac, then I looked up at his violet eyes and I don't know if it was because I was, like, totally delirious or what but suddenly I wanted to kiss him instead of Danny.

–What are they doing in there anyway? Playing Ouija board? Light as a Feather?

–No, I said. Spin the Bottle.

–Oh, he said. Well, then, maybe we should play Spin the Bottle since that's what all the cool kids are doing.

–There aren't enough of us, I said hesitantly.

–Sure there are. All you need is two and we've got three.

–Um. Okay, I said, thinking that now was my chance to kiss Shawn, which was cool, especially now that my Dorito breath had been washed away by the wine and the cigarettes.

Jason grabbed one of the wine bottles, said, I'll go first, and then he spun it and it landed on Shawn, and the three of us started laughing and Shawn said, Do-over, and I said, No way, you two gotta kiss, and they both scrunched up their noses, and I said, Whatever, I'm not going to tell anyone. And then they did it anyway, and I was surprised that it wasn't actually a short peck like all the other kids inside had been giving each other but a real one and I felt a weird feeling in my stomach that wasn't painful but actually kind of good, and then they weren't kissing anymore and Shawn was spinning the bottle again. It landed on Jason again and we all laughed again, only maybe not so much this time, and they kissed again, only this time they didn't act like they didn't want to anymore and then I pulled them apart and said, All right, all right, it's my turn, and we all started laughing and Jason gave me the bottle and I wanted it to land on Shawn because he had prettier eyes but actually Jason wasn't bad either and it was then I realized that it doesn't matter what parties you get invited to, they were only cool if you found a way to make things happen yourself, and I was so glad I found the boys, even if they were weird, and when I spun the bottle it landed on Jason and I wasn't scared or sad about Lea and Danny anymore and I leaned forward and smelled the cigarettes on his breath and pushed my lips against his and then he pushed my lips open with his tongue and then our tongues were touching and I felt the weird feeling in my stomach again and then I felt a hand on my shoulder which wasn't Jason's because both of Jason's hands were on my hips, so it must have been Shawn's, which was okay too, and then I heard.

–Alex! Alex Rossi, are you out here? Your mom's here! I jumped up and without looking back I opened the doors to the pool house.

–What are you doing out there? I thought everyone had moved inside. Mrs. Andrade squinted her eyes to detect other signs of life in the pool house.

–I know, I said, I had to go to the bathroom.

–We have two bathrooms inside, said Mrs. Andrade. Why didn't you use one of them?

–I would have, I said, I just get a little . . . shy.

She smiled. I can understand that, she said. We just didn't know there were any kids out here.

–Oh, there are no other kids out here. Just me. I like my . . . privacy.

Mrs. Andrade laughed out loud. Well, don't we all? I can't blame a woman for wanting her privacy, she said, but next time, use the one upstairs.

I thanked Mrs. Andrade, who was way nicer than her skank of a daughter, and said good-bye. I sprinted down the driveway to my mom's car waiting out front, opened the door, and climbed into the passenger seat. When she asked me what happened at the party, I said nothing much, because really, it was nothing much.

Lea and Danny broke up over the summer because they lived too far away to get to each other's houses by bike, and before I knew it, he was dating Alaina again, a relationship that would last well into high school, and was still going strong at a party years later when I lured him into the bathroom with the promise of a joint. After we smoked it, I asked him how he could be going out with someone so skanky. By then I'd gained a confidence that can only come after you've gotten your braces removed. He shrugged and said, When she calls me, I just let her talk. Most of the time she doesn't even notice I'm playing video games. And I don't know, Alex, she lets me, you know . . .

–I don't want to know, I said. And then I kissed him. And he kissed me back. And this time, I knew exactly how to do it, and this time, I knew what the weird feeling in my stomach was, and this time . . .

–Danny O'Shaughnessy, where are you?

It was Alaina. I kissed Danny quickly on the cheek and he tried to grab my wrist but I was already half out the window that opened up into the backyard, and as I was running away I heard someone shriek, *There* you are. Have you been smoking *pot*, you dickfuck?

And as I rounded the corner to the front yard, I almost tripped over Jason, who was passed out in a pile of his own puke. He'd been doing that a lot lately; both him and Shawn had turned into total stoners. I guess I kind of had too, but the difference was, I wasn't failing classes and getting caught with pot in my locker and stuff.

I checked to see if he was breathing, and then I woke him up by slapping him on the face. Come on, I said, before someone finds you.

–Alex, he said, trying to stand up with my help. You look like an angel.

–If I'm an angel, Jason, then, boy, are we in trouble, I said, as he fell from my arms.

beat it

BEN

I'm so fucked. Seriously, I mean, what kind of best man leaves his speech in his hotel room? I'll tell you what kind: the worst kind. I am the worst man in the history of best men. I am so utterly not worthy to stand before Dan the man, Dan the groom, may he rest in peace till death do us part . . .

All of a sudden my thoughts are rudely interrupted by a sharp pain in my thigh. Good Christ! Why, it appears that someone has just poked my leg with a fork. It doesn't take me long to discover the source of the four-pronged attack: Alex. Well, well, well, isn't this an interesting turn of events? I mean, I might not have gone to a fancy school like NYU but I know phallic symbolism when it is thrust into my leg. That cutlery is a cry from the depths of her unconscious signifying that, in addition to loving her father and hating her mother and being scared of horses and bicycle seats, she wants to *do me*. I raise my eyebrows, but only slightly—be cool, man; be cool—to indicate that if tapping that ass is what is required of this worst of best men, then so be it. That ass shall be tapped.

But instead of returning my gaze, she rolls her eyes and issues a most filthy response from her dirty little mouth: You fucking dipshit! The DJ called you up to give your goddamn toast, like, five hours ago.

–Don't hate a playa. Hate the *game*, I say, before throwing my napkin down in defiance. Unfortunately, it lands in Cort's salad, which is not at all what I'd intended to happen. I try to apologize, but before I can utter a word, Alex says, Way to go, fuckface. She's a vegetarian. You just ruined the only thing she can eat.

Cort shrugs. Nah, it's cool. There's, like, bacon dressing on here or something.

Sweet girl. I smile at her and scowl at Alex. She will be sorry for her insolence later.

I clear my throat, pick up my glass of champagne. I'll admit, it is not my first, but then, neither is it my second, third, or fourth. As I glance out into the crowd, a blurry mess of boring, I decide that what this room needs is an icebreaker. Forgotten speech, be damned.

–*Ahem. A-hehehe-hem.* Thank you. Thank you. Well, they sure do know how to put on one hell of a shotgun wedding here in Galestown, don't they?

Silence.

–Erm, um, sorry about that, wrong speech! Shotgun wedding? What a joke! Wait . . . it *is* a joke, right, Danny? (Embarrassed nod.) *Phew!* Buuuttt *seriously*, folks, you don't need me to tell you that this matrimony has nothing to do with an attempt to spare unwanted children from bastardy, and everything to do with a love that first blossomed between children.

Silence.

–Um, you know, cause Dan and Lea were *children* when they met. *Crazy*, right? It just goes to show you that children are a lot smarter than we give them credit for. I mean, you should have seen some of the skanks Dan dated in high school. Actually, you *can* see them because some of them are here.

I point at Alex twice and wink at the audience and she gives me a look of death.

–Kidding!

Silence.

–Boy, is this a tough crowd! Lighten up, people, it's not a funeral. . . . Anywhooo . . . *To the bride and groom!* I scream.

–To the bride and groom, they say.

–Now bring on the virgins, battle the calves, man the steamrollers, and slaughter the fatted wenches!

As I take my princely seat, I am met with more than a few scowls from the old women in the general vicinity. As if I care about them. There is only one woman here worthy of me and that is the mother of the groom. Pardon my Dutch, but all I've been thinking about since we got to the church was how bad I want to hit that. I know, I know, it's wrong, but she's dope. Straight up. I've been wanting to hit that since I was, like, twelve, for real, and you fucking know it, you dirty little bitch, don't you? You'd fucking like it, too, wouldn't you?

–Cut that out, Benny boy, or Wally will kick your ass.

Fuck . . . Dan just caught me checking out his mom's ass. I snap my head around and I'm like, What'd you say, bro? Sorry, man, I missed it. It's just, this jam takes me back, yo.

Dan, good old Dan, grins because he knows I am full of shit but, really, his mom's hot so he is accustomed to such behavior by now. In fact, he probably knows that the ass I was checking out was the very reason we became such good friends in the first place.

Okay, so I'm exaggerating. It was the ass, but it was so much more than the ass. It was also the Atari, the Nintendo, the PlayStation. It was the cable with its healthy dose of scrambled Skinemax which, if viewed with the right amount of squinting, allowed one to see all kinds of things, but mainly tongue-flicking and fake tits. And as if these creature comforts were not enough to satisfy my adolescent cravings, it was also the fact that Kelly made french fries for dinner.

All divorced moms did.

And I was not lying to the man of the hour when I told him this jam takes me back. Dan doesn't know it, but it was this song that set the scene of the afternoon in which my virgin eyes first beheld the sight of a woman in the throes of passion, and a fine-ass woman at that, my Venus in sweatpants, my Diana wielding arrows of perfectly fried Ore-Idas, my Kelly Pawlowski, also known as the mother of the groom, also known as the woman who is pining for my di-dick. I know, I know, I am one lovesick puppy, but look at her over there, nursing her G&T. You can tell she likes it dirty just by the way she's smoking her cigarette, and Oh My Fucking God, are those garters? Oh my Lord, does she want it Benny-style? I think she does, I think she most *definitely* does.

–Yeah, those were the days, Ben.

–Huh? Oh, right . . . Word. The days, those were. I can't believe Kel . . . erm . . . your mom sold that house. Misty watercolor memories, my man.

–Word. But, you know, with me gone, she and Wally didn't need all the extra rooms.

Wally. Man! Talk about rubbing salt in a fork-inflicted wound. What has that fool Wally got that I don't? I mean, besides, like . . . a house, a car, and a bachelor's degree from an accredited college. Wally is like a seasonal flu, but I am Kelly's plague! Back when me and Dan first started chilling, Kelly was newly divorced from Chuck, lonely, and all eager to be a part of her son's life, which meant she was always there, bringing us sundaes and hamburgers and shit, and walking around in tight pants, knowing she still had it, but perhaps not quite ready to bring it to the world yet. We were, like, the dress rehearsal for her glorious comeback into the world of dope bitches.

I spent more time at Dan's house than I did at my own—it was that kind of place. Most days I'd take the bus straight to his house. Other days we'd cruise around town first, checking out the local scenery and what have you, usually ending up down at the Reservoir where you could do wicked jumps, cascading over the tires and piles of garbage, reimagining ourselves as the Dirt-Bike Kid and the guy who boned Lori Loughlin in *Rad*. Oh, the glory of it all! If my moms knew I was going down to the Reservoir, she'd have roasted me, carrot-style, alongside her famous pot roast, mostly because that's where they found Kenny Castalucci and that other kid no one remembers five years back, facedown in the water, throats sliced open from ear to ear. It was also the place Jason Lane died but . . . on to happier subjects, for today is a day of making merry!

My point is simply this: The Reservoir was a bad place and everyone knew it; everyone, it seemed, except for Dan's mom, who had other things to worry about, like working two jobs, making sure Dan's dad paid alimony, and keeping her ass tight enough to find a new husband, not that Wally deserved a wife with a nice ass—but that, my friends, is also a topic for another day.

The day Kelly and I shared a moment, a brief moment that has linked us forever in stolen glances and nasty longings, started out with Dan and me down in his basement, watching a Michael Jackson retrospective on MTV. Homeboy was already hurtin' back then, no doubt, but back in the day . . . nobody could hold a candle to Michael, so we felt it was only right to pay homage to his former greatness. Kel had brought down some hot dogs, mac and cheese, and Tater Tots just as Vincent Price warned us that Michael Jackson was about to go all zombie on our asses, and so, of course, Dan busted out his trademark White Boy Moonwalk which made me and her laugh, and then she said, Lemme try, and she tried but she couldn't do it, so we all started laughing again and then she said, Your turn, Ben, but all of a sudden it hit me that Michael wasn't Michael anymore and all the moonwalking in the world couldn't change it, so I said, No way. I'm a gangsta and gangstas don't dance.

–Come on, Kelly said, laughing at me, and then she grabbed my hand and tried to pull me up, but I would not be moved.

–Oh, you guys are no fun. I'm going back to my story.

I almost lost it when she said that. *Story* is what all the little old grandmothers called their favorite soap operas and it killed me that Mrs. O did too. I wanted to scream, Save yourself, good woman, before it's too late! Before you start crocheting caftans! Before you start taking in stray cats! Before you start pickling whatever foods cannot be fermented or stewed!

But in addition to not dancing, gangstas apparently do not rant about things pickled nor about the dangers of watching *Santa Barbara* so I just sat there like a dumbass and watched her walk her fine ass away.

–I'm out, I told Dan a few minutes later, because I'd had enough Kennedy and Kurt Loder and good women just *giving up* for one day. I popped the remaining Tater Tots in my mouth in a decidedly gangsta fashion, but Dan totally missed the *power* of the moment, as he can be known to do, because he was too busy trying to pull off the switchblade moves from "Beat It."

I stormed up the stairs, past all the pictures of Dan, on family trips to Niagara Falls and Disney World, in school photos, at the Little League World Series. They were like those pictures of Jesus or the pope or Elvis whose eyes follow you as you pass by, burn into your very soul, and seem to say, I know what you're thinking about doing to my mom. I tried to ignore them as I scaled the stairs and just when I'd almost reached the top, I heard something emanating from the third floor. A kind of creaking, maybe even a muffled voice. A woman. A damsel in distress.

Mrs. O!

I cupped my hand over my ear and there it was again. She was crying for help!

The O'Shaughnessys never locked their doors. Nobody

in our town did—at least, none of the parents did; the kids knew better. Maybe somebody got in after she went upstairs; maybe he'd been waiting for her in her bedroom. I did my best fight-or-flight and gave the place the once-over, then grabbed the closest thing to a weapon I could find in the living room: a statue of a naked chick perched on top of the piano. I almost left it there, telling myself gangstas don't even need weapons; they can kill with their *eyes*, but I didn't believe that. I was terrified, and it didn't help that as soon as I picked up my makeshift weapon, I felt like a perv on top of it, as the deadliest way to use it was to wrap my fingers over the statue's tits, my thumb snug inside her hairless marble pussy.

I tiptoed up the stairs, regretting that I'd never let Dan teach me his silent glide. When I reached the summit, I put my back to the wall and slid around the corner, expecting to find myself face-to-face with some thug trying to have his way with Mrs. O. I took a deep breath, as I began to channel the moves imparted upon me by one Mr. Miyagi some years before—PAINT THE FENCE, PAINT THE FENCE—and swung around the corner and peeked in the bedroom door, which was open a crack, ready to unleash a formidable assault.

But there was no thug. There wasn't even a story. Mrs. O was all alone. Lying on her bed with her eyes closed and her hand down her jeans. Holy fuck. The statue fell out of my fingers; miraculously, before it could crash to the floor, I caught it with my knees and stood there for a moment, doubled over, mouth gaping, ruined for life.

It was so hot. It was so . . . I'd never seen anything so

hot. And even now, after years of banging all types of dope bitches and what have you, I still have never seen anything quite so hot. Kelly, man, she fucking ruined me for life.

I only watched for a few seconds, because almost immediately the most intense boner of my life began threatening to explode all over the place. I debated jerking off in the O'Shaughnessys' bathroom, but they only had two—one upstairs, one downstairs, steps away from Dan. It was too risky. Besides, if I did it here, I'd have to do it quick, and I didn't want to do it quick; I wanted to savor every moment of it.

I had but one choice. Get home as quick as possible, run up the stairs without my moms seeing me, into the bathroom, shut the door and . . . then it was just me and Kelly.

I snuck down the stairs, as quiet as before but much faster, the image of Mrs. O fingering herself burned inside my brain. And then it hit me. She was lying there, engaged in autoeroticism, with the door wide open . . . or, at least, sort of open . . . she'd moaned loud enough to wake the dead or, at least, I think she had . . . she'd wanted me to see her. . . . She wanted me to . . .

No, no, no, no, no. Don't even think that or you'll blow your load here and now, I told myself. I needed to clear my head. When that didn't work—turns out that a clear head is a head just waiting for an image of Dan's horny mom to appear—I climbed onto my bike and sat there for a second. I willed my boner down to a respectable level by thinking about the grossest thing I could—Weird Al

Yankovic, Weird Al Yankovic, Weird Al Yankovic—and started pedaling like mad back to my house.

There was no way I could take Main Street; we'd had gym last period and I was still in my shorts, which meant my dick had pitched a tent in the mesh that I didn't exactly want anyone to see, were they to roll down their window and say hi. On top of that, passing through the woods by the Reservoir cut ten minutes off my trip; as Mrs. O popped back into my head, replacing Weird Al with his Hawaiian shirt and white man's Jheri curl and sending a sharp pain from my toes to my groin, I knew I couldn't afford to waste a minute. I pedaled harder.

As I came to the part of the road that turned into woods, I could hear the rushing of the water, see the thick of the pines, but that was it. I had no idea if anyone else was on the path; the water and wood made sure of that, which is why it's such a dangerous place to be. You can't hear a damn thing, can't see a damn thing, either.

Except when you can, when that damn thing is loud enough to overtake the water, when that damn thing is as alien enough to these parts as a junked Volvo or blown-out tire.

Like when that damn thing is a kid's scream, like when that damn thing is a bunch of kids around that screaming kid. Kids I didn't recognize at first, but by their JNCOs and 8-Ball jackets, I could tell that they probably lived on the North side of the Reservoir, where even Dan's mom wouldn't let him go.

When I squinted my eyes I saw that there was one kid among them I did recognize: Shawn Riley. He was the one on the ground, he was the one screaming, and the other kids—three of them in all—were beating the shit out of him. I was still frozen in place, staring at Shawn, who wasn't exactly my friend, but who was someone I chilled with now and again because we'd been in the gifted program together and because Dan sometimes played drums with him. Truth is, he was a little, *you know*, even back then. And it's not like I've got anything against f . . . I mean, gay dudes; I don't, I really don't. I just, I just didn't know what to do about gay dudes back then, you know?

–Ben, will you get the fuck over here and help me fend off these fucking assholes? No sooner did the words leave his mouth than one of the bigger kids looked up and saw me.

–This isn't about you, Reardon, so don't fucking make it be. Better beat it while you can.

Eddie Contardi. What a fucking dick. I wanted to help Shawn; I didn't like Eddie Contardi and his crew any more than the next guy, and three against two was much fairer than three against one.

But then I looked down at my pants. My cock didn't seem to understand the urgency of the new situation we were threatened with, and I couldn't blame it much; I hadn't masturbated in a week, ever since Father Leo said it was a sin to defile the body and afterward I asked Dan what that meant and he laughed and called me a retard and I felt dumb for not knowing, only now I don't feel so dumb because clearly Dan knew so much about the sin because body defilement obviously ran in the family.

There was no way I was going to let those guys see my boner; I knew exactly why they were kicking Shawn's ass; it was on account of how he'd had a boner in the locker room earlier that week and that scumbag Anthony Lepporio called him a fag, when everyone knew that everyone got boners in the locker room; everyone got boners everywhere. It had nothing to do with being a fag, even if Shawn *was* a f . . . gay guy.

And besides, I didn't see how I was going to put up a good fight anyway, the condition I was in. Shawn would understand; I'd explain it to him tomorrow. He'd understand.

I sped by the boys, trying not to look at Shawn, but looking anyway, and seeing the look on his face just as Anthony kicked him in the side. He wasn't just wincing; he was pissed.

When I got home, I threw down my bike without locking it, just as I planned. I ran past my moms, just as I planned, and up the stairs, just as I planned, and into my bedroom, just as I planned.

But what I hadn't planned on was that after I dove into bed and pulled up the covers, hard as I tried to picture Kelly O'Shaughnessy, her perfect tits and tanned stomach, her tight little ass, and the pussy that I knew was blonde, even without getting a good look at it, the only thing I could see as I wrapped my left hand around my cock and clenched my eyes shut—the same thing I see pretty much anytime I'm getting ready to blow my load— was, is, and forever will be goddamned Shawn goddamn Riley.

smells like teen spirit

SHAWN

–If he doesn't stop looking at me, Alex, I'm going to have to do something about it.

–Oh, Shawn, don't be so dramatic, you're a lover, not a fighter. Alex takes a small bite of her chicken in a way that would look elegant if she wasn't grinding her jaw long after she finished chewing. Besides, she adds, he could sit on you and snap you in half.

I laugh. He is a fat fuck, all right.

–Oh, admit it. Don't you think he's actually a little cute? Like, in a Fred Durst kind of way? Alex rubbed her bare foot on my leg.

–I wouldn't know.

Now Alex laughs. What do you mean you wouldn't know? The last time I checked you weren't exactly the poster boy for heterosexuality.

–Just because I'm gay, Alexandra, does not mean that every man I see automatically makes his way onto my radar. Especially not ones that look like bloated Eminem knockoffs.

–Oh, he probably just figured out it was you fucking with him all that time.

–*Me* fucking with *him*? You know full well that he started it.

–Shawn. You put *acid* in his Gatorade.

–If he had a cool bone in his body he would have thanked me for it. It was excellent acid. I mean, do you know how difficult it is to get liquid LSD?

–As I recall, he was too busy flashing the entire football team. I have half a mind to tell him it was you.

–Oh, you're just being a shrew because you're sexually frustrated. Look at the way you're pulling the label off your beer bottle.

–That has nothing to do with sexual frustration. I just hate Coors, you know, them being Republicans and everything.

–Riiiiight. Seriously, how long has it been?

–I don't want to talk about it. Speaking of, do you realize what sluts we all are?

–Speak for yourself.

–I'm serious. Between the two of us, we've hooked up with everyone in the wedding party including the bride and groom.

–That's not true. What about all the relatives?

–They don't count. We just met the Guidette cousin, her sister is jailbait, and Danny's relatives are subhuman.

–That doesn't seem to be deterring your former paramour Luke Goldenrod from carousing with the little DeAngelis. What is she, like, fourteen? Luke's a way bigger slut than either of us.

–He's not a slut. He's a pedophile. And an asshole. Big difference.

–Anyway, what about Ben? No one's hooked up with Ben.

Alex doesn't say anything.

–You? Ohhhhhh. Noooo. No! Gross. Was he good? No, wait, don't tell me. I don't want to know. Okay, yes . . .

yes, I do. What's his cock like? And don't play coy with me. Is it crooked? Of course it is, you don't even have to tell me. I know a crooked cock when I see it. Or wait, wait, no, no, wait. I bet he's got one testicle.

–Oh, Shawn, give me a break. He was actually . . . It was actually kind of . . . nice.

–Ew. I am sooooo not sharing a room with you tonight. You're dirty. Did the bride know how dirty you were when you two explored your bi-curiosity on graduation night?

–That was Truth or Dare!

–*Life*, my dear Alex, is Truth or Dare.

Which meant that, yeah, between the two of us, we had pretty much hooked up with everyone in the bridal party that counted, although the thing is, it's not like I'd even wanted to. It's just kind of the way things worked out. Like, I bet in most schools there are only four or five kids that anybody actually ever really wants to make out with. But we all need to make out. So we settle.

Take my kiss with Cort as an example. Don't get me wrong; she's a cute girl, I guess. Looking a little unwashed these days, like she was just puddle jumping at a mud festival, but still . . . if you're into that kind of thing, cute. And by "that kind of thing," I mean girls.

It was at my own birthday party, and Alex was hosting because she knew I was too embarrassed to have it at my own house, which was small and a little dirty thanks to all the stray cats my mom let in. I hated living like that, hated that my mom didn't have time to keep the house clean like Jason's or Alex's or even Danny's, a place I hung out at only if I knew Ben wasn't going to be there.

I hadn't spoken to Ben since he'd been too pussy to lend a hand when I was getting my ass kicked by the Future Garbage Collectors of Galestown. Not that I avoided him completely; for years I'd been playing little tricks on him, only he'd grown too stupid to figure out they were tricks and was instead convinced that there was some kind of plot initiated against him by some angry, hungry ghosts or whatever. That's what I'd overheard him telling Danny one day in the locker room, anyway. It was hilarious to watch him, looking over his shoulder every time he rounded a corridor at school, making the sign of the cross before he got into his dad's minivan. But I especially loved riding my bike by his house real late at night and discovering that he slept with the light on.

It wasn't usually major things I did, just spooky stuff to freak him out. Like leaving a shrunken head I'd ordered from the back of a comic book inside his locker. I'd gotten the combination from Steve the janitor, who liked me because we were both from the same part of town and because he owed Kyle a lot of money, for what, I had a pretty good idea by now.

I'll admit I went a little far with the acid in the Gatorade thing, but look, from what I'd heard about him hugging all the other jocks and telling them how beautiful they all were, he was having the time of his life. And the fact that he was wearing nothing but his jockstrap or whatever, well, that's just icing on the cake. And it's not like anyone kicked his ass or anything; they were too fucking stunned to do a thing. It's not my fault that his trip went bad after that, is it?

Okay, okay, so it was. We all make mistakes.

But, Cort. Back to Cort.

So Alex was having this huge soiree at her place for my birthday and I was happy about that; so happy that I was almost willing to get over the fact that I wouldn't even see her or Jason all night because they'd be too busy sucking face. Or the fact that she'd gotten it into her head that Cort and I would be perfect for each other because I'd yet to break it to Alex that the person I thought would be perfect for me was currently trying to do everything in his power to get her to go down on him.

–Alex, the girl doesn't even *speak*.

–No, you're wrong. She does! You know I never liked her when we were at Peterson, but she's my lab partner and so I have to talk to her or whatever and she's actually totally sweet and funny . . . (And now for the famous Alex pause . . .) even though she *could* definitely use a decent haircut, and what's with those Birkenstocks? Ick. But, really, those things are so fixable because she is just such a doll. She got our whole class out of dissecting frogs because she said that there wasn't anything else we could possibly learn from animal testing that hadn't already been discovered through the corporate-sponsored torturing of amphibians.

–How very *E.T.* of her. Seriously lame, though. Dissecting a frog was the only cool thing about biology.

–Actually, we got to watch a movie instead.

–A movie about dissecting frogs? That's even lamer.

–No, actually, it was *Back to the Future.* They let us sit in with ninth-grade physics.

–Well, still, it's not like she's pretty.

–She totally is pretty.

–You're just saying that. Girls think every other girl is pretty.

–That is not true. I think Amy Santangelo is an ugly skank.

–That's because you're just jealous that she knows how to give blow jobs.

–Whatever . . . Alex considered this. Does she really know how to give blow jobs?

–Oh, how the fuck would I know?

–Because you're a skank too.

–I'm hanging up on you right now.

But I didn't. I could never hang up on Alex. Could never hang up on Jason either. I spent more time talking to them on the phone than they spent talking to each other. When they got together, they were like magnets, but when it came to the phone, they were mine, mostly because that's how they found out things about each other.

–Shawn, do you mind if I ask you something serious?

–Shoot. (Here we go.)

–Is Jason mad at me?

–Why don't you ask him yourself?

–Oh, yeah, sure. Like I'd do *that* when I can just ask you.

–You know, maybe he is. Yeah. Yeah, come to think of it, I think he is a little mad at you.

–Whatever, she said. Wait, are you being serious?

–Well, I don't know for sure . . . it's just that I saw him flirting with Elly Kim after school today, so I guess I figured something was up with you two.

–You're so full of shit. Elly Kim has mono and you know it. Anyway, why would he be mad at me?

–Why do you *think* he's mad at you?

–Because . . . I don't want to talk about it.

–Join the club. Listen, Alex, I gotta go. I got things to do before the party.

–No you don't. *Talk to me!*

–Why don't you call your boyfriend? Then you'll see he's not mad at you and you're just being a crazy girl.

–Okay. Whatever, she said, huffing. Hey, Shawn, she added in a softer voice.

–What?

–Happy birthday. I love you, you know.

Girls were like that, so loose with love—it made me nervous. They said it to boys, to their girlfriends, to girls they didn't even like. It was totally weird and made them all seem so fake, even girls like Alex who weren't fake but felt they needed to fake up all their real feelings for you with some lame words that some dude invented, like, however many years ago English was invented.

I mumbled something in return, then hung up the phone and lay down on my bed, staring at the guitar that was sitting across the room, taunting me about how long ago it had been since I'd last practiced.

I had about two hours to kill before I had to start getting ready so I decided to work on my English assignment so I would have the whole weekend to myself. A Nirvana song was on MTV but the sound was off and I promised myself I'd practice the guitar tomorrow even though I knew I wouldn't.

I had to memorize the prologue to *Romeo and Juliet* and recite it in front of my entire class, which sucked because I hated getting up in front of people. I didn't bother asking myself how I planned to be in a band if I couldn't face a crowd, but I figured at least it would be a lot darker in clubs than it was in Mrs. Petrossian's class.

I plopped the huge Shakespeare book down on my bed and began reciting the lines. Though I was one of the last kids in the class to go, since my name began with an *R*, my time had finally arrived. It had been pretty boring to watch everyone recite the same things over and over again, at least it had been until Ben Reardon turned around the Shakespeare cap Mrs. Petrossian made us wear and rapped the prologue to the tune of A Tribe Called Quest's "Scenario." I loathed Ben but I had to admit: He had his moments.

I tried to pay attention to memorizing the lines but before I knew it I had a massive hard-on thinking about Ben of all people, in his backward hat of all things, and then all I could think about was this porno tape I'd stolen from Kyle called *Foul Balls* which featured two baseball players jerking their huge cocks off over this girl's asshole. By now, the porno chick had completely disappeared from my mind and was replaced with Ben and the other baseball player who, I had to admit, looked a bit like Danny, and though this hadn't happened in the video, the one who looked like Danny told Ben to bend over and take it. Ben did as he was told—he was begging for Danny to fuck his ass now—and just as I was about to come, I imagined Alex giving Jason a blow job, which wasn't even something that had actually happened, as far as I know, and before I forced it out of my head I came real hard and then felt terrible that I was the kind of pervert who whacked off to Danny O'Shaughnessy in his baseball uniform, not to mention his two best friends and Ben Reardon in his stupid Shakespeare hat. I put my pillow over my head.

When I woke up three hours later, I realized I was already late for the party. I kicked off the covers, looked down at the dried jizz all over my belly, and scanned the floor for a semi-clean towel. My room wasn't exactly neat, but it was a lot cleaner than any other room in the house because I wouldn't allow the cats in. I wrapped a towel around my waist, wondered why my mom wasn't home yet, and stepped into the shower, turning the water on hot enough to burn away all the bad things I'd thought and done that day, too numerous to count.

As I stepped out and looked in the mirror I had to admit that I liked what I saw. I was still tan from the trip to Florida to visit my dad and though I wasn't nearly as big as any of those jocky guys, I knew I looked good.

When I got back to my room I saw that the answering machine was blinking. I pressed Play and heard a very shrill Alex: Where *are* you? I dialed her number and before I could get a word in, she said, Shawn, how can you be so late for your own party? This is waaay beyond fashionable. Everyone is asking for you and Cort has an early curfew so if you don't get here soon, you're going to blow it.

–Is she there yet?

–There are so many people here, I can't keep track. But I'm sure she is.

After we hung up, I threw on my baggy jeans with the chain around the belt loop that linked to my wallet and I pulled on a green T-shirt and a gray sweater because Alex once told me that there is nothing sexier than guys in green T-shirts and another time she said the same thing about guys in gray sweaters, so I thought I better be prepared for any kind of weather. It was April, so you never knew. Before I turned off the TV, I noticed yet another Nirvana song on and thought for a second that maybe MTV wasn't as lame as I'd thought it had gotten.

As I stepped outside, I almost knocked over my mom coming in from work.

–Hey, hey, there, she said, grabbing on the door frame to keep from falling backward. Where are you off to in such a rush?

I wanted to just keep on walking to spare myself the third degree but I've never been much good with that.

–Alex's. Is that okay? I won't be late.

–It's fine, hon, of course it's fine. I just never see you around here anymore.

–That's not true and you know it, Natalie. I knew she hated it when I called her that but I couldn't stand the guilt shit.

I looked at her, scowling, which was a hard thing to do with someone like my mom. She was so pretty, so young-looking in her nurse's outfit and the Mary Janes that girls my age wore. But, you know, she wasn't too much older than I was then when she got pregnant with Kyle.

–Hey Nat, I'm already late . . .

–Okay, sweetie, it's just, I bought a cake. I thought we'd said we were gonna celebrate before you went off with your friends. She held up a little bakery box tied together with this heartbreaking green-, red-, and white-striped string and I felt absolutely terrible for leaving her.

–Yes . . . we *did* talk about hanging out at six . . . but it's already eight.

She lowered the box and looked down at the ground, the way girls do when they're feeling dumb, and said, Shit. I know, hon. It's just, by the time I finished up at the hospital—it was a madhouse today, it's not even a full moon but people were freaking out all over the place—Calvito's was closed and so was Solitro's so I had to drive to Johnston to find a decent bakery.

At that, one of the cats came out and started rubbing itself against my leg. So typical. I want nothing to do with them and they can't get enough of me.

–Tomorrow, we'll, like, have cake for breakfast, I said. And you can even sing and everything.

–I have the early shift tomorrow Shawn, so I won't wake you. But you'll be around tomorrow night? Her eyes were big and hopeful.

–Sure, Mom, that sounds great, I said and gave her a

quick hug, knowing full well that she'd be late as usual and I'd probably be out by the time she got home.

As I rode my bike to Alex's house, I was glad I'd taken the sweater. The air was cold and heavy, wet with rain. I wondered for the millionth time if I should ask my dad to let me come down and live there where it was sunny and warm all the time; even when it rained, it was only for a few hours and you were guaranteed a rainbow. Not like here where you were just guaranteed to be sorry you left your jacket at home.

Before I'd even fully set foot in Alex's front door, I knew something was wrong. There was just that kind of feeling you get that something really heavy has happened, like your dog got run over by a car or your brother got busted again or your parents are getting divorced. Something not just heavy, but also unchangeable.

–What's up, Sexy Lexy? I said. She was standing at the kitchen counter with her back to me.

When she turned around I saw that she was crying. And then she said something but she was crying so hard it made it tough to hear what she was saying.

–Dead. Dead, I can't . . .

–Dead? What? Who's dead? What are you saying?

–Cort's dead! She sniffed and looked at me, her face all puffy.

–What? Did you say . . . *What??* What are you talking about? Are you for real?

Cort? Dead? Whoa. It was so . . . so completely unexpected. I'd never known a kid who died. I mean, there

were those kids who got murdered down by the Reservoir—
I played Little League with one of them, but I didn't know
him, or anything about him outside of the fact that he usually pulled to left field.

–Yes! Isn't it, like . . . the end of the world . . . or an
era . . . or something?

I wasn't so sure about that. I mean, Cort was a nice girl
and everything, particularly if you were a frog, I guess, but
I wasn't sure her death signified the end of anything other
than her life. Still, it was weird to have the girl you were
supposed to hook up with up and die on you the very
night you were supposed to hook up. It was actually, well,
when you thought about it, it was actually a little cool.
I thought back to seeing her in the hall yesterday when
I'd caught her staring at me before she looked away.
From what Alex said, she was really, really into me. Which
means, she went to her grave with thoughts of me on her
mind. Even though I'd never felt anything remotely resembling attraction to Cort before, I felt a little orgasm af-
tershock shoot from my knees to my cock. Pervert.

–Listen, Alex, how can Cort be dead? Did it happen
tonight? At your house?

–A shotgun, suicide . . . what? What are you talking
about? What do you mean at my house? It was in Aberdeen or Seattle or whatever. . . . Alex had taken her
head from her hands and was looking up at me, her eye
makeup all smudgy.

–Wait, wasn't she supposed to be here tonight? What
was Cort doing in Aberdeen or Seattle or whatever?

–Not *Cort*, you idiot, she said, *Kurt*. As in, Kurt Cobain! You know, like, the lead singer of Nirvana? The reason you have a guitar you never play and only wash your hair once a month?

–Oh. Jesus. That sucks, I said. But, well, at least it wasn't Cort.

–At least *what* wasn't me?

I turned around and there was the formerly dead girl standing in the doorway, wearing some quilty-looking skirt and top in about seven shades of brown. What on earth did Alex think I had in common with this girl? Didn't Alex know that the only reason Kurt Cobain wore a T-shirt that said CORPORATE MAGAZINES STILL SUCK on the cover of *Rolling Stone* was because they told him not to wear one that dissed the Grateful Dead?

–Did you guys hear about Kurt Cobain? Shot himself in the head. Jason emerged from the staircase looking so cool with his ears all stretched out with those big barrel things that Alex told me I shouldn't bother getting myself. You should ignore what everyone else is doing and rock that disaffected-prep-school-kid look, Shawn, she had once said, while plucking an oversize Oxford shirt from the sale rack at Filene's and handing it to me. You know, like, little rich boy lost. It would be so *ironic*—you being so . . . you know . . . not rich. And anyway, that body mutilation style just wouldn't work for you the way it does for . . . other people.

And by *other people*, she meant Jason. But of course, I knew she was right. Alex was smart about that stuff. She wanted to be a designer, was always talking about people like Vivienne Westwood and Jean-Paul Gaultier.

–What a pussy thing to do, I said.

–I don't know, said Jason. You gotta admit, it takes guts, he said, walking up to Alex and putting his arm around her. Then he added, Hey, shit. I almost forgot. Happy birthday, man. He let go of Alex and came over to me and gave me a big hug. I did my best to return it, patting him lightly on the shoulder.

–Thanks, Jay, I said weakly.

–Oh yeah, God. I'm such a dick! Alex added, wiping her eyes with her sweater sleeve. She rushed over to me and threw her arms around my neck and I noticed that she smelled uncharacteristically sweaty underneath her signature baby-powder scent. Let's go downstairs. We've got presents and everything.

My presents turned out to be a bottle of Jack Daniel's and small bag of seedy pot, which was a little pointless when you considered it was probably bagged in my own basement by my own brother, but it was still a nice gesture, I guess, so I promptly proceeded to break it up and roll it into a neat little joint. There were a good number of people there, but everyone was sitting in front of the TV as Kurt Loder gave details about the suicide. My birthday had turned into a memorial service. So typical. When everyone started breaking off into little couples and cliques, Alex and Jason nowhere to be found, I slipped out the basement door which opened onto a little patio. It was raining, but the patio was covered by a tin roof, so I didn't get wet.

I took a few puffs and looked out into Alex's backyard, which was full of trees that seemed to go on for miles. It pissed me off that Jason thought there was something cool about what Kurt Cobain had done; he was such an idiot like that. And it doubly pissed me off to think that he'd say that kind of thing around Alex. She could be so impressionable. I often caught her repeating lines verbatim that other people had said to me the week earlier, something girls did all the time, but something Alex was way too smart to be doing.

–Hey Shawn, someone said and I turned around quick, startled. I had my back turned to the house so I didn't see the door and the rain was coming down so hard it was almost impossible to hear anything else. It was Cort. Fuck.

–Hey, I said. I wished she's just go away but, not wanting to be rude, I handed her the joint.

She stepped closer to me, took the roach tentatively, and raised it to her lips. I'm sorry Kurt Cobain had to go and die on your birthday. That totally sucks.

–Nah, actually it's okay, I said. Especially because, when Alex first told me, I thought she said it was you who died: Cort, you know, instead of Kurt. Now, that would have totally sucked.

Her eyes got wide. Why?

–Because if you were dead, I would have never gotten to do this. And then, God knows why, I leaned over and kissed her. And she kissed me back.

But the thing is, I felt nothing.

So I kissed her ear. And she kissed my ear back.

Again . . . nothing.

So I put my hand up her shirt. And she didn't protest when I unhooked her bra.

And yet, nothing.

So I put my hand down her skirt. And I could feel that her underwear was really wet.

And still, I felt nothing.

And she put her hand down my pants. But instead of getting hard, I felt nothing.

–What is it? she said, as if not expecting this, as if expecting anything but this.

–I feel stupid, I said.

But that wasn't it. What I felt was . . . nothing. Because normally pot made me feel horny enough that I could get over my usual lack of attraction to girls, made me feel whatever everyone around me was feeling, which was just how I liked it, but this time I felt incredibly alert, hyper-aware of everything around me; every sight, every sound, every smell was there right in front of me and nothing like me. The air looked like rain, the rain sounded like bullets, Cort smelled like Teen Spirit.

And I felt . . . nothing.

lover lay
down

CORT

It's weird sitting here with all of them, like there's nothing strange about it, like everything's cool. And maybe everything is, maybe no one else is thinking about how little we have in common these days, or how little we ever had in common outside of above-average IQs. I mean, the last time I saw most of them was years ago, before I met Uncle John, before I let Uncle John convince me to blow off college and go on tour with him instead

–because that was real life, man, not what they're selling you on them college brochures

–because who wanted to live the straight life your parents had mapped out for you

–because you can't save the world from the Ivory Tower.

A touch on the shoulder interrupts my thoughts, which I'd begun to think in a voice that sounded a lot like Uncle John's stoned drawl. Lea. You're not dancing, she says, slurring slightly, though not in an unbecoming way. Of course, there aren't too many things unbecoming on a bride, especially when that bride is Lea.

I look down at my untouched chicken marsala and give it a little poke with my fork; there had been no vegetarian option on the invitation. At least the wine was good.

–I don't like dancing.

–Oh, please. You, like, dropped out of humanity to tour the world with dirty musician boys and you're telling me you don't like dancing. She is trying to pull me onto the dance floor. By my hair.

I don't want to dance with these people; I hardly know

these people and, anyway, no one's dancing, except some drunk uncle and I don't feel as if we should encourage him. But it's Lea's wedding, and she was my first friend, so I can't say no. I down my glass of red wine and chase it with what's left of the watery vodka tonic I got during the appetizers and I join her on the dance floor.

Lea is still, as ever, a completely-comfortable-in-her-own-skin dancer, much like so many of the girls I see at festivals. Only they're usually barefoot and muddy and wasted, while Lea looks expensive and shiny . . . and also wasted.

Lea's right, I don't hate dancing—but it's never come effortless to me, so I usually need to enlist the aid of psychedelics infused or mixed together with Chex, Rice Krispies, and chocolate and handed out by lost little girls in paisley or men who look more goat than human.

—I'm really sorry about the bridal shower, Lee, I say. The cameraman is pointing his flash in our faces because nothing makes for good video like a drunk bride. I worry that he'll pick up what we're saying, but then I remember they'll probably play some song like "True Companion" or "Wonderful Tonight" over the whole video anyway.

—Oh, who gives a fuck about that? She's gone floppy in my arms, surprisingly heavy for such a petite girl. I would have rather been at a concert, too.

—Lea, you are so full of shit. The one time she came to a Phish show, Lea put on a happy face, but I know she hated it. Porta-Potties and hippie boys are about as much her scene as French manicures are mine.

—I'm allowed to be full of shit. It's my wedding day. But I mean it. You don't belong here, in Galestown, with these people. You never did. And I liked seeing you in your, you know, element. She hiccups, then adds, You know, for a long time I was mad at you for leaving me at that show, for just announcing that you were taking off with some complete strangers and making me drive all the way back to Rhode Island *alone*, but then . . .

I want desperately to know what she is going to say next, but Lea's attention has already been pulled away by the flower girl tugging at her dress. Lea whisks the kid up in her arms and begins twirling her round and round and round. I stand there on the dance floor, my arms pulled tight around my chest, not sure of whether to return to my seat or join in the dancing. With my fuzzy brain unable to decide I just watch as the children lead and the adults do their best to keep up.

I wish there was someone here that I could talk to, but I have nothing to say to any of these people. Lea had put Alex on one side of me and Ben on the other, which means that I had the option of discussing two vastly different lines: Valentino's Fall or the Patriots defensive. Not that having a conversation with Alex was actually possible, what with her slipping into the bathroom every twenty minutes for some lines of a different kind. God, I hate cocaine. In the last year, you were every bit as likely to find hippies selling coke or heroin as you were mushrooms or acid, and it worried me.

I could talk to Shawn. But I always found him such a disappointment. He looked so sensitive with his long hair and purple eyes that I always expected us to have some kind of life-altering discussion about the meaning of life, but we never did. Plus, before Alex told the whole world he was gay, I used to follow him around like a lost puppy.

I look around the room once again. Surely among all these former classmates who Lea and Dan kept in touch with long after I'd let them go there was someone who could make this night more than just a huge mistake. Just as I'm about to give up and plot a way to sneak back to my hotel early, I see him.

Luke Goldenrod.

What on earth is Luke Goldenrod doing here? And more importantly, why didn't Lea tell me that Luke Goldenrod was going to be here?

And *that's* when I see who he's dancing with.

Amanda.

Lea's sister Amanda.

Lea's *sixteen-year-old* sister Amanda.

And *that's* when I remember why things didn't work out between us in the first place.

Before I even met Luke, he was the stuff of legend. His parties were famous for their lack of parental guidance and all that came along with it. I'd heard all about the last one—his biggest ever—from a couple of the girls on the field hockey team.

—Melissa Robechaud puked all over Ken Geary. I think she drank a fifth of vodka or something.

—Gary Paola and Andrea Potter had sex on Goldenrod's washing machine! I think they had taken ecstasy or something.

–Jennifer Stansfield stripped in front of a whole room full of people! I think she was sober but, you know, she, like, takes *theatre*.

But that wasn't all. No less than three of my field-hockey teammates, all juniors, had warned against his advances. One day, while we were waiting in line to take shots against the goalie, the starting left wing, Jackie Donadio, explained it to me. He's got a *major* freshman fetish. It's like everyone else knows he's a scumbag, but he's got a blank slate with the fresh meat or something. No one from his class or ours will touch him with a ten-foot pole, and only the most desperate sophomores are still into him so he's already been cherry-picking from your class. All I'm saying is, Watch out.

When Jackie pointed him out to me at the game the next week, I didn't see what the big deal was. I mean, he was cute and everything, with his blond curls and tan, but so were a lot of guys. That's why, the day before his first big party of the year, when the only thing anybody could talk about was the party, who was going to be at the party, who was going to get wasted at the party, I was still set to do what I did just about every Saturday night: go to the movies with Lea or stay home and watch TV with my parents.

Even with no real plans on the horizon, I couldn't wait for the clock to hit three that Friday. Coach Vargas had given us the day off from practice, which meant I could finally catch an after-school Eco-Club meeting.

But when I got to Miss Danvers's classroom it was

empty. A piece of paper on the door said the meeting was canceled because Miss Danvers was out sick.

–Damnit! I said, and spun around, colliding into the person who'd been standing behind me.

–Oh, shit, I said, I'm so sorry. The person was more than a head taller than me, so I had to tilt my head to see who it was.

–Don't be sorry. Accidents happen. Canceled, huh? Bummer. The body I'd bumped into was attached to the curly head of none other than Luke Goldenrod.

–What do you mean, "Bummer"? I said, a little rudely, then caught myself. I mean, like, why do you care? You're not a member.

–*Like*, yes I am. I was president last year, actually. What are you, *like*, a freshman or something?

–Yeah. Um, I'm, um, sorry. I just never saw you at any of the meetings.

–Well, you know, I'm still working out some kinks in my schedule. What's your name, freshman?

–Cortina.

–Cortina. Nice. *¿Se habla español?*

I shook my head no. Italian, I said, but I actually think my parents made it up or something.

–Well, wherever it came from, it's cool. So, you're coming to my party tomorrow, right?

–I am?

–Well, I don't know. That's up to you, isn't it?

I cleared my throat and tried to act cool. Now that I knew Luke had been president of the Eco-Club, everything had changed. Yeah, I guess so, I said. What time does it start?

–I don't know. You know, regular time.

–Should I bring something? I asked. Oh, God. Why did I say that? That was something my mother would say. Kill me now! But did I stop there?

–That all depends. What do you want to bring?

–I don't know, Doritos or something?

He laughed out loud and said, Just bring your beautiful self, baby. He turned his back to me and sauntered down the hall, then called out over his shoulder, without even turning around. And some beer, if you can get some. But if you can't, that's cool. My brother's getting a keg.

–What do you mean, you can't go? Of course you can.

–I can't, said Lea. It's my grandmother's birthday.

–Your grandmother's birthday! I'm talking about, like, the biggest party of the year.

–Wait. Like, hello? Is this Cortina I'm talking to? Since when do you care about things like the biggest party of the year?

–Since I found out Luke Goldenrod was president of the Eco-Club last year.

–So do you like him now or something?

–No! I mean, yes. Like, not like *that*. I just, I don't know, feel like it would be a good opportunity to meet some people with, you know, similar interests.

–You know he's a senior, right?

–And you don't think a senior could like me?

–Sure, I think a senior could like you. But you know he's had a·lot of girlfriends, right?

–Yes! Jesus! I'm not, like, a complete idiot. I know he's had a lot of girlfriends. I know he's probably had a whole lot of sex with a whole lot of those girlfriends. And I don't care. He's nice.

–What, you, like, *know* him now?

–I met him, yeah.

–What was he like?

–I don't know, a little cocky, I guess. But nice. Come on, Lea, there are, like, *no* boys in Eco-Club and he was the *president*.

–Did you ever think that maybe that's *why* he was president?

–No. Though she had a point. Maybe he just likes seals, I said.

She sighed. Of course, she said. Why hadn't I thought of that? The man likes seals. And coral reefs . . . and . . . pussy.

–Lea!

–Don't be such a pervert. I meant *endangered* pussy . . . like . . . snow leopards. So, what time is the party, anyway?

–He didn't say.

–I can probably get there by ten. My parents will take us home whenever.

–I love you! I love you! Really. I love you. But I'll meet you there, okay? Because I gotta be home by midnight.

–They're still giving you a midnight curfew?

I didn't remind her that the midnight curfew was a vast improvement. She wouldn't understand. Ever since Lea's mom got sick, the laws in her house had pretty much disappeared.

–Yeah, but if I'm late, I'll just blame you.

–Don't blame me. Blame your endangered pussy.

There was no way I was going to let my parents anywhere within ten blocks of Luke Goldenrod's house, so I'd used the Eco-Club as a cover, said we were having a "get-together" afterward, and asked my mom to drop me off at the library near his house.

–There's an Eco-Club meeting *today*?

–The environment doesn't stop getting destroyed on weekends, Mom.

–For someone who wants to go out so badly, you're sure not acting like it.

–You're right, I said, I'm sorry.

–Yeah, you sound real sorry, my mom said and walked away.

We drove to the Elm Library in silence and I counted the houses absentmindedly. My mostly rural neighborhood of Farm Hills soon gave way to the center of town, Gardenville, and its pathetic suburban longing for urbanity: white-marble city hall, gray-granite post office, and red-brick high school towered over the dental offices and hair salons, steamy hot-wiener joints, and ubiquitous Dunkin' Donuts. Miraculously, Nelson's five and dime was still in business, as was the old-lady-underwear store with its window full of old-fashioned yellowing girdles, and Brown Bakery with its mostly-blown-out neon sign. The movie theater didn't have much time left; its white walls had gone gray and the robin's-egg-blue border that once gave it a royal bearing was chipping away. The black-iron war-memorial cannon across the street was covered in pigeon shit.

As we drove farther east we passed the copy store, the hardware store, the auto-parts store, and the cobblestone bridge that might once have covered a creeky offshoot of the Reservoir but now arched over a sad stretch of a 45-mph road that wanted desperately to be a highway. Just as I was almost overwhelmed with the ugliness and sprawl of my town, we mercifully emerged in Elmhurst, the oldest and most beautiful part of town, both richer and poorer than Farm Hills, because of its proximity to Providence. There, some houses had little bronze plaques near the front doors, as proof of their historic status, and others housed three or four families. The regal old houses by the water stood in stark contrast to everything else in Gales-town: the iron eagles and Madonna shrines you found in the Italian neighborhoods to the center and north of town, the faux urbanity of Gardenville, the rusted farm equip-ment that adorned the porches and backyards of Farm Hills, and even the McMansions of the gated communities to the far west.

I think it was then that I realized how small, how in-significant, my town really was. Before then, Galestown had seemed immense; in typical suburban fashion, neigh-borhoods were closed off from one another; off-limits. There was no sense of community, no bike path, no com-munal garden. Just row after row of nuclear families in small enclaves and subdivisions shut off from one another, slowly pulling away from the old days when second cousins were like brothers and no food went to waste.

I don't think this newfound sense of space, the discovery of the way time has a knack of folding upon itself, turning from an endless thread to a taut elastic so that a half-hour car drive, what once felt like an eternity, now seems only a second, was simply the result of growing older. It was more than that, otherwise every single Galestown resident would decide to leave the place the moment they drove across it. It was that for the first time I was experiencing my existence for what it was: sheltered, suburban, limited, differentiated only by architecture and the food served on Sundays. As a child, taking the bus from Farm Hills to Peterson, each neighborhood we passed seemed to extend forever in the other direction. They all seemed endless, out of reach. But now that I knew people who lived in all these neighborhoods, now that I'd driven down most of the streets, except for the few that were off-limits thanks to growing threats of gang violence flowing over from Providence, I realized their finitude. The minivan had barely come to a stop before I hopped out without so much as a word to my mother.

After a few hours of unfocused studying and a dozen trips to the bathroom to check my hair and teeth, I packed up my books and stole out of the library. Terrified that my parents might have me under surveillance, I walked quickly, and prayed that I'd beat the rain I could infer was on its way from the frizziness of my hair. In about twenty minutes, I was standing in front of a white house atop a steep hill I knew bordered the bay on the other side. As I smelled the salt in the air, I was reminded that the ocean was mere miles from my house—unbelievable, when you considered that my parents always made a trip to the water seem like such a hassle. Of course, I knew there was no real beach here, just grass leading into murky water oiled by the yacht club around the corner.

I took a deep breath and began my march up the driveway, which was weirdly empty. Luke must have asked people to park on different streets so that neighbors wouldn't be able to tell that he was having a party. Not that you could really hide that kind of thing once it got started.

When I got to the top of the steps I checked the paper in my pocket on which I'd written the address. The ink was blurry from my rubbing it between my fingers so many times as I committed it to memory, just in case I lost the slip in the time it took to get from my house to the library to the party.

But sure enough, the address was the same as the one on the plaque in front of my eyes. I took another deep breath and rang the doorbell. I waited for a minute or so, then became convinced I hadn't actually gotten a sound out of the thing, so I went for the knocker instead. As I reached up to take hold, the door opened.

On the other side was a tall blond guy who looked enough like Luke for me to conclude it was his brother. Is . . . is . . . Luke here? I asked. I think he's supposed to be . . . I stopped myself before I announced the party, in case this wasn't the brother who was getting the keg, but a young uncle or visiting priest.

–You're a little early for the party, but he's here. Come on in.

–I'm early? Really? I was . . . um . . . at the library. . . . I thought it was at least nine, I lied. I can come back . . .

–I'm sure Luke won't mind. He's upstairs.

Oh, shit. This was sooo much worse than bringing Doritos.

–Ooookay . . . you sure I shouldn't come back in a little while?

–Nah. People will be here soon, anyway. LUKE, some-one's here!

Oh, God. This was beyond mortifying. Why hadn't I just gone with Lea at ten? I should have known a high-school party wouldn't get started before eight.

–Oh, yeah? Who's the early bird?

–Me, I mean, it's me, Cortina.

–Cortina? Eco-Club Cortina?

–Yeah, I said weakly.

–Well, come on up. You can help me pick out a shirt to wear.

Oh my God, Luke Goldenrod wanted me to help him pick out a shirt. I finished walking up the stairs, followed the voice, and walked into his room, where he was stand-ing, bare-chested, in front of his mirror. He was holding up a yellow T-shirt and a blue one, but all I could see was his stomach. He had a six-pack and a perfect tan, as if he'd done nothing all summer but play shirtless soccer in the sun. Of course, that's probably exactly what he'd done.

He shook the shirts at me. Come on, you're a chick. Which one?

Okay, wait, how long have I been standing here? And did he just ask me something? There was music playing softly in the background.

–What are you listening to? I finally said.

–Dave Matthews Band. You don't know them?

–Oh, sure, I lied. Sure. I just didn't recognize them at first.

–Well, they're the best. I saw them play last summer, and man, it was the craziest time of my life. You should come see them next summer with me when they play.

–Totally, I said. Since when do I say words like *totally*? I sounded exactly like Alex and all those other girls who spent all their time talking about boys they totally loved and girls they totally hated. I was out of my mind. Finally, I spoke, The yellow one, totally. I'd totally go with yellow. Definitely.

–Thanks, he said, pulling the yellow T-shirt over his head. There was a picture of a skull with an arrow running through it, a pot leaf, and the words CYPRESS HILL. I wondered if that was a place in Jamaica or Amsterdam or something, but I didn't want to ask another dumb question. Then Luke broke the awkward silence, saying, Look, people aren't going to be here for at least another half hour. What do you feel like doing until then?

–Whatever, I said. I'm totally cool just hanging out up here.

–Why don't I get us both some beers?

–Excellent, I said. I'd love one. Totally.

Okay, girl, get it together. He's just going to get some beers and I'm going to wait in his room. Totally normal.

And I am totally not going to snoop. I tried to force out of my mind everything that wasn't Dave Matthews or my hands nervously braiding a thin strip of my hair, but as soon as I'd plaited and unplaited several sections, bitten an entire nail down to the skin, and started in on a second, I decided that there was no harm in looking around, as long as I didn't touch or open anything. After all, I'd never been in a boy's room before.

After scanning the room, searching for signs that the former Eco-Club president lived here and finding none, I decided I never needed to see another boy's room again, so representative of boyness was this one. I counted nine soccer trophies then moved on to the posters, one of John Belushi in *Animal House*, another for a movie I'd never heard of called *Reservoir Dogs*. On the floor was a mess of CD cases—Pink Floyd, Led Zeppelin, the *Dazed and Confused* sound track, The Who, Bob Dylan—tangled in a pile of blank tapes with big bubbly letters, obviously a girl's. Peeking out from beneath the bed were soccer cleats, beaten-up Adidas Sambas, and a glass bong with swirly yellows, pinks, and blues, filled with yellow-black water. On the bedside table was a photograph of Luke and a girl I didn't recognize, in a silver frame engraved with the words ALWAYS AND FOREVER, GALESTOWN HIGH JUNIOR PROM, 1994.

The disarray of the room was making me nervous; nothing was where it should be. I couldn't stand to look at it anymore so I picked a copy of *Rolling Stone* off the floor whose headline read:

WHAT'S THE FREQUENCY, MICHAEL?

R.E.M.: SEX AND NOISE

I heard the doorbell ring and voices outside.

–Goldenrod, open the fucking door, bro!

–Yoooooo-hoooo, Goldennuts, let us into your pants. I mean, your party!

–Yeah, dude. Open the door. It's fucking raining out here.

–UH, UH, let me INSIDE, Goldenpussy, let me COME inside. OPEN your LEGS, I mean, open your door!

I heard the front door open and Luke say, What the hell's up, you fuckers! Come in, come in.

I didn't recognize the voices so I assumed they must be seniors. God, I hoped some other people I knew showed up soon.

–Dude, what the fuck? Don't tell me this is gonna be another sausage fest, Goldenrod. . . . Where's all that sweet freshman pussy you promised us?

Freshman pussy? Luke promised them pussy? Oh, Jesus, Lea was right. What an idiot! And the worst part of it was, Luke didn't even want my pussy. I mean, me. He just wanted to pass me off to one of his loser friends. I should have known this was going to happen. I mean, I couldn't even get a boy my own age. No, wait, to be more accurate, I turned boys my own age *gay*. Did I really think a senior was going to like me? What was *wrong* with me?

I let out a deep breath and fell back on his bed and saw something that could have exposed Luke for who he really was long before those voices did. There, just a few feet from my eyes, on Luke's ceiling, was a picture of a model in a red bathing suit that hardly covered her breasts or her butt. Her hair was soaking wet, her body was dusted over with a layer of sand, and she was smiling in a way that made it look as if the sand actually felt good, when everyone knows there is nothing worse than getting sand all over you; it's scratchy and gets stuck inside your suit and I hated that someone made the poor model smile as if it felt good. God, boys were so gross. I hated Luke then. Even if he didn't put the model into the bathing suit or roll her around in the scratchy sand, the fact that he owned the poster just encouraged it. God, why couldn't he be more like Shawn? Suddenly I didn't care that he was gay anymore or even if he'd made up the whole gay thing to get out of hooking up with me; at least Shawn wasn't a total pervert who somehow found me repulsive enough that he needed to foist me off upon his friends.

What was I thinking to come here, to like Luke, to *like*-like him, despite all the warnings? If this was what high-school boys were like, then you could have them and their sausage fests. I was so totally outta here. . . .

–Cort? I got your beer.

–Um, don't worry about it. I'm not really feeling that great . . .

–Wait. Don't tell me you're punking out on me. Is it because of those idiots downstairs? Listen . . .

–It's not that. It's just I'm not . . .

–It's just that you're not a fan of being treated like a piece of meat. Well, I don't blame you. Look, I don't even *like* Thibodeau, Wayne, and Molloy. I mean, they're, like, total hockey guys, you know?

I laughed in spite of myself. The hockey team could be found on an evolutionary scale somewhere between chimpanzees and slugs.

Luke added, I bet you field-hockey girls could kick the hockey team's ass.

–No way. I don't skate.

–Well, neither can they. And you've got better-looking uniforms.

I laughed again but before I could say anything else, the doorbell rang again. Look, he said, we should probably head down, since everyone else is going to be coming soon. Besides, I probably shouldn't leave those guys unattended. You want to head down with me?

–Sure, I said. I hadn't forgiven him exactly, not completely, anyway, but that didn't mean that I couldn't use this as an opportunity to meet some new people. I could think of the party as a, you know, grassroots environmental outreach social networking event. . . .

–Follow me, Luke said and then grinned his soccer-star grin. I followed.

I was happy to see that the group at the front door included Jackie Donadio, who raised her eyebrows at my opening the door, but dropped them once I explained to her how I'd managed to make it past my strict parents. Jackie was Italian too. She understood. As the party started filling up, I did my best to mingle, which was easy to do because as big as the house was, the party was contained to three rooms: keg in the kitchen, bong in Luke's room, and music in the living room. But no matter who I was talking to, my mind was on Luke. I kept him in my sight as he talked to other girls; when he'd touch their arms or make them laugh, I'd squeeze my eyes shut momentarily. Upon opening them, I'd watch him walk over to another group and I'd tell myself that it was harmless flirting; he was just being a good host.

By the time I began to refill my keg cup for the second time—or was it the third?—I felt like anything was possible. I didn't even feel like it was necessary to talk to Luke; it was enough to know he wanted me there. I followed him in the most discreet way I could imagine: by leaving the room whenever he entered it. I knew it was only a matter of time before he'd end up where I had disappeared to. And in the process, I moved through clouds of smoke, crowds of people I only knew from reputations that preceded them, various stages of drunkenness, and rumors that the keg was about to be kicked, so drink up now.

At 10:34, with no sign of Lea, Kevin Frederick shoved a beer funnel in my face and told me, Suck it, freshman. I pushed it away and said, Suck it yourself, Frederick, and everyone laughed, including Kevin.

At 11:01, Karen Lyons from the field-hockey team asked me if I wanted to smoke pot, and I said yes, should we go up to Luke's room? And she said, no way, then we have to share, so we went out to the back porch and smoked and watched the rain come down. She must have been really wasted because she started telling me about how her boyfriend, Michael Jansen, wanted to have sex with her, only she didn't want to, not because she doesn't want to have sex, just because she doesn't want to have sex with Michael Jansen. I didn't ask why she was going out with him in the first place, because it seemed like I should know. Not long afterward, Michael found us outside and I could tell Karen didn't want me to leave them but that

Michael did, so I just kind of hung out there for a bit, frozen in stoned awkwardness, until I realized all I needed to do to gain my freedom was finish my beer and say I needed a new one.

At 11:28, after I finished filling up my cup, Marissa DiCecco, a senior I'd never met before, dragged me outside to share a cigarette with her, and after professing how beautiful my hair was, how natural, she turned her head, puked over the side of the porch, checked around to see if anyone noticed, popped a stick of gum, lit another cigarette, and said she was going inside to refill her beer.

At 11:39, there was still no sign of Lea and I had no idea how I was going to get home. As it was, I'd already be late. I walked into the kitchen, stepping over a passed-out Daria Michelson, and picked up the phone.

–I'm so glad you called! I didn't know how to get in touch with you.

–Where are you? How come you're not here?

–I just got home a half hour ago and my dad said it was too late to go out. I didn't feel like arguing with him.

–Can you tell him I need a ride?

–Look, Cort, my mom just had chemo yesterday, which means the next week is going to suck. I really don't want to piss off my parents tonight, okay?

–Yeah, that's cool—I understand. I'll find a ride. And, Lea, I'm really sorry about your mom.

–That's okay. I'm really sorry I couldn't make it.

I hung up the phone. What was I supposed to do now? I couldn't call my parents. Not with the music blasting and people passed out all over the house, maybe even outside on the front lawn, I thought, looking at Daria. Shit. I slid against the walls, closed my eyes, and put my face in my hands. A few seconds later, someone—a boy someone—pulled my hands away.

–So, Cortina, why have you been ignoring me all night?

–Wha . . . What? Luke. I haven't been ignoring you.

–Yes, you have. Every time I walk into a room, you look at me, then you look away, then you disappear.

–I do?

–Yeah. Why? I thought we were cool.

–We are. I mean, I just figured you had a lot of people to talk to cause it's your party and everything.

–Yeah, and you're one of them. So, where are you going to run off to now?

–Home.

–You want to leave?

–I don't *want* to leave. But I told my parents I'd be home around midnight. (Why was I *saying* this?) And I don't want them to worry. (Oh, please, kill me now.)

–Damn. I thought we'd get more time to get properly acquainted. Who's your ride?

–I'm her ride. I felt an arm on my shoulder. Jackie.

–You can bring me home?

–Sure. I'm leaving in five minutes. No offense, Goldy, but your party is lame.

–None taken. Especially coming from you, Jackie baby.

–Cort, I've got to find Anthony. He and Seamus Keane ate some mushrooms an hour ago and ever since Seamus took off for greener pastures I've been stuck on babysitting duty. But I'll meet you outside in five?

–Cool. Jackie, I totally appreciate it.

–You're *totally* welcome. She raised her eyebrows and walked away.

–So, you got your ride. And now you're leaving me.

–I'm not leaving you, I'm just leaving. Besides, I'll see you on Monday.

–You're coming over?

–No. I mean, at school, I said. Wait, do you want me to come over?

–Do you want to come over?

–Ye . . . yeah. Sure. Why not?

–Okay, cool. Why don't you come by after field hockey?

–The thing is, we've got a game.

–That's cool. So why don't we meet up afterward? Sound good?

This was totally moving too fast. I knew it, he knew it, even Jackie knew it. But did that stop me from saying, Sounds good?

No.

I was never the type to get nervous before a game. It wasn't really all that important to me, all that competition stuff, you know? Field hockey was just something to put on my college applications. Funny thing is, I was actually pretty good at it, mainly because you didn't need coordination, talent, or experience. We weren't like the basketball girls who went to camp in the off-seasons, or the cross-country team who regularly ran 5Ks. We didn't have the bodies of athletes, nor the minds. And you didn't have to. You just needed to be angry. Before I joined the team I never knew I was angry, but as it turned out, that's exactly what I was.

But I still didn't care if we won or lost, you know? So when Jackie noticed that I looked unusually nervous before the game—I was so busy trying to count the number of people in the stands that I was missing practice shots like you wouldn't believe—she wanted to know what was up.

–Just nervous, that's all.

–No offense, girl, but I've never seen you nervous before.

I couldn't tell Jackie where I was going after the game, not after what she'd told me about Luke. Maybe someday, I mean, like if I started dating him or something, then I'd tell her, then I'd tell everyone, but until I knew exactly what was going on, I wasn't going to risk anyone finding out about it. If it got back to Luke that I was telling everyone I was going to his house, or worse, if the rumor got around that I liked him and he didn't like me, I'd be mortified. I didn't want to lie to Jackie, especially not after our ride the other night, which was hilarious, because Anthony kept talking about Smurfs and how much he'd like to be one, and didn't Jackie and I, with our luscious hair, look like Smurfettes? And wasn't everything great in Smurftown, which was just south of Galestown, he said, and didn't we wish we had taken shrooms too, because they were the magic key that unlocked the gateway to Smurftown? I did, but I didn't say so, because before I could open my mouth Jackie said seeing what an idiot Anthony was acting like made her realize she never wanted to take shrooms, ever.

Then she said that she felt stupid enough by association, and I remembered what Alex's mom's weird friend Ramona had told me last July, that I was super-susceptible to intoxication, that I had thin skin, that the spirits of this world and others could slip in and out of me at will. She said I needed to beware the poisons, for they would find me and take me away, whether I wanted them to or not. Alex had rolled her eyes and said, She says stuff like that to everyone, just ignore her, but I was spooked all the same.

I didn't want to lie to Jackie, but I didn't want to be like her either. The way she treated Anthony like a mother, the way all the other Italian girls did with their boyfriends—it was like they were their own mothers in training. I didn't want to lie to her, but I didn't want to tell her the truth, either, because telling her the truth would bring me one step closer to her, and one step further from freedom. Anthony might have sounded stupid that night, but at least he was free.

After the game ended, and I don't even remember if we won or not, I ran out to my parents and told them some of the girls were getting a bite to eat, either to celebrate our victory or drown our sorrows in Pepsi, can't recall. The point was, I was getting a ride home. I knew they wanted to argue, but I was either wearing my warrior face or crying tears of loss, so they couldn't.

When they pulled away, I could not believe I'd gotten away with it. And I wasn't completely sure I was even happy about that.

There was no sign of Luke so I walked back to the benches and sat down. Fall had definitely kicked in; it was already dark and I needed a jacket. Some of the girls were still hanging around with friends and boyfriends and for a moment I felt jealous, jealous of all these kids who grew up together in this neighborhood, who never needed to be bussed to some school across town the moment they started making friends simply because they were smarter than everyone else. Sure, I had Lea, and sometimes I had Alex; mostly, though, I was alone.

As I watched the last of my teammates drive off, I looked at the trees that surrounded the field, watched them standing motionless, despite the breeze that was trying to coax my hair from its French braid pigtails, and I wondered if they felt as lonely as I did.

–Cort! Hey, Cort! I'm freezing my ass off over here. Come on!

I turned my gaze from the trees to the parking lot, where Luke was standing outside his Jeep—oh, God, why does he have to drive a tank?—in his soccer shorts and a long-sleeved T-shirt—oh, God, why does he have to have *that tan*? I slid on my backpack, and trudged through the muddy field to the place he was standing.

–Rough game, eh? he asked, pointing to my muddy shin pads.

–Yeah, they don't really take such good care of this field, I said. We were slipping all over the place out there.

–Sounds hot, he said. Get in. He held the door open for me and I stepped in, hoping that I'd forget he was driving a war machine once I was inside.

I didn't.

As we pulled into his driveway, I noticed it was free of other cars. Are your parents home?

–Nope. They're in Mexico. How else do you think I managed to have that party?

–Oh. And your brother?

–Nah. He doesn't live here. He just came to the party to cherry-pick. He laughed then looked worried. From the senior girls, of course. He's not interested in jailbait, you know what I'm saying?

I didn't.

As soon as he opened the door, he started up the stairs. So why don't we go up to my room?

–Okay, I said, nervous. It was one thing to go to a party at a guy's house when no parents were home, but another thing altogether to be there when the party was over. Still, I followed him upstairs, unsure of what exactly to do when we got there.

–Have a seat, he said, pointing to the bed. The room was cleaner than it had been the night of the party, but I tried not to look around too much, too afraid that I'd find more evidence that Luke was the kind of guy everyone was telling me he was.

–You mind if I put on music?

–No, of course not.

I sat at the edge of the bed, untied my cleats, and began to take off my shin pads. Hey, let me help you with that, he said. I was embarrassed. I'd been running around for hours and I knew I probably smelled gross. The last thing I needed was for the hottest guy in school to think I was a pig. I can manage, I said, plucking off one cleat, then the other.

–Don't be shy, he said. I just came from playing too, remember? He grabbed a piece of his own shirt near his chest and held it out. Besides, he added, I think sweat is sexy.

I scrunched up my nose as I peeled off my shin pads. You do?

–Sure I do. It's natural. Healthy. He sat down next to me and touched my braids. Like your hair, he said. Curls are so pretty, so natural. Can I take it down?

–If you do it will be all frizzy.

–I don't care, he said. No. In fact, I do care. Everyone's hair should be frizzy. Frizzy is natural. I hate all those girls that think they have to look like they're thirty years old or something. Makeup, hair spray, all that stuff is just so . . . toxic . . . don't you think?

–Yes! I do! I think it's totally toxic and fake, and terrible for the environment.

–You're so beautiful, Cortina, Luke said, and touched my knee, just below where my field-hockey skirt ended. With his other hand, he cupped my chin. I looked at him briefly, then I scrunched my nose up, knowing he was going to kiss me.

His mouth felt good, warm—no, hot. He tasted like watermelon Jolly Ranchers, like he was keeping one inside his cheek. I put my hand on his stomach, over his shirt, and he pushed it underneath, so that I was touching his skin, which was even smoother than mine, and warm. Boys were always so warm.

And then he pushed my hand lower, on top of his shorts, which were warm too, and I could feel, even through his shorts, that he had a big dick, that he was hard. He sighed a little, even though I hadn't done anything but let my hand be moved. Instantly, I felt terrified, partly terrified that I was in way over my head, but mostly terrified that he was going to discover at this very moment that what he really liked was boys.

–Sit on my lap, he said.

–What?

–Sit on my lap. Please, he said.

So I did. Thank God it had been cold enough outside that I never broke a real sweat, I thought, as he put his hands around my waist, and I sat down on his lap.

–I love these fucking skirts. You look so fucking hot, he said, pulling his mouth away from mine, then pushing his lips against mine hard, and using his teeth a little to bite my lower lip.

I didn't know what to do, now that I was sitting on him, but it felt so good that I didn't want to move. So I just sat there, frozen.

–Move back and forth, he said.

–Huh?

He spoke louder now. Move back and forth, over my lap. Trust me, you'll like the way it feels. It will feel really fucking good.

So I did what he told me, even though it made me nervous for us to be this close. He was wearing mesh shorts, and I was wearing cotton underwear. Could sperm get through?

–Oh, I said, and Oh, again, surprised that I had allowed myself to make any noise.

–It's good, right, he said and I nodded. It was good, like, ridiculously good. I'd never felt anything so good in my life. Just keep doing that, he said, and then he pulled off his shirt.

–Can I take off your shirt? he said. Your skin is so beautiful. I want to feel it against mine without all the artificial layers in between. I didn't answer, just pulled my jersey over my head.

–Oh my God, he said. That is so hot.

I liked hearing that, that I was hot or, at the very least, that what I was doing was hot. It was not something I'd ever heard before, and that Luke was saying it, well, that made it even better, even if he was probably just saying it to be nice.

I expected Luke to take off my bra, but he didn't seem all that interested in feeling me up. Instead, his hands went lower, first to my thighs, then to my hips.

–I want to look at you, he said, and laid down on his back, taking me with him, before rolling over so that he was above me. I want to see you, he said, then got down on the floor. He touched my knees, then moved his hands up my legs, giving me goose bumps, and then said, Will you take everything off so that I can see you? See you as you really are without the, um, constraints of . . . uh . . . synthetic fibers?

I laughed, nodded slowly, and started unwrapping my skirt. No, wait, he said. Leave that on, okay? But take off everything else. I pulled off my bra and my underwear and put them in a little pile at the edge of the bed. Luke sat at my feet, his hands on my legs, his long hair all messy. Good, he said. That's good, Cort. You look so fucking beautiful. Do you want to see me too?

I nodded again, and waited for him to climb out of his red shorts, which said GH in the lower right-hand corner—Galestown High. He was wearing blue boxer briefs and his dick was up so high, it was showing at the top of the waistband. He looked much taller, much bigger with his clothes off, and I could see hairs on his chest that I hadn't noticed the night of the party.

Feeling ridiculous in my stupid plaid field-hockey skirt, I said, Are you sure you don't want me to take this off?

–Yeah, I'm sure, he said. Because I want to experience what you're, uh, like on the inside, while you're, um, wearing what you wear, you know, like, on the outside . . . in, um, the nature, I mean, in the environment. Is that okay?

–I . . . I don't know. I said. I want to, it's just, I haven't showered.

–You can shower here, he said. I mean, you don't have to, but if it will make you feel better, you can. . . .

–I can't, I said. My parents will wonder why my hair is wet.

He chuckled. Okay, Cort. Your call. Come here, sexy girl, he said, and jumped onto the bed with me. He grabbed my face and kissed me hard. I felt an ache in my belly, and wanted to tell him I'd changed my mind. I wanted to sit in his lap a little longer, or, like, you know, forever, but I was too nervous now that he was in his boxers and I wasn't wearing any underwear. I was also thinking of the time. The game had ended at least an hour ago; my parents would be wondering why I wasn't home yet. I had to leave soon, and there simply wasn't time to lose my virginity, or so I thought. There wasn't time for anything, not for anything good. But I couldn't stop, couldn't leave. If I left now, Luke would tell everyone that I was a cocktease, or worse, that I didn't know what I was doing. Lord knows, Shawn had probably already warned people about me. Besides, I had heard about blue balls and I didn't want Luke to be in pain. So I lowered my head, or maybe he lowered my head, I don't remember.

The way I remember it is this, he put his big strong arms around me and laid me down on the bed, which was soft, like the earth should be. There was no pain, there was no girl in a red bathing suit, there was no driving home in silence.

That's not the way I remember it at all.

The way I remember it is this, the song was about love, or about lovers, at least. It wasn't about things ending, it wasn't about seeing him in the hallway the very next day, kissing Alex Rossi, holding her hand. It wasn't about the week after that, arm-in-arm with some other girl.

That's not the way I remember it at all.

The song was about laying down together, about sleeping, it wasn't about things being over before they'd begun.

That's not the way I remember it at all.

my mind playin' tricks on me

BEN

The Windham really is a pretty sorry excuse for a mansion, if you ask me, but I guess back in the day it was pretty swank; now it just looks sad to me, and it makes me mad, too, when I think about how good the Windhams had it compared to all the little people piled up on top of one another in all the little mill houses behind it, where my mom and dad both grew up, where their parents grew up, too, and, you know, so forth. This place gives me the willies, but at least out here you can see that Main Road is just a few feet away. At least when you're outside you're still inside this century.

The reception is still going on, but the DJ is on a Tony Bennett kick, so I snuck out here to spark a blunt before they even brought out the coffee.

I see the limo driver standing outside his ride, smoking a stoge, and he nods in my direction and I figure, what have I got to lose, it's not like he's a law-enforcement officer, so I mosey on up to him and ask him if he'd mind if I got a little lifted in the limo, and he says, Mind? and holds up his stoge, which isn't a stoge at all, and passes it to me. It smells good, better than the schwag I got off Seamus Keane and yeah, yeah, I know Kyle Riley's got better stuff but as long as I've got beef with his brother, I figure it's best to bring my patronage elsewhere.

We hop in the front seat of the limo, and I reach over to the backseat where I got all my CDs stashed in my pack and ask him if he minds if I put on some old-school Geto Boys. He's, like, I prefer East Coast stuff, and I say, Who doesn't, but this song's the bomb, and he nods and says, Whatever, man, and closes his eyes and I must say I'm glad he's not driving me home. I light my blunt on the car lighter, blow on it to even things out, and pass it to my man. Then I slide in the CD and hit the Forward button five times.

The year Jason died, Halloween fell on a weekend. Me and my boys were too old for trick-or-treating, so we decided to cause a bit of a rumpus instead. You know, waking the dead, hallowing the eves, cracking some jack-o'-lantern skulls and what-have-you.

All I could think of during football practice was what was gonna go down that night. I loved Halloween, man, always did. Not the dressing up part, really; that was for pussies. Not even the candy, either. We lived next door to this Italian bakery called Delvecchio's and Mrs. D always used to bring over piles of sugar-dusted wandies and zeppoles; I guess she was afraid the Reardons were going to choke on some dry soda bread if we didn't get our daily dose of mascarpone. If you're used to a cannoli with every meal, Twizzlers and Milk Duds kind of pale in comparison, you know what I'm saying?

No, what I loved about El Día de los Muertos was how they let all us kids run loose on the neighborhood, even when we were little and shit. It was just us in the dark, freaking each other out, equally convinced that something was about to creep up on us and pretty sure that nothing would. And after my bedtime, whatever it happened to be that year, I'd stay up real late, looking out the windows at the older kids walking by, some of them not wearing costumes at all, but soaking up the freedom the holiday gave them anyway.

But that year, for the first time, I *was* the older kids. Not old enough to have a car—and let's face it, if you had a car, who needed Halloween?—but old enough to stay out late enough to make things, you know, interesting. And with it being a Saturday and all, there wasn't much our parents could do but stand at the door waving good-bye nervously as we crept into the night. It was going to be *awesome.*

The anticipation was making football practice even more heinous than usual. Coach had us doing sprints because we'd lost the night before, 33–6, fucking up something royally against St. Ray's. Not that we could help it; those fuckers were fast and huge. They were way out of our league but some asshole in the interscholastic league decided per-capita income per town was a better way of demarcating divisions than average height, weight, and, oh, I don't know, roid-spiked Pop-Tarts consumed each morning.

Not that Coach Z saw it that way. Reardon, he screamed, don't think I don't know that you were out chugging beers in the Aquaduct Woods last night after the game. Let's see you sweat the alcohol out, eh? You boys think I don't know what you're up to? I have eyes and ears all over the city. You're athletes! Do you think Drew Bledsoe was out getting drunk after last week's game? No! He was thinking about *this* week's game!

–While getting his *dick* sucked, Kevin Frederick said to me, under his breath.

–Tell me about it, I said. If Coach wants to hook us up with postgame knobbies, I'll never touch another sip of alcohol in my life. I gave myself the sign of the cross, as best as I could, seeing as Coach had upped the ante on the torture by making us run with a helmet in one hand, ball in the other.

God, Coach Z was such a fuckwad. I'd never been so happy to hit the fountains. The team limped to the locker room, but I made a detour to my regular locker first because I always put some Gatorade in there before practice so no one would steal it. And believe me, steal it they would. The water Coach brought tasted so much like the old school containers it sat in you'd have thought that plastic was a fucking electrolyte or whatever.

As I walked into the empty corridor, I let out a little whistle to push all the creepiness out of the space. Being in school on a Saturday just feels . . . wrong. Like, there's nobody there, you know there isn't, outside of maybe some math dorks or whatever who come in on the weekends to solve equations. But even when the place is empty, it's full. In fact, it feels even fuller than when you're sharing the hallway with a hundred other kids. It's only when they're not there that you can see what a truly fucking heavy place it is, full of kids even when it's empty. In spite of it being ballsin' hot for October, my body was overcome with middle-of-the-night-in-winter toilet-bowl chill.

I walked up to my locker and tried to open it but, for the love of Christ, I'd forgotten the combination again, still stuck on last year's 38-24-18. Fuck. Why was it so fucking cold in here? There was no AC in the school that

I knew of and it was at least 80 outside. After a few more tries, finally, bingo! I grabbed the bottle of Gatorade, slammed my locker shut, gave the lock a quick spin, and ran as fast as my legs would take me after two hours of sprinting.

And then I heard something weird, like footsteps running in the other direction. I stopped in my tracks, swung around, but the sound was gone. Who's there? I called, but heard nothing but the echo of my own voice. Dumbass, I thought, it's probably just one of the other guys. Ever since some asshole broke into my locker last year and put a mail-order shrunken head inside, I've been acting like a total *bitch*.

Still, when I have nightmares, and I have them a lot, it's always of this place. This place between locker and gym, between classes, between weeks. I never know my combination, I've forgotten to study, the bathrooms are filthy, I've forgotten my clothes. Someone's watching me, I'm all alone. It's silent, there are echoes. I'm burning, I'm cold. I'm running fast, I'm stuck in place.

Walking faster now, I started humming Sir Mix-A-Lot's "Baby Got Back," completely convinced that anyone trying to kill me would be so amused by this choice that he'd set his bloodthirsty sights on some smooth-jazz fan instead. It was only when I got to the gym and heard the sounds of my teammates that I knew the ordeal was over. I chugged the bottle of Gatorade, tossed it in the garbage can next to the bathroom stalls, and walked into the locker room.

There was a line. Lots of days guys just wait to shower at home, but after practices like today's, the faster you could get the grimy sweat off, the better.

–What's up, Joey? I said to our tight end, all terror forgotten.

–Man, what the fuck is up with Coach today? It's like he's fucking possessed or something.

–He's upset because Ms. Leon tore down the banner in the gym, Lou DaSilva chimed in.

–Why did Ms. Leon tear down the banner in the gym?

–Because "Chiefs" is racist . . . you know, to Native Americans. Ms. Leon is trying to get them to change it. Even Coach wants them to change it.

–To what?

–Fuck if I know.

–So why's Coach so pissed if he wants to change it too?

–Because Ms. Leon called him racist.

–Oh, that's retarded. Coach Z's an asshole but he's not racist. His wife is Chinese!

–Cambodian.

–Whatever.

–Hey! said Rithisak Choeun.

–Oh, don't get mad, Rithi. You know what I mean.

–No I *don't*, white boy. And anyway, how would you feel, Lou, if I called you Irish?

–I'd kick your ass.

There were still, like, ten dudes ahead of me, so I left the crowd waiting in line and slunk deeper into the locker room where it was quiet and cool. I lay down on the bench and stared up at the ceiling which was chipping and peeling in all kinds of ways. I shut my eyes and listened to the sound of the water coming down, the other guys' voices a steady buzz beneath the drips. Before long, I was asleep.

I was jolted back to reality by the sound of my name. Bennnnn . . . Bennnnnnnnneeeeeeee. The soft voice rose above the showers and knocked me out of my brief slumber. I stood up, tightening my towel, and then nearly fell backward. Something was wrong. I couldn't see straight. It was like there was a thick fuzz in the room, not steam, but something else, something heavier. I figured maybe I was dehydrated or something, but wait—I'd just finished, like, a liter of Gatorade, so that wasn't it. I wondered if I had a concussion, so I held my hand up to my head. When I took it down, though, I almost lost it. Instead of its normal color, it was bright blue and, I don't know, kind of shimmery. What the fuck? The voices were gone, but the showers were still on, so I crept in there. Maybe if I just got under the water, I'd feel better. I walked into an empty stall and turned on the faucet, my right hand now bright red and shaking. I turned the water on and gave out a yelp, confused until I realized what was going on. I'd only turned it a little. Cold. Mighty pleased with myself for figuring this out, I turned it a little more and felt a lukewarm rush of water flooding all over me. I looked down and realized I was still wearing my towel, which for some reason struck me as goddamn hilarious. I started laughing my ass off, took it off, and hung it on the hook next to the curtain.

–Who is that? someone called from the stall next to me.

–Yeah, what's so fucking funny?

I didn't recognize the voices. The water was changing them somehow, absorbing them, making them bigger and growing right along with them.

I looked down at my hands, which looked so strong to me all of a sudden, both true blue and really fucking beautiful if you got right down to it. They were the hands of a quarterback. Fuck yeah, I said, I am the fucking king!

–Ben, is that you? What's up, man?

Did I say that out loud? Fuck. Except well, fuck it. Yeah, it's me, I said, and I am the fucking king!

–Whatever, man. If you're the fucking king, why did you throw three interceptions last night? You're the fucking king all right, the King of Suck.

–I . . . I . . . I started to protest until I realized the voice had hit the nail on the head. I *was* the King of Suck. I looked down at my hands and saw that they weren't strong and blue anymore, they were withered and green. I looked down at my cock, shriveled and tiny, and suddenly realized the water had gone cold.

I grabbed my wet towel and started running. Out of the shower. Out of the steam and the fog and toward the lockers. But as soon as I got there, I realized I couldn't remember the combination in here either. Numbers flew all around my head, but I couldn't hold on to any of them long enough to pull one down and take it into my hand and make it fit into the little lock before me. And where was I gonna find another towel?

I sat down on the bench and put my head in my hands and then I heard it again, my name, only this time the voice speaking it sounded kind, warm. I opened my eyes

my mind playin' tricks on me

and standing there in front of me, naked except for a towel, was Dan, grinning.

–Hey, King.

–Dan, I'm fucked up, man. I think I got a concussion or something. I feel wicked out of it.

He looked down at the towel that had caused a big black grimy puddle to form underneath the bench. I can see that. What happened to your towel?

–It's wet, I said. I just forgot . . . and before I could say anything else, I could feel my eyes watering until a big fat green drop fell onto my shriveled-up little hands.

–Hey, man, don't . . . look, I'll get you a towel. I think I got a spare in my locker.

Dan disappeared, leaving me alone and shivering on the bench, clinging to my wet towel. The sounds of the shower had been replaced with the clanging pipes of the ancient water-heating system, but to me, they sounded like a funeral march.

And then he was back, a big fluffy towel in his hands that he tossed to me. I looked up gratefully, grabbed the towel, and let the other one fall to the ground in a wet heap.

As soon as I dropped it, I looked up at Dan. He looked fucking beautiful. Like a fucking prince . . . only, let's face it: The only touchdown we'd scored last night had been on a pass I'd thrown to him—and not a long pass, either. He was the one who'd run fifty yards for the touchdown. He was no prince. He was the fucking king, man. Too bad those St. Ray's kids kept him locked up for the rest of the game or we would have scored eight more like it. I jumped up, gave him a huge hug, and said, I'm not gay or nothing, Dan, but you're fucking beautiful. I love you, man.

And with that, I darted out of the locker room in nothing but my towel. I had to get outside, into the sun.

Standing out front were three guys from the O line. As soon as they saw me, they started laughing their asses off. I didn't care. They still looked fucking beautiful. The sun was behind them, so the edges of their hair blurred into the sky behind them. The way the light was putting rainbow edges on everything was like looking at the three-dimensional world with 3-D glasses, enhancing things that didn't need enhancing, so that instead of jumping out at you, everything faded into the background, flattened into color.

−You save my asses every week, guys, and I fucking love you for it. Seriously, guys, you are fucking knights!

−Dude, you're tripping.

−Yeah, man, what the fuck's wrong with you?

−What is he on, is more like it?

−You all right, man? Dan, fully clothed now, had run outside. He grabbed my arm.

−No, Dan, it's like I'm losing my mind or some shit. I looked up at him and saw that his face was twisting into something else entirely. What the fuck was wrong with me? And then it hit me. Larry was right. I think I *am* tripping!

−Did you take anything?

−Nah, man. Nah. It's just . . . I know I've . . . I'm tripping, man.

–What do you feel like?

–Well, right now, I feel . . . It's like, everything is fucking funny one minute . . . and the next . . . shit, man. And there's this weird smell like something is burning. Whoa. Do you think my brain is on fire?

–Um, no. How could you be tripping, bro? You didn't take anything.

–I know. That's the crazy part! I started giggling.

Dan shook his head. Did you have any Robitussin this morning? I heard that stuff can fuck you up.

–Nah, man. All I had was some Gatorade. But I put it in my locker during practice. No one could have gotten it.

Dan spoke slowly. It's not that tough to get people's locker combinations, he said. Anybody who works in the principal's office could get them. And, hey! Didn't someone break into your locker last year?

I started laughing, even though shrunken heads are far from funny. Still, the thought that the herbs who work in the principal's office would have acid was fucking laughable.

Danny went on. Hey, doesn't Jason Lane work the front desk? That dude is fucking tapped. He'd totally do something like this.

I thought about it for a moment and it seemed like a good idea, but still fucking laughable so I just sat there, geeking.

–Dude, why don't you get some clothes on? We can go back to my place and chill or whatever till you sober up.

–Yeah! That would be awesome. I tugged up my towel

and followed Dan back into the locker room, grateful that the other guys had laughed their asses home already.

As Dan and I walked, he'd ask what I was seeing and I'd tell him, as best I could, and he'd shake his head and say he wished somebody had played the same trick on him. By then we'd pretty much figured out it was Jason who did it—well, Dan did; the concept of walking was mysterious enough for me at that point. The thing is, I never really had beef with Jason. I made fun of the stupid shit he did to his ears, clicked at him in Swahili and shit, but so did everybody else. Okay, and maybe once in gym class I didn't do anything when Gary Paola called him a pussy when I should have told Gary to shut the fuck up. I'm bigger than Gary—but everyone's bigger than Gary, which is why he feels he's gotta call everyone pussies. I mean, I can be a dick, but I'm not really that bad a guy.

When we got back to Dan's house, I noticed there was no one there. Where's Kel . . . your mom? I asked, before collapsing on the floor and staring at the breathing carpet and the plants waving at me from the other side of the room.

–She and Wally are in New Hampshire this weekend. Foliage and whatnot.

I tried to hide how much of a letdown this was, because the best part of being at Danny's was the fact that there was always a chance his moms would pop by. But I didn't feel bad for too long cause the second best part was Super Nintendo—and Mario and Luigi could give a shit about foliage.

At first, I thought my super-heightened senses were gonna make me the baddest Mario Kart racer ever. But instead I just continued my reign as the King of Suck. I was jonesin' for the old-school control pad, when A and B, up and down, left and right, start and select were the only choices you needed to make. Now there was all this X and Y bullshit, and things were only going to get worse. I mean, I could remember the secret code for Contra that would give you thirty-three free lives, for chrissakes, and now speeding up and slowing down was too fucking complex. In the end, I threw the controller down and asked Danny if I could just watch him play. He laughed and said sure.

–Can you, maybe, put on something a little, I don't know, like with elves or something like that?

–You mean something lame?

I started to say no, then Dan started laughing. I'm just kidding, Ben. If it's elves you want, then it's elves you'll get.

Dan pulled out some quest game whose name I didn't recognize cause I didn't really play that shit that often. Still, it was nice, just sitting there with Danny, watching him set off into the woods. I closed my eyes and let the flute music creep up into me, finding it sounded a lot better than it ever had before. It, I don't know, made sense or something.

And then something weird happened. I was in Dan's basement, but I wasn't *just* in Dan's basement. The flute was playing but it wasn't just the flute. It was dark and not dark. I was walking around and something was pulling me. I was moving and completely still.

I was in the game. And outside. In the woods. Down by the Reservoir. Looking for something. Only that wasn't it. Something was looking for me. The fact that Dan had the controller in his hands didn't mean shit; someone else created the game, mapped out every possible move before we could take it. We could only follow. There were choices. Into the sunlight, underground, home. But none of them our own, see.

When I opened my eyes I realized I'd never left Dan's couch. And it hit me that Dan's the one playing, I was just sitting there doing dick and that's when I knew I had to get out of there. I didn't know why. I just did.

I told Dan I was going home.

–Dude, let me walk you.

–Nah, man, I slept it off. And before he could say anything else, I was ghost.

I had to do this alone. This was my quest, not Danny's. I didn't need him today the way I needed him out on the field. It was like what happened in video games. Jason was, like, a dude who lived in one of those little straw huts that's hidden from view, the kind that you only find out about by doing something nice for some little old lady or by slaying a dragon. The dude working those shops isn't always cool, and he might not be giving you the treasure you deserve cause he wants to, but if you've got the rupees, the dragon heart, the scroll, he's got no choice but to give it to you. Jason might have been trying to fuck with me, but all he'd done was give me supreme fucking knowledge. There was something out there in those woods that somebody bigger than Jason wanted me to find. And

Jason, man, fucking beautiful shaman wannabe with his stretched out ears, fucking beautiful, man, maybe he'd been in on it too, maybe he hadn't cared that I called him a pussy once when he struck out at fucking softball in gym class, maybe he knew that was just the way the game started off.

This is what I'm thinking as I'm riding my bike—no, *flying* my bike—to the woods, ready to collect my treasure. It was getting dark outside and all the little kiddies were out, tiny pumpkins and pirates all shiny, shiny, felt and glitter, angels, ballplayers, chickens, fucking beautiful, every little kiddie so goddamn beautiful. I want to pick them all up, all the little kids, and swing them around in the air and say, stay there little guys. Don't grow up. Stay glowworms, stay goblins, stay goonies, stay freaks. Hold on tight to your little pumpkin pails and keep a lookout for the straw huts hidden behind the Volkswagens, that's where you'll find the good candy, none of this Jolly Rancher shit, I want fucking king-size Snickers like Mrs. Hughes gives out because I don't care if Dan's better than me, I am the fucking king.

I am racing, racing, and the woods are in sight and none of the kiddies out at this hour dare go close, they got mommies on their back, daddies trailing behind them in wood-paneled station wagons. They don't know that the real candy's out in the woods, they don't know that Rithi and Beans are rolling a keg in there tonight and that after we have the PARTY OF THE YEAR we are gonna wreak some serious havoc around G-Town.

I'm flying, right, *E.T.*-style, fearless, baby, dragon heart in the front basket except I don't got a basket. Fly, fucker, fly, sun going down, kiddies gone, trees there, still there, but when I trade in this dragon heart I'm gonna buy me some fire to burn 'em all down, to tear shit up tonight. I want to burn these woods down because bad shit goes down here, Shawn pussy Riley getting his ass kicked, stop, don't think of Shawn, don't think of Shawn, dragon heart, Benny, dragon heart, you are the fucking king in training, and there are branches all around the ground but at least it's dry, so my bike's still flying—no mud, too hot, trees are gonna burn, dragon heart, fire ahead—are the guys there early? Fire ahead—homeless dudes?

I pedal slower to the fire, which is really just smoke, and someone's sleeping next to it, one of my boys? Nah, couldn't be, too early for the woods, really, these woods are strictly 10:00 P.M. woods, it's fucking suicide to come into these woods any earlier than this, for real, too risky with cops circling—fucking asking for it, man.

I'm closer, so close that I can smell the fire and for a second I think it's my brain burning but that's stupid. Cause the fire's right there in front of me and I see that the dude is Jason, and he must be waiting for me, ready to welcome me into the clan of the fucking shamans and I'm half ready to offer up my earlobes, for real, and I hop off my bike and call out his name and he's still laying there and I'm like, Jay, dude, what's up? But he's still not moving and something's wrong because the smoke from the fire isn't just rising like it should be, it's swirling all over Jason like he's inside it or something, and I can hear the flutes and I see bottles pill bottles four fucking pill bottles five and no rupees no fire no blue bottles no gilded shield no enchanted map something's wrong and I'm shivering, dragon heart, and I lean over and see that his eyes are shut which is better than the alternative, but I lean over and hold my hand under his nose, dragon heart, and there's so much smoke swirling over him choking me making me cough and tons of it under his nose, just standing there, cause there's no breath there to push it away.

I back up, I start to run away, except I can't leave. I can't leave him there the way I left Shawn years before. I can't leave him there, so I scream. I scream and scream and scream and scream and scream and scream and scream and scream and scream and scream and scream and scream . . .

Until they find me, screaming and burning and screaming and burning, my dragon heart all dried up.

uncle john's band

CORT

It's not even 11:00 yet, but the dessert is out and the old people and the couples with kids are gathering together shawls and purses and cameras and silver picture-frame souvenirs. I can leave now, I guess, except Lea mentioned something about an after-party in Ben's hotel room, and I should at least show my face.

My table is empty—the rest of the wedding party is either getting high in the bathroom or out back. Nobody bothered to ask me to come with, so here I am, alone. Someone taps me on the shoulder, a guy tap, and I tense up, mostly hoping that it isn't Luke Goldenrod, partly praying that it is. I turn and am initially disappointed but ultimately delighted to see Jared Epstein where Luke might have been.

–Jared! What are you doing here? I haven't seen you all night.

–Well, I wasn't the only one missing in action. From what I heard, a bridesmaid missed most of the ceremony, he says. Wasn't you, was it?

–No!

–Didn't think so. I actually just got to town this afternoon. I was at this conference this morning in Cambridge. So . . . man, you look great, Cort. Your hair is awesome!

Jared Epstein was a year younger than me: sweet, smart, funny, took over as Eco-Club president after I graduated. I didn't remember him being friends with either Danny or Lea, and I said so.

–I wasn't, really. I mean, not like you were. But my mom was good friends with Danny's mom in high school. . . .

–Oh, I say. So are your parents here too?

–They were, he said. But they already left.

–I wish I'd seen them. They were always so nice to me. And I loved hanging out at your house too.

–You did? Why?

–All those books. I thought it was so cool that your parents were professors. It was, just, like, another world to me.

–Well, not anymore. How'd you end up liking Vermont? I almost went there too, you know.

–Well, the thing is . . . I didn't end up going to Vermont either.

–Really? I could totally picture you there. Where'd you end up?

–Actually, I didn't go to college, like, at all . . . I just thought there was more work to be done in the real world, you know?

Jared gives me a funny look, but then nods slowly and says, I can see that. I can totally see the benefits of working from the inside. Like, this morning, I was volunteering at this sustainability panel, and the discussion was just getting nowhere. It was, like, the academics just weren't speaking the same language as the panel members from the private sector.

I nod, but I don't really get what he's talking about. I'm sorry, Jared, I say, what exactly is sustainability?

He laughs. You know, that's what I love about you, Cort. You have the sense of humor that most environmentalists lack. Seriously, we're not going to get anywhere if we focus on the gloom and doom. So where are you working?

–Well, I'm not technically on the payroll, per se. Just

kind of networking with other . . . um . . . like-minded individuals. I spent some time, like, touring with Phish and now, you know, I'm considering what to do next.

–Oh, cool. So, you're, like, doing leaflets for environmentally responsible concert-going?

–Kinda like that.

I need to sit down. The painkiller is either wearing off or really kicking in, because suddenly my legs feel completely fucked up, and not in a good way.

–Jared, do you mind if we sit down?

–Of course not. I'd love to find out if there are ways we might be able to partner in the future. So what exactly are you working on right now?

–Oh, lots of stuff, I say. Lots of really good, good stuff . . . really, really . . . good. So, um, you said your parents were here, right?

–Oh, that reminds me. I forgot to tell you what they said when I said you'd be here.

–What?

–Well, when I mentioned your name and my mom said, Cortina Capotosto, Cortina Capotosto, wasn't she the one who was always running away from home?

I start to laugh, and Jared does too, until it hits us.

–I guess, he says softly, it wasn't all that funny, was it?

–Because you're grounded, that's why.

–I don't even understand why I'm grounded. I manage to lower my voice to a respectable level, to show that I am rational, mature, willing to negotiate.

But my mother just glared at me and walked back to her bedroom, which pissed me off more than anything she might have said. I didn't understand why my imprisonments were steeped in silence. Why didn't I have the chance to argue my own case? When had our household become a police state? I thought of Mumia Abu-Jamal. The circumstances surrounding our imprisonments were dissimilar, but in our desire for justice, for *life*, we stood in solidarity.

It was mid-August and I'd already been grounded four times that summer. The offenses included:

1. Threatening to cut my wrists with a steak knife and bleed all over my mother's fur coat.
2. Kicking in the windshield of my father's gas-guzzling SUV which, true to the manufacturer's safety promise, did not shatter all over the seats, but rather spun out into a spiderweb of cracks, as if my Doc Marten had been a bullet.
3. Calling my father a fascist cannibal when he asked me why I refused to eat the chicken cutlets my mother had worked so hard to cook.
4. Staging a nonviolent direct-action protest against my incarceration by handcuffing myself to the American flag outside our house. You must be held accountable, I told my parents. If you are ruling this house under martial law, at least have the honor not to hide it from the neighbors.

The summer before I was supposed to go to college was one long, steady grounding to which my parents would add a day here, a weekend there for each minor infraction. This particular day, with only three days remaining on a fourteen-day-long sentence, I'd woken up thinking maybe they would let me see Phish after all. After the initial tussle outside the bathroom, I put on my slippers, walked downstairs, and began making breakfast for the entire family. A half hour later, my mother walked into the kitchen to tofu bacon sizzling (well . . . simmering) and a pitcher of wheatgrass smoothies. I said brightly, Good morning, Mom! I thought you all might like a healthy breakfast . . . for a change. She ignored me completely, still angry about whatever I'd done to cause them to be pissed off at me in the first place.

She wouldn't even glare at me. She just grabbed a particularly toxic-looking doughnut from a box my father had bought earlier that week, though with all the preservatives, the powdered blobs of bleached flour and animal fat might have been a decade old, and walked away, leaving me in the kitchen, alone with my sad looking skillet full of soy.

I called after her, Where are you going? Why won't you talk to me? Why are you being so EVIL?

Couldn't she see that things would just be a whole lot easier for everyone if we could just talk? That giving me the silent treatment was only going to make things worse? My parents' lack of communication skills wasn't going to be something I was going to fix in a day, I knew that. But surely they would understand my desire to go to the concert that weekend. Lea had bought the Phish tickets months ago for my birthday and we're talking about a girl who sees nothing wrong with listening to R. Kelly, so needless to say, this was monumental.

I decided to try one final appeal. After dropping the spatula and turning off the burner, I chased my mother into her bedroom.

–Cortina, this is not up for discussion.

–Mom, Lea and I have had this trip planned for months. It's, like, a once-in-a-lifetime experience.

She snorted. If everything is a once-in-a-lifetime experience, then nothing is.

–What's that supposed to mean?

–It means that this isn't the first time you've asked us to lift a punishment because of a once-in-a-lifetime experience. And yet, time after time, you always manage to disappoint us. Do I have to remind you of your little trip to Vermont which, as I recall, was supposed to have something to do with environmental-farming practices. . . . You conveniently left out the fact that the most popular crop on the farm you visited is illegal in this country.

I rolled my eyes. I told you, that wasn't my pot. I was holding it for a friend.

My mother glared at the mere mention of the word.

–I don't know why you can't seem to get it into your head that we're not budging on this. We can't trust you to make good decisions, Cortina.

I ripped off the apron I was wearing and threw it on the floor at my mother's feet. You'll be sorry you were such an asshole when you don't have a daughter anymore.

–Well, you'll be sorry *you* were one when you don't have a mother anymore.

When she said things like that, I'd feel this kind of jolt in my side that said, Stop now, stop now, stop now, just walk away. Of course, the jolt wouldn't stop in my side; it would stay there for a second, then shoot directly into my arms, my fists, which would send a message to my brain that said, Don't stop now! You've already gone too far to turn back now; go in for the kill! And that's when I'd say something like,

–No, I won't. In fact, I *hope* you die. Why don't you have another doughnut and speed up the process?

And that's when she'd do something like grab my wrist and twist it, which is really all I wanted in the first place, and the jolt of heat would move from my fists to the place where she'd grabbed me, but the heat would feel good now, because now it could escape, and I didn't have to push it out myself by using my hands to break things or punch things, and my breathing would become regular, and I wouldn't be angry anymore, just sad, and I'd start to cry and fall to the floor and she'd shake her head and walk away, leaving me crumpled in a pile on the hard-wood floors that had probably been stolen from some endangered forests, cut down by locals who would never see a decent cut of the profits that would instead go to the American corporations who rape their land and steal their livelihood.

I lay there with my eyes closed, breathing slow and deep, enjoying the calm that can only come after a storm, for I don't know how long, until I heard my brother calling my name.

–What!

–Geez. Phone. It's Lea.

I really didn't want to talk to Lea right now. I'd told her the night before that I was pretty sure my parents were going to let me go, seeing as Lea had spent so much money on the tickets and all, and I didn't want to come clean about the fact that they were most definitely not budging.

But we were scheduled to leave that afternoon, so I didn't have much choice. I stood up slowly and walked over to the phone.

–So, are you almost ready?

–Um, yeah. Almost.

–And you say your parents aren't cool. God, I'm so glad they're letting you go. I really didn't want to have to go to this thing with Danny. I kind of hate him right now.

–Why?

–Why else?

–Alex?

–Of course, Alex.

–Why are you even friends with her when she is so obviously after your boyfriend?

–I don't know. Maybe because I know Danny would never do anything.

I didn't agree. Danny was nice and all, but I didn't trust Alex. It's not that I didn't like her . . . no, actually, that's exactly what it was. I knew that I was supposed to love everything and everyone and not judge the young souls among us, but Alex was superficial and cruel and liked to think that she was sophisticated because when she'd visited schools in New York City she'd had foie gras and bought an alligator purse at Prada. Now, before you think

I'm overreacting, let me say that I wasn't even a vegan then—leather shoes and free-range turkeys were fine by me—but I could smell the bad karma on that girl a mile away. She didn't care about where things came from as long as they looked good on her.

–Maybe you should take Danny instead. Maybe it would be good for you guys. . . .

–No way! Are you kidding me? I bought those tickets for you and me! Next year I'll be at Villanova and you'll be at Vermont and we'll only see each other, like, a few times a year. This is for us, okay?

How could I tell her the truth when she put it like that? I mean, eventually I'd tell her, like when we crossed over into Maine, when we'd already passed the point of no return, then I'd tell her, then I'd let her know the sacrifice I'd made.

–So should I pick you up?

–Nah, I'll ride my bike over.

–With all your stuff? Are you crazy?

–What do you mean? The tent's already at your house. All I have is a backpack.

–That's it?! I have, like, three suitcases.

–That doesn't surprise me.

But actually, I wasn't taking my bike over because I'd sold my bike. I'd also sold my computer, my skis, and my rare coin collection, which meant that, along with my graduation money, I now had $5,047.83 in my bank account. It would soon be transferred into the housing and meals program at Vermont, but until August 28, it was mine.

I finished packing my sack with the essentials: trail mix, jar of peanut butter, loaf of bread, eighth of kind bud I'd bought from Shawn's brother, tank tops, Birkenstocks, rolling papers, tie-dye RIP JERRY GARCIA T-shirt, and waited until I saw my mother's car pull out of the driveway before I tiptoed down the stairs. She had her weekly hair appointment on Fridays and it would be a good two hours before she'd be back. Luckily, her hairdresser was on the other side of town, so my walk to Lea's would be a relatively safe one. I'd take the backroads, only veering onto Reservoir Boulevard to withdraw $500 from my account. At least I told myself it was only going to be five hundred. Whether I wrote in the extra zero or the bank teller, eager to close her window for the weekend, made the serendipitous mistake that set the next stage of my life in motion, I can't recall. I only know that when she handed me fifty crisp $100 bills, I didn't hand her back forty-five of them.

–Look at all the fireflies! I told Lea, and she murmured her approval. According to the directions we'd gotten in the mail along with our tickets, we were only ten minutes away from the festival grounds.

–I can't believe I'm doing this! Lea said, her straight brown hair whipping into the backseat. This is so unlike me! Camping! I can't believe it.

–Well, believe it. You're an honorary Phishhead now, I said, looking in the mirror to see how the braids I'd put in my hair at the last rest stop looked.

Lea laughed. So who did you say is going to be there again?

–I'm not exactly sure, really. It doesn't matter though. You don't really need to know anyone going in. Everyone's just so friendly.

Lea looked a little nervous so I kept talking until I found myself stretching the truth a bit. I did meet these boys from Barrington at the Allman Brothers show, I said, and I bet they'll be there.

–Were they cute?

–Not your type.

–What do you mean, not my type? Who says I have a type? I don't have a type.

–Okay, you don't have a *type*, you have a *boyfriend*.

Lea waved her hand. Yeah, and his type is girls with pink hair.

I laughed. Her hair's pink now, is it?

–Oh, I don't know. Probably. I don't see what her deal is.

I started to say something like, Her deal is that she's a total bitch, but remembered what that old Rasta dude said to me at the Burning Spear show, about how the days of nonjudgment were upon us. Or did he say the days of final judgment?

–Well, then, why are you making a big deal about it? I said. Listen, Lea. Forget Danny. He does not exist for the next forty-eight hours. Nothing exists. Not boyfriends, not girls out to steal boyfriends, not parents.

–Wait. Why did you say, not *parents*? Cort . . . do your parents know you're here?

–I'm sure they've figured it out by now.

–Oh, shit. Shit! They're going to call my parents. Jesus, Cort, you know how sick my mom is. She can't deal with this kind of bullshit. Why didn't you tell me?

–Because you never would have let me come.

–Why would you say that? I'm not your mother, Cortina.

As she said that, something green and glowing splatted against the windshield. It was a firefly. Lea and I both stared at it without speaking, and after a few seconds, she turned on the windshield wipers, so that we wouldn't have to see the glow fade away.

–I didn't mean . . . I just meant, I didn't want you to have to make a choice. Hey, there's the exit.

Lea swerved the car and pulled off into the wooded exit. You don't have to protect me. Just be honest, okay?

–Okay, promise.

–Do you think they're going to show up looking for us?

–No way. My parents would never admit to yours that they couldn't control me. They care way too much about what other people think.

–Are you sure?

–One hundred percent sure.

It was the main thing I hated about my parents. They were completely obsessed with what everyone else thought about them. Like when I turned ten and my mom gave me deodorant but I refused to wear it because I found out it was made from aluminum chromide, which gives lab rats breast cancer, and why did we need to give rats breast cancer just to make ourselves smell pretty, and anyway, I liked

the way my armpits smelled without deodorant, my mom
barged into my room holding up my T-shirt, saying, Is this
yours?

And I said, Yeah, why?

And she said, You're disgusting.

And I said, Why?

And she said, Get over here.

And I said, Mommy, why?

And she said, Don't Mommy me. Get over here!

And when I went over there she bent over and smelled
my armpits and said, Did you go to school smelling like
this?

And I said, Smelling like what?

And she said, Answer me!

And I said, Yes, I went to school like this.

And she said, I did not raise my daughter to be dirty.
GET INTO THE BATHROOM!

And when I didn't go, she dragged me by the neck of
my sweater and pushed me into the hallway until I stumbled on my sister's shoe and onto the black granite. When
I touched my nose, there was a drop of blood.

But my mother wasn't paying attention to this. She was
bent over the sink, which was gushing water so hot that
steam had already fogged the mirror and the windows.
Get over here, she said.

–But Mom—

–*Get over here.*

She put a stick of Lifebuoy under the water, then lath-
ered up her hands. As I walked closer, she grabbed my left
arm up over my head and started rubbing the soap vigor-

ously into my armpit. No one is going to say that I have a filthy daughter! She reached for the other arm and started scrubbing, and then when she was done, she looked at me and said, Stop crying. And hold your nose. It will stop bleeding. After she was finished, she pointed to a towel hanging from the rack. Get yourself together. And then she reached into the medicine cabinet and pulled out a tall blue and yellow can of Sure deodorant and thrust it into my hand. And if you say anything about chorofilo-carbos, she said, I will make you quit the science team.

She slammed the door before I could correct her.

As Lea pulled into the field where the festival was being held, I already knew I'd made the right choice. Standing around with flashlights in their hands were boys with stringy hair and girls with dreads; they wore tie-dye and hemp and none of them, *none of them*, looked like they were wearing deodorant. One of them motioned for us to roll down our window. Lea and I did as we were in-structed.

–You guys have any drugs on you?

We shook our heads no.

Instead of asking us to step out so he could search the car, he said, Don't worry. There are plenty in there. He pointed to the north side of the field where there were rows upon rows of RVs, updates on the Volkswagen bugs, and sedans obviously on loan from parents. He grinned and we got a flash of a mouth full of white teeth, except for the places where they were missing.

He waved us ahead and we drove through the dark, our headlights illuminating the dust other people's tires were kicking up. A girl wearing a short white slip of a dress waved us in with a lazy flip of a purple flag in her hand. As our car passed her, I couldn't help but notice how unsettling her gaze was, as if she was seeing something completely different than the rest of us, and it wasn't good. I shivered and rolled up my window, telling myself it was just because I was cold.

Once we'd gotten our tent and sleeping bags set up, Lea looked at me and said, Now what?

–Now, we sleep.

–I'm not very tired.

–Well, neither am I, but just try. You've got three days ahead when stuff is actually going on, so you might as well sleep when nothing is.

Lea mumbled something and turned her back to me. But she was right. How could we sleep when there was so much ahead?

–Do you want to smoke? I asked her.

–Yeah, she said.

I got out my little one-hitter; my mother hadn't found it in any of her exhaustive searches of my room because I kept it in the hollowed out sole of my old Nikes, which I stopped wearing once I found out the company used sweatshop labor. I plucked off the stems from the pretty green bud and stuffed it in the glass tube. Then I pulled my lighter out of my pocket, lit the bud, and took a deep hit. I passed it to Lea and she did the same, coughing.

And that's when the rain started. Sprinkles at first, then

a full-out pouring. Our tent was secure, and we'd made sure to pitch it on high ground. Still, I really wished we'd had an RV right then.

Lea and I passed the pipe back and forth soundlessly; after three hits, I knew I'd had enough but I didn't feel like stopping there. I wanted to knock myself out, sleep soundly and well so that I'd wake the next morning refreshed. So long after Lea held up her hand to tell me she was done, I kept on packing and smoking.

· But instead of feeling tired, my mind was racing. What was going on? Normally, I'd be out cold by now. Lea's eyes were looking heavy, but I knew mine were bugging out of my head. That didn't mean the usual effects were absent. It wasn't long before I felt, as often happens when I'm stoned, all kinds of liquidy and numb. I thought of how I'd fooled around with that guy from Barrington at the Allman Brothers show who never even told me his name. I'd thought I was so cool for letting him put his hand up my skirt during "Sweet Melissa," but now I just felt disgusting, dirty, like I was exactly what my mother thought I was. Like every person who ever touched me from now on would know exactly how I'd been touched before. I felt as if I was oozing, or worse, as if I had peed all over myself. I looked at Lea, who was flicking my Zippo open and shut and looking impossibly beautiful in the on and off of the light. I wished that I had her shiny straight hair or her flat stomach and dancer's legs. I know she couldn't be feeling like I was feeling right now: fleshy and globular, my hair a tangle of snarls, my features too big, my skin too loose.

I tried to tell myself it was just because I was stoned that I was thinking these things, but I knew that wasn't it. The pot was bringing me closer to the truth of the universe, and the truth of the universe was that I was too big for myself, too messy. I needed to be smaller, to take up less space. I needed to tighten myself up, to flatten myself out. I needed . . .

–I need to go to the bathroom, I told Lea.

But Lea didn't respond. She was asleep.

Shit. There was no way I was going out there by myself. I'd have to wait until morning, or until Lea woke. I knew there were porta-potties less than a hundred yards away, but Lea and I had made a pact to stay together.

I could hear someone playing a Grateful Dead bootleg not too far away. "Uncle John's Band."

It was like listening to a ghost, hearing his voice like that, clear and strong through the rain. Dead songs never felt recorded; they were so raw, real, alive. I couldn't believe Jerry had gone and died before I'd even been old enough to like his music, to follow him, to live the gypsy life I knew I'd been meant to live. Phish was fine and everything, but they were just trying to do what the Dead had already done. This thing had already been done before, years ago; it was like all of us were trying to live something that was already dead, only it was too late, for me, for Jerry, for everyone.

Jerry's voice trailed off and mingled into the sounds of someone strumming their guitar, off-key, and someone else banging a drum to a rhythm too complicated to try to count. It wasn't good music, but it was live music, and that was something. Maybe I was wrong. Maybe the death of the Dead didn't mean things were over. There were people out there, and most of them were here for the same reason I was, to expand our minds, to experience oneness with the earth, to meet like-minded souls. Why had I been so scared to just be where I was?

More important, why was I so scared to leave the polyester confines of my tent?

Because, my mind answered in my mother's voice, it was dangerous out there. There were killers and diseases and rapists and sin. There were bad men and nasty germs lurking around every corner. And there were tons of bugs—grasshoppers mostly—trying to get inside the tent. As hard as I tried not to reach into my pocket and pull out the hand sanitizer, resistance was futile. I pulled it out and began rubbing it furiously into my skin. I knew that not everyone was as clean as I was, or at least as clean as my mom wanted me to be. The little bottle of gelatinous goo was my talisman against the diseases my mother spent so much time lecturing me about.

Of course, there were other illnesses, I knew, that had nothing to do with germs lurking on toilet seats or faucets. I envisioned my bladder exploding from the now-painful pounding of the three bottles of water I'd drunk on the way here. Why had I told Lea earlier that night that I didn't need to go, when that's exactly what I needed to do? Why did I just stand there, frozen in place with my eyes on the door she'd stepped through? Why was it so difficult for me to do such simple things, to take the most basic of actions? As I agonized over my terribly useless mind, I noticed the tent roof wasn't black, as it had been earlier. It was still raining but morning was approaching. I didn't have Lea to brave the journey with me but at least I had some light.

I slipped out of my Smurfs sleeping bag—the only one I owned, a bit snug these days—and unzipped the tent, trying not to let in the rain or the grasshoppers. I reached down for my windbreaker, prayed that it was waterproof, and pulled on my sneakers. I made my way out into the dirt, which was still dirt, thank God, and not yet mud. I looked at the cars around us and made a note where we were in relation to where I was headed. I remembered taking a right, then past four rows of cars, then another right, then a left. Piece of cake.

When I got to the porta-potties, I was pleased to see that there were ten of them and no line. I checked my pocket to make sure I still had my hand sanitizer. It was there, but that didn't make stepping into the green closets of filth any easier. I unlocked the door farthest from the center, figuring it would be the least used. But as soon as I walked in I was horrified to see the state of the thing. Shit on the toilet seat, on the floor. I slammed the door closed, and took a step to the next one.

Thankfully, this one was cleaner, so I went inside, forcing myself not to think of what it must have looked like before its last cleaning, then pulled out the hand sanitizer and doused my hands to remove any germs I'd picked up from the door handle. I squeezed the water out of my hair and peeled down my cargo pants, which were already drenched with rain, careful not to let them touch the ground where God knows what lurked. I clenched the muscles in my upper thighs to keep from falling over, and spent a few minutes willing my bladder to cooperate; filled as it was, it had higher standards than this.

When I was done I pushed open the lock with my shirt-sleeve and kicked it open with my foot. As soon as I stepped out into the rain, I began applying the sanitizer. And I started to walk right, but then couldn't remember if that was the way I'd come. Yes, my last turn was left; I was sure of it. But as soon as I walked straight ahead, I realized I didn't remember which turn I was supposed to take to get back to my tent.

I took a guess and turned left at the second aisle. I could've sworn I'd seen the purple balloons attached to that car's antenna before. I faced the row ahead, unsure of how far in we'd parked, then I kept walking. What cars had we parked next to? I remembered a Volkswagen bug full of people unpacking their stuff when Lea and I were pitching the tent but it had been too dark to tell the color. Green? Yellow? I walked some more, then pulled my hair back into a ponytail to keep it from covering my face.

As I walked through the RV Village, I noticed little groups of people securing their tents to keep out the rain. One woman smiled at me, her muddy little kid running around at her feet. I tried to smile back, but I was too nervous to look sincere. I wondered if I should tell her I was lost, but I shook the thought away, telling myself that there was nothing to be afraid of. I'd find my way back.

I decided to turn around and go back the way I'd come. If I could get to the porta-potties again, I could at least try to retrace my steps from there.

But the problem was, I couldn't remember exactly how to get back to the porta-potties. It wasn't as if the aisles around me were the kinds you find in supermarkets, neat and orderly. Some RVs took up three or four spaces. And some people had spread their camping stuff far back enough that the aisle was partially obscured. It was also apparent that people had moved their cars in the middle of the night, making a mess out of the attempted order created by the festival organizers. There were spots where cars had obviously been parked and now were filled only with muddy tire tracks that were becoming puddles. A smiley-face balloon tied to a freshly parked RV, a good omen I'd remembered seeing when we drove in, looked sinister now in the early morn, mocking my lack of direction. It was a maze, a terrible labyrinth of metal and steel and rain, nothing like the magical corn maze rumored to be set up within the stage grounds, and I was much too out of my head to attempt to solve it.

I crouched down and tried to think straight. The smiley face, evil though it was, wasn't too far from my starting point, so I decided to move off the larger aisles and start weaving in between the cars, in the hopes of finding Lea's car. At the very least, I'd recognize that.

As I stood up, I heard someone call out. I looked up and saw a short man with a beard and a Bud can. He was walking toward me quickly.

–Hey lady! he said, I got something to tell you! He stumbled forward.

I squinted my eyes to see if I knew him and instantly realized I did not. He was drunk, and he was potentially dangerous. I started running in the other direction.

–Hey lady! Why are you running? I've got something to show you!

Whatever he wanted to show me, I didn't want to see. There were cars all around me, but I realized, as I ran from this man, they were all filled with strangers. And there was no way of telling whether they'd be harmless like me, or dangerous like him. Oh God. What if he catches me? He's going to catch me and rape me behind one of these cars and people will have no idea what's happening. The rain was heavy, loud enough to obscure the screams of a girl, the grunts of a man. I looked over my shoulder, but he'd obviously tired of the chase. I stood there for a second, put my hand up against a stick that had been propped up to delineate parking aisles, and tried to catch my breath. What if I never found the car? My mind started racing. Maybe I should head toward the stages and find Trey Anastasio and ask him to page Lea. Or maybe he'd even let me catch up on a little sleep in the band's Winnebago. That's the kind of guy he was, right? That was the vibe here, wasn't it?

Finally, in the distance I could see the porta-potties once again—an unlikely salvation, but at least I'd be safe there, with all the people coming and going. I wiped the hair that had come loose from my ponytail out of my eyes and trudged through the mud, my sneakers sinking deeper with every step. I didn't know what to do once I reached the line. I certainly didn't want to go back into the porta-potties, so I just sort of stood there next to the line and watched as people tried to keep themselves dry.

–Don't worry; it'll clear up by afternoon. A slow, deep voice interrupted my racing thoughts, all involving some form of death, none of them peaceful like the Tibetans promised. I looked up and saw a tall hippie boy, tanned, blond, dreadlocked, big blue eyes. He didn't seem bothered by the rain; it seemed to just melt into him. Then again, he was a lot less drenched than I was.

–I guess, I said. I didn't really want to talk to him. He might be cute, but that didn't mean he didn't have the same thing in mind as the guy who'd been chasing me before.

–You okay? he said. You look a little freaked out.

–I'm fine, I just, I just don't really exactly remember where my tent is.

–Oh, shit. That sucks. That totally sucks. Maybe I can help you find your way.

–That's nice of you, but really, you don't have to . . .

–It's cause I'm a guy, right? That's cool. I understand. But, look, my friend's girl is here with us. She's in one of the stalls right now. She'll come with us, cool?

I couldn't believe it. He was totally saving me. Really, I said. You wouldn't mind?

–Of course I wouldn't mind. He pointed up at the sky. Look, the sun's almost broke through. Morning's just around the corner. Things are looking up . . . Look, there she is . . .

I looked over at the stalls, where a small girl with freckles and hair as white as cotton was emerging from one of the stalls. Kyrie, girl, he said, over here.

She trudged through the mud, unfazed by it, thanks to her big green rain boots. Whatchu want, Uncle John? I'm freezing out here.

–This girl needs help. She's lost her way.

–Join the club, she said and laughed. Don't worry, mama. We'll get you home.

–Hell, said the boy called Uncle John, real slowlike, his bright eyes the same color as the blue poking through the storm clouds. You're home already.

pictures
of you

SHAWN

–What do you mean you don't have any more coke? You always have more coke.

–Not in Galestown, I don't.

–Can you call someone?

–Um, isn't your brother a drug dealer?

–He hates coke. You know that.

–I don't blame him. It's a terrible, terrible drug. So, can we leave now?

–I think we should probably wait until the photo slide show is over.

–I can't believe they picked "Pictures of You" as their slide show song. Do they not realize this is a *sad* song?

I look over at the real Danny and Lea, embracing and smiling at the photographed Dannys and Leas on the big white screen, who are, not surprisingly, also embracing and smiling.

–Not everyone listens to lyrics, Alex.

–Still. What, did the DJ, like, not have "Girlfriend in a Coma"? Alex kicks off both her heels and stretches her calves. What a weird night.

–Yeah, but you know what was even weirder? Danny's friends from college were, like, totally normal and nice and they *liked* Rhode Island. A few of them even stayed here after they all graduated. They kept talking about how beautiful it was. They must have used the word "revitalization," like, fifty times.

Alex snorts. Ha! Because of the *mall*?

–Yeah, it was totally creeping me out. They started

building some mall in Syracuse my senior year and everyone went crazy about that, too.

–Revitalization via mall construction is soooo eighties.

–Wait until they realize that everyone's going to start buying things online.

–Yeah, but you know what? They were probably just being nice. They didn't want to hurt your feelings or whatever since you grew up here. I mean, when people ask me about Rhode Island, I always give them this line of bullshit, like how if I didn't grow up there, it would be a great place to live, and blah blah blah, but it's total bullshit. I wouldn't live here if I grew up in Kentucky. I don't know, I guess once you've lived in New York you can't picture living anywhere else.

–What made you first decide to go to New York anyway?

–I don't want to answer that.

–Why?

–Because my answer is lame.

–Tell me!

–Okay. You have to promise not to laugh.

–I promise.

–*Friends.*

I almost spit out my beer I'm laughing so hard.

–Like, as in the show? I didn't even know you watched it. It's so . . . *hetero.*

–Shawn, *I'm* hetero.

–Not like them you aren't. I point to Danny and Lea. And believe me, I mean that as a compliment. Do you know how fat they're probably going to get?

Alex smiles. Anyway, do you remember how *Friends* used to be on the same night as *My So-Called Life*?

–I guess. But I didn't really watch either of them.

–Well, naturally I watched *My So-Called Life*, but that was when Danny and I were kind of, you know . . .

–Fucking?

–*Seeing each other*, and he kept going on and on about how great *Friends* was and so I started watching it and I don't know, I remember him saying that we were kind of like Ross and Rachel and maybe we'd move to New York someday, and . . . God . . . I realize how lame that sounds. But still it was the first time I thought maybe New York made sense for me.

–New York *does* make sense for you. But not for Danny. He was never going to leave here, Alex. And you never could have stayed.

–I know that. I think I knew it then. And anyway, I hated that show. But I watched it so we'd have something to talk about.

–Because you didn't have anything else to talk about.

Alex looks at me and nods.

–Because you have nothing in common.

She doesn't nod this time but I know she knows it's true.

–You just don't like it when other people get stuff that you want. And it kills you that Lea got him because you think it means you lost or something which is ridiculous because you . . . won.

–Okay, that's enough, Shawn. Thanks. I appreciate it. I

really do. But . . . enough. Alex puts her feet up on the empty chair next to us. So do you think you'll stay in New York?

–I don't know. I guess I became a musician so I wouldn't be stuck in any one place.

–And yet you spent four years of your life in the most depressing place in the continental United States. I was only there for a weekend and I wanted to shoot myself.

–Um, that was possibly because we smoked opium the entire time you were there.

–Still.

–It wasn't that bad.

But it was. And my reason for picking Syracuse had been much lamer than Alex's for moving to New York.

Not that you could blame me. I mean, how exactly was one supposed to pick a college in the days before the Internet gave you a rundown of every program, faculty member, and course you might possibly take over four years? My guidance counselor, Mrs. Montecalvo, was nice enough, but can you really fault me for not wanting to take life advice from someone masochistic enough to work as a public-high-school guidance counselor?

–So have you thought about where you'd like to go to school, Shawn?

–Not really.

–Well, if you're as smart as your mom, you could go anywhere you like. I never understood why she didn't go to school somewhere far away.

Mrs. Montecalvo went to high school with my mom. What she'd obviously forgotten was that high school was when my mom had gotten pregnant with my brother, a turn of events which needless to say put a bit of a damper on the college-application process. Why my dumbass father got to escape while she got stuck in Rhode Island dealing with us—that's what *I'll* never understand.

And so I applied to schools that were good but not *too* good, schools that would be pleased at my grades and SAT scores but wouldn't bemoan my lack of extracurricular activities—and sure enough, I got into them all.

I couldn't be bothered to visit any of the schools—judging by the photos in the brochures they sent, they all looked about the same. The same sunny quads, ivy-covered old buildings, and state-of-the-art facilities. And why should I care where I was going as long as I was getting out of Galestown?

But while I can usually avoid making a decision long enough until my options disappear and the decision makes itself for me, in this case I actually had to make a choice.

Mrs. Montecalvo had given me printouts of demographic information at all four schools that had accepted me—average class size, male to female ratio, percentages of various ethnicities, religions, and hometowns, stuff like that, but one piece of demographic information, the most important to me, was curiously absent.

Though a ridiculous number of people seemed disproportionately interested in my sexual orientation, I'd only told two people in Galestown I was gay—Alex after she demanded to know what had happened between me and Cort; and Danny when we were fucking around with his drum set in his basement.

–I don't know, dude, I'd said after he asked, I guess, wondering if he noticed my voice was shaking.

–It's totally cool if you are. I was just curious. So how did you know?

–I don't know, I said, you just know.

He nodded thoughtfully and said, Yeah, that makes sense, and we never talked about it again, but after that, he treated me differently. We'd always gotten along before, but after that day his behavior toward me started to border on flirtatious and I knew it wasn't because he was gay or even curious (you just know) but I wasn't sure what he was doing—until it hit me. He was treating me the same way he treated all the girls in school who knew they'd never have him. He wasn't teasing us or being cruel, on the contrary—the way he acted was I imagine the way celebrities treat normal people. They know they're out of our league, but they also know that without our adoration, they'd be nothing.

My mom had been harping on me for weeks that the decision deadline was fast approaching and so one day I went to my room, put on some music, and spread out demographic information and brochures before me. Villanova promised a community that was, as reflected by the rule of St. Augustine, "of one heart and mind." Interesting. Naturally, I imagined an illicit tryst with a golden-haired choirboy in the balcony of the St. Thomas of Villanova church.

Next, I dreamed of seducing a serious-minded young Jesuit-in-training at Boston College's Center for Ignatian Spirituality. After that, I considered the scandal that would erupt were I to get caught screwing a Young Republican in the bathroom of Georgetown's Intercultural Center.

And then I picked up the brochure for Syracuse, the school that seemed the least likely candidate because of the high percentage of student involvement in Greek life. I was flipping through the supplementary material absentmindedly—it was tough to pay attention to the words with all those images of self-flagellating Jesuits running through my mind—when I saw him.

A boy, the most beautiful boy I'd ever seen, sitting with a small group of students in what appeared to be a wooded amphitheatre. The sun was shining through the trees and seemed to illuminate his face more than any of the others. With his slim frame and dark tousled hair, he looked like a young Keanu Reeves, only much, much more beautiful.

The people he was sitting with were also beautiful, multicultural, happy. One couldn't tell if they were gay or not, but they looked, above all else, tolerant. I knew they were probably hand-picked for their attractiveness, for their diversity—for all I knew, they weren't even students—and yet, I knew that someone at Syracuse knew that putting this picture, this boy, in the brochure sent a message to boys like me. I closed my eyes and imagined a world with him in it, with no mother in the next room, no cats, no trashy kids threatening to kick my ass for merely existing, and smiled.

I'm not sure who was more excited the day I left for college, my mother or me. Though I'd tried to convince her I could just take the train, she insisted on taking the day off and driving me all the way up.

I'd talked to my future roommate exactly once on the phone; his name was Chris and he was from outside Philly and he'd seemed nice enough, though I'm sure I didn't endear myself to him by asking him the question my mother had insisted upon:

–Uh, my mom's buying me a blanket and wanted me to check what color yours was so they don't . . . um . . . clash.

–Oh . . . I don't know, blue?

–Thanks, I said. I mean, I don't really care about that, you know. She just, you know, made me ask.

I, of course, knew that asking questions about decor because your mom wanted you to was just as gay as asking questions about decor for yourself, if not more.

After hanging around our room for way too long, my mom finally got the hint, or else she was so creeped out by Chris's staring at her tits—whatever the reason, she finally left and I was stuck having to overcompensate for making such a lame first impression.

Luckily, there are benefits to having a drug dealer for a brother.

–Do you smoke? I said, unpacking the kind bud my brother had given me as a going-away present.

–Not cigarettes.

–Yeah, me neither. He walked over to my side of the room, stood there for a moment, sized up me and my stuff, and then sat on the chair next to my desk as I unwrapped my bong.

–Wow, that's sweet, he said.

–Yeah, I take good care of it. Hey, man, about that blanket thing. I know I must have seemed like a total freak, but my mom . . .

–Nah, it's cool. My mom's like that too. You're lucky she's already gone or you would have gotten the third degree.

After I packed the bong and handed it to Chris first for courtesy's sake, I reached over and turned on my stereo. I wondered if I should change The Cure to something more outside-Philly-friendly, but decided that it was my side of the room, my pot, and my bong, and if Chris didn't like the music, then fuck him.

After Chris took a big hit—too big, if you ask me—and started coughing like an old woman, he passed the bong back to me. I relit the bud, took a hit, then put it on the ground and laid back, hoping he wasn't one of those people who was going to talk about how high he was.

–Dude, that's some good shit. I'm totally stoned.

Here we go.

I didn't respond, so we sat there in silence for a moment. Clearly unsettled by this space, Chris blurted out, What's with this music? It's a little gay, no?

I tensed up but let it go. The Cure wasn't for everyone.

–Shit. I . . . hey, you're not . . . gay, are you?

I turned the music down a little and looked at him and realized the answer he was looking for was not exactly the one I'd given to Danny. I didn't want to lie, didn't feel like I had to, but I also didn't feel like it was any of his business. I mean, there was more to me than that, and once he got to know the rest of me then maybe I'd tell him about that one specific part.

–Fuck no, I said. I just like Goth chicks, I guess. Girls who hate themselves give the best head.

Chris laughed. Tell me about it. The ones who cut themselves, though . . . that's a little out there for me. I'm not into that.

–You're missing out, bro, I said. Those are the ones who like you to come on their face and shit like that. Total freaks. (Where did I come *up* with this stuff?)

And thanks to this little performance, I became more of a theatre fag than the queeny blond kid on my floor who could constantly be heard singing "*Would you light my candle?*" at the top of his lungs or the Puerto Rican diva who made it a habit of vogueing in the dorm cafeteria, because unlike them, my entire life became a performance.

Which is not to say that I was not interested in searching for underground gay life on the most heterosexual of campuses. Because I was a liberal arts major, I was able to take classes like Camp Poses in The Hollywood Musical and The Queer Novel from *The Picture of Dorian Gray* to *The Front Runner*. But my sexual exploration never left the classroom and I couldn't bring myself to attend the GLBT club's Wednesday-night meetings which I assumed would be filled with a lot of man-hating womyn who were nothing like the girls I preferred to spend time with—girls like Alex or her Syracuse stand-in, Adelle. (Naturally, Alex and Adelle loathed each other and I would not have it any other way.)

My social life was a farce. I allowed Chris and the other

guys on my floor to drag me out to keg parties and the
dingy basement bar Hungry Charlie's, which was most le-
nient on IDs; I loathed these places and the people who
frequented them. I was jealous of the straight people, for
whom such evenings had a purpose: Getting wasted was
simply a prerequisite for getting laid. But I hated the ones
who were out even more, mainly because they were so
"We're here! We're queer!" that they seemed to me a par-
ody of gayness. I wondered if there were other people like
me who didn't feel like they needed to flaunt their sexuality, who didn't think that who they wanted to sleep
with should, like, define their entire identity.

I loathed Syracuse because the school hadn't provided
the demographics on people who acted like total poseurs:
whether it was the frat guys who considered *Animal House*
their bible, the gay guys who were all "Oh, no you didn't,
girlfriend," or the stupid sorority girls who all wore the
same uniform of black pants, blow-dried hair, and Tiffany
jewelry.

And alongside the blind conformity there was the
whole ridiculous emphasis on multiculturalism and tolerance. In Galestown, we didn't talk about multiculturalism
or tolerance; you either accepted that people were different or you were an asshole. Sure, there were racist kids,
and I have my share of scars to prove that not every kid
in Galestown was tolerant, but I didn't see why having
forums, talks, and discussions about tolerance was going
to make anyone more tolerant. All it did was make some
people feel really fucking special about being tolerant and
make other people really fucking paranoid that maybe

they weren't tolerant enough. As for the assholes who weren't tolerant, you can bet they weren't going to the forums.

Of course, I also hated myself because I knew the reason I chose this place had everything to do with my sexuality which meant maybe Foucault was wrong and sexual preference does drive everything we do and everything we are and all we are is fucking monkeys looking for someone to fuck and because there were no gay monkeys I had any interest in whatsoever I was going to die a sad stupid gay virgin monkey and . . .

I started to think about transferring. After all, wasn't Alex complaining *all the time* that everyone at NYU was gay and no boys wanted her and if only I was the kind of person who could make those kind of decisions but I'm not . . .

Then one day you see him. The boy from the brochure. You're in that dingy bar and you're buying a pitcher of beer for your stupid roommate and his stupid friends and the boy from the brochure is buying a pitcher of beer too, and the bartender slams the pitchers down in front of you both so hard that a bit of beer splashes up from the pitcher of the boy in the brochure and lands on his upper lip and it's all you can do not to lick it off but then he does exactly that, and you're dying, you're seriously dying, because he is so beautiful and you would be so good to him, so good, and as you're thinking all this, all of a sudden a girl walks up to him, and she's tiny and she's blond and if you were a stupid breeder like your roommate you would want to hit that but you don't want to hit that, not at all, and then she reaches up and moves a lock of hair out of the eyes of your Keanu and you want him to send this harlot for the hills but instead his eyes light up and he turns to her and they kiss, drunkenly and sloppily, and you're dying, you're seriously dying, and your idiot roommate screams across the room, Shawn, bro, you got weed right, and of course you have weed, you always have weed, having weed is like your fucking job, and the boy and girl are walking away and your heart is breaking, like, seriously breaking and . . .

You go back to your dorm room with your idiot room-mate and bring out the pot and the next year you go back to your apartment with your Keanu and his girlfriend and bring out the mushrooms and the year after that you go back to your house with these art students you met at the pizza place where you work and bring out the acid and the year after that you go back to the frat house where your band regularly plays and you bring out the X. You called it E but the frat boys called it X and that was okay. When it was around, it made it okay to lay on the bed with them, to hug them, even. They let you stay there some nights even though you weren't in the frat and it was okay that the way you loved them was different from the way they loved you. You thought about Jason a lot those days but only in this floaty faraway kind of way and you may have started crying once except then Scott was rubbing your shoulders and Kevin was blowing Vicks inhaler into your eyeballs so you could play the tears off as a side effect of the Vicks and then you realized that this is how straight boys justified crying and touching one another and then you wondered whether Jason would have been gay or straight and you think how sad it is that he never got to become either one. Except then you realized you hadn't become either one yet either.

Those days you hovered between many different ways of being. And you thought that this was how things might have been for Jason, too. One of the frat boys, Kevin, he even looked a little like Jason. But it was different with Kevin than it was with Jason because the way you loved Kevin was exactly the way he loved you—or at least that's how it seemed when he told you to stay after the other frat boys went to their rooms.

Or maybe it wasn't so different at all. Because before you would leave Kevin's room, he'd tell you you couldn't tell anyone. And you were okay with that, really, you were, because it wasn't who you were, it was just a small part of a much bigger picture of you, and you told yourself that when you got to know people better then you'd tell them everything but right then it was nobody's business but your own.

And you were okay with that.

Really.

fake plastic trees

ALEX

I can't sleep. And not just because of the coke, I don't care what Shawn says. I'm pretty sure it's because I'm dying—you know, like, from that disease where you can't sleep for ninety days and then you die. The coke is only something I've taken up to dull the pain in the moments prior to my impending death.

Shawn and I are sitting in the bedroom we're sharing, watching this documentary about mental patients. This one guy, who's wearing a plaid flannel shirt and horn-rimmed glasses with Scotch tape on the bridge, is walking up and down the halls of a stark white asylum, repeating this totally deranged mantra: Nothing works here. No one listens. I've been here for sev-en yeeeears. Nothing works here. No one listens. I've been here for sev-en yeeeears.

We're both fucked up, Shawn and me, so we laugh. But the truth is, I feel bad for the guy. It's mean to laugh at him, I know, but it's just that he doesn't feel like a real person; it's like he's a TV character or something. I guess I'm kind of, you know, rationalizing my behavior with my own mantra, one that I've stolen from Bastian, the kid in that movie *The Neverending Story*:

It's only a story. It isn't real. It's only a story.

But it isn't only a story and I've had about enough of the flannel guy. Can you change this, I ask Shawn. It's depressing me.

Sure, he says and starts flipping . . . acne infomercial starring some blonde singer of bad music . . . bad movie starring Sylvester Stallone (not *Rocky* or *Rambo*, not that either would have been better) . . . better than a diamond! sparkling cubic zirconium on the Home Shopping Network . . . Home Shopping Network's stepchild QVC hawking special dirt-removing fabric softener for the spin cycle . . . sad spin-off of *Xena: Warrior Princess*, something about her friend with Sapphic tendencies; sadder rip-off of *Xena: Warrior Princess*, something about a samurai chick and her plucky sidekick with Sapphic tendencies; even sadder spin-off of rip-off of *Xena: Warrior Princess*, something about the samurai chick's plucky sidekick's ability to cast spells, shrivel up testicles with a mere glance or whatever else market researchers felt would be similarly enticing to the growing yet underserved late-night TV-watching lesbian demographic . . .

And then, mercifully, Thom Yorke singing about Fake Plastic Trees. Shawn shouts Hallelujah!, jumps up and opens the blinds, flooding the room with sun and, like, totally killing any chance I might have had to excuse myself for being up this late yet again.

–Shawn, what are you doing?

–Just checking to see if it's raining frogs. MTV is playing a music video, so I assume the Apocalypse is upon us.

It does seem weird so I pick up the channel guide from under my pack of cigarettes, several of which are now only filters, which we tore off when creating makeshift rolling papers for Shawn's weed. I'm not really a big fan of pot—it's such a sloppy drug; who wants to be even *more* lazy and slow and paranoid and hungry than they

already are? Sometimes, all it takes is for me to see someone smoke weed on TV and I get a huge stomachache and
a feeling like the world is coming to an end. Tonight,
I foolishly thought it would help me sleep—but, then,
I'd done enough blow over the last twenty-eight hours to
counteract the effects of anything depressive. I squint to
see the channel on the TV and when I match it to the one
on the guide, I realize we have our answer and say to
Shawn, It's MTV2, that's why.

–Oh, he says. MTV2 is even *more* depressing than the
Apocalypse. It's like, they play nothing but the Gorillaz,
as if anyone even fucking listens to the Gorillaz when
they're not watching MTV2. Fucking cartoon mother-
fuckers! Shawn's screaming now.

–Shawn, are you insane? They're not even playing the
Gorillaz, in case you hadn't noticed.

–Thom Yorke only encourages the fucking Gorillaz.

–Okay, I don't know what that *means*, I say, and I don't
think you do either. Will you chill out before we get
thrown out of here? I turn down the volume. Isn't the Gorillaz just, like, the lead singer of Oasis or something?

–Oh my God, NO. *Blur*, for Chrissakes, Blur.

–What?

–Not Oasis. Blur. *So* much better than Oasis.

–Whatever. I thought a second ago you, like, hated them.

–I don't *hate* them, Alex, Shawn said, sighing dramati-
cally. I'm *jealous* of them. Why don't *I* have a cartoon side
project?

–You can have a cartoon side project someday, Shawn, I
say helpfully, then add, Maybe MTV2 is British.

-MTV2 only encourages the fucking British.

I sigh and roll over to face him. Shawn is back on the bed, twitching now, but at least laying down. I rest my head on his tummy just as the opening strains of "Karma Police" begin.

-They must be doing a Radiohead block or something, he says, calmer now.

-Mmmm, I say, that makes me happy. I decide to be out with it. Shawn, I think I really fucked up my karma.

-Oh, join the club, he says.

-No, I mean it.

-Why?

-I fucked Danny.

-Well, duh, you bitch. And you can spare me all the gory details. I've heard them more times than I'd care to recount. Dick like an arm, I get it.

-No, I mean, I fucked Danny, like . . . after that.

-After what?

-After . . . Lea's mom died . . . before they got engaged, I'm not that bad . . . but . . . not that much before.

-Oh, Alex.

-I know, I know. I look down at my plastic bottle filled with water from Fiji or Poughkeepsie or wherever and start to cry.

I had, like, no intention whatsoever of sleeping with Danny when the weekend began. Ben had called to say that Danny was bummed because Lea dumped him again, something about being too fucked up with her mom dying and everything to think about a relationship. Okay, look, I should have called Lea, I know I should have, but the fact is, after the funeral, I didn't call her at all. I couldn't. I mean, I didn't know what to say. I always ended up saying the wrong thing, like, It was for the best, when she needed me to say, It's so fucked up. Or, Life just sucks, when she needed me to say, Everything's going to be okay. That kind of thing. I'm not, like, good in a crisis.

So I told Ben, sure, come on down. We'll have an amazing time. Totally. I didn't think my New York friends would like them much, but the thing was, I didn't much like my New York friends by then—their pretentious habit of peppering their speech with French phrases, the way they always picked restaurants where even the water was out of my price range, the fact that they had their parents call fucking Tom Ford or Miuccia Prada to get them jobs while I was stuck answering phones at a law firm. I was looking forward to a weekend with real-life people. People who paid their own student loans, people who'd worked as waiters and landscapers, people who didn't make fun of people who had to buy their clothes at Filene's Basement because they bought their own clothes at Marshall's.

I had no intention of getting fucked up, either. Danny and Ben liked to drink, but as far as I could tell, they didn't touch anything harder than the occasional joint, not since they, like, both totally freaked when they saw a vampire on a skiing trip or an alien at the mall or something like that, or, more accurately, since Shawn sent Ben on a trip to hell and back. So, I, you know, put on my jeans and a tank top, pulled my hair back into a ponytail, dug out some old Nine West shoes I reserve solely for places with icky floors, and suggested a pub crawl at all the little dives in the East Village.

And it was fun . . . for, like, five minutes. But a night out with the Irish boys at stupid McSorley's reminded me how little I liked drinking in the first place. Alcohol should be an appetizer, not a main course. I was dying for something a little more civilized, a quail's egg kind of buzz as opposed to a four-cheese omelette with home fries and bacon. A drug that doesn't leave you feeling puffy, nauseous, and fiendin' for diner food the next morning. A city high.

So on Saturday, I took them to one of those velvet-rope clubs on the West Side that I usually hate but, I mean, what other options did I have? They were, like, wearing khakis and striped shirts, so I really couldn't see how I could take them to Williamsburg. Besides, my roommate Caitlin was doing some modeling back then, so we didn't have to wait long. I could tell this impressed the guys, or maybe it was just Caitlin that impressed them, with that slinky shirt she wore that let you see her entire shoulders and back. It was like they didn't even care that *my* dress was a Stella McCartney when she walked out in that thing. But, whatever. As soon as we got our first drink, I spotted this dude that I'd gotten E from before, so I told the guys I'd be right back.

The DJ was playing that kind of terrible techno that only exists because it sounds good when you're on drugs. If I were a wiser woman, I'd catch a clue there, that there's something wrong with ingesting substances that make the most plasticine hollowed-out drum-machine beat topped off with the obligatory whistle-inducing apocalyptic crescendo sound like God's little side project with Debussy, Bach, and Beethoven. Instead I've convinced myself that trance DJs are fucking geniuses who make everyone endure a whole lot of monotonous, soppy crap just so they sneak in those moments, those golden fucking moments that send you on your teeth-sucking dope-smile descent into transcendence, into those eyeballs-rolling-into-the-back-of-your-brain inhalations of ecstasy, and down those whirling-dervish dives into drum-and-bass deviancy deep, deep, so motherfucking deep inside those purple vortexes of mirror-world splendidness so unimaginable to the uninitiated that it just doesn't seem right that all that remains after you emerge from the genie-bottle world is a curiously three-dimensional awakening the next morning complete with an aching jaw, sweaty pajamas, mascara clinging to the circles under your eyes, and an all-consuming sadness that you just slept through another day, a day that might have been better than any other old miserable Sunday, if only you'd given it the chance.

As I shoved my way through the New Jerseyites, the song playing was some kind of cheesy progressive house thing, the most notable thing about it a sample from a Samantha Fox song, a girl's sexy breathy voice asking *"Are . . . you . . . ready?"* and a tinny rolling-drum snare. Despite the lameness of it all, I was ready. A little too ready. I pumped my fist in the air exactly four beats before the bass drums exploded in climax, signaling the crowd to go wild, destroying any chance I thought I'd had of looking cool.

I lowered my arm slowly, then stretched up the other one, as if I'd just been yawning. I walked up to the dude.

–You got any rolls?

–Nah, not tonight. Just greed.

–Greed? I asked dumbly. I'm sorry, I've never heard of that.

He laughed. That's my name for it. He held his finger to his nose as if snorting.

–Greed, you know? A little bit only makes you want more.

Ugh. There were few things I hated more than philosopher drug dealers. Just give me two small, okay? He gave me a price, I asked him what he was drinking. He said, Sprite, so I ordered him one, then handed it to him with a wad of bills. He nodded his approval at my smoothness, then he told me to meet him at the bathroom.

I wasn't sure yet if I was going to share with the boys. I mean, they didn't need it, you know, not like I did. I didn't want to bring them down to my level, but then, I didn't really want to do it alone, either.

As I waited for the dealer near the bathroom line, I looked out into the crowd. Ben and Caitlin were grinding on the floor. I could tell she was loving the attention, but was she actually going to sleep with him? Gross. I mean, I'd fooled around with Ben before, but that was in high school, when he was on this "I love eating pussy" kick and was dying to show us all how skilled and sensitive a lover he was. And, actually, he wasn't half bad, but there was a big difference between high-school losers and real-life losers, and if Caitlin wanted to go there, fine, better her than me.

Danny was at the bar. Some skank was trying to talk to him and he was laughing politely, but then I saw him looking around for me, and just as it was about to be my turn in line, I felt a hand on mine, slipping what I could tell were two bags into my hand.

Thank the Goddess. As soon as I closed my fists around my purchase, I walked into the farthest stall, pretending not to listen to all the other people sniffling in the stalls next to me—I'm nothing like any of you, I'm so much better than every fucking one of you, I'm a bona fide genius, an artist, ahead of my time, and I'm sacrificing myself for my art, a devoted student of fashion and its discontents, and why is it so bad to want to actually *fit* into the clothes I sew . . . aw fuck it. Open door, scan seat, not too gross, throw down wads of toilet paper, hike up dress, pull down tights, take out bag, take out key, dip in key, stick key in nose, breathe, repeat,

> repeat,
>> repeat,
>>> repeat,
>>>> re . . .
>>>>> fucking . . .
>>>>>> peat

You open the door

    You walk outside

        You smile

           Or is that a sneer

               You are beautiful

                  You are beyond

                     You need nothing

                        You want everything

                           He's yours if you want him

                     You want him

                        You want everything

                     You need nothing

                  You are beyond

               You are beautiful

           You are mine

    You are

Mine

I don't want to even talk about how disgusting Caitlin and Ben were being when they got back to my apartment, all slobbering and falling all over each other and generally acting like total schoolchildren. Caitlin insisted on putting on Depeche Mode, a band I usually like, given that they make me feel all '80s and cokey and lurid, but it pissed me off that Caitlin was trying so desperately to act sophisticated and sexy in front of my friends so I folded my arms and forced myself not to nod my head to the music.

I was getting beers from the fridge when Caitlin got up to use the bathroom and Ben, in her absence, turned to me and Danny and *actually* said, Um, so I'm gonna, like, hit that now so . . . whatever . . . I'll, uh, check you guys tomorrow. He walked into her bedroom and shut the door and when Caitlin came out, looking coked-out but still hot—being rich helps—she stumbled into her room without even saying good night.

Danny and I looked at each other and I said, Ew. And he laughed. I handed him his beer and tried not to get excited that it was just him and me alone for the first time since we broke up over something stupid like me making out with Ethan Garrity at the junior prom or whatever but, I mean, I was, like, totally wasted and Ethan needed consoling cause his Labrador retriever just died or maybe it was his sister (who died, not who I made out with) but Danny obviously didn't understand the power of human grief or else he wouldn't have abandoned Lea after her mom died and everything, and if you thought about it, wasn't he just a little bit of a prick?

–So what do we do now? he asked.

–I don't know. You wanna watch *Austin Powers* or something? I think it's the only tape we have.

–Seen it.

–Well, duh. So have I. The point is, it doesn't get good until you've seen it, like, at least eleven times.

–Eleven, huh?

–Eleven, though ten might do it, but definitely more than nine.

–Are you on something, Alex?

–On something?

–Yeah, like, I don't know, diet pills or something?

–You think I need diet pills?

–No, I think you're talking really fast and don't chicks do that when they're on diet pills?

–I wouldn't know.

–Shit, I'm sorry. I always say the fucking wrong thing.

Oh, here we go, the point where I feel all bad for him. Well, it wasn't going to happen. He was a prick. We'd established that already. But instead of telling him he wasn't getting my pity, I said, No you don't, Danny.

–Yes, I do. Lea broke up with me for just that reason. Why don't girls realize that guys are stupid and what we say doesn't mean shit?

I wanted to say something about how the oppressors frequently hide behind stupidity—didn't he ever listen to George W. Bush?—but instead I said something like, If we did, then time would fold in on itself and the space-time continuum would be, like, totally fucked.

–It's just that, what do you do when you're dating someone who's so fucking . . . so fucking perfect when you're so fucking . . . not. It's like . . . you're just bound to fuck things up, you know?

–It's not like that, Danny, I say, because I know how he feels because that's the way Lea makes everyone feel and it isn't fair. You're just as good as she is . . . better, even,

I say and I mean it, because Danny's great, he's fucking great, and if Lea understood how great he was, half as much as I do, she'd never have been stupid enough to let him go.

–I just love her so much, he said. And then he put his head in his hands and started crying. Oh, God, I was so not equipped to handle that.

All I could say was, I know, I know. I love her, too.

I mean, how couldn't you love her? The truth was, there's been a time when I thought I was, you know, *in love* with her. I'd even told her so the night we graduated from high school, after we made out on a dare, while I was helping her puke up the bottle of Southern Comfort she'd drunk after the ceremony. As I held her long hair back and told her I loved her, like, *really* loved her, she lifted her head up from the bowl and opened her mouth— I thought to say something. But then she dropped it back into the bowl and puked even more. The next morning, she gave no indication that she remembered anything about the night, and I don't think she was faking it.

I got over it as soon as I remembered how much I loved boys, even ones I didn't, like, really love—or even really like, for that matter. But still, when I saw poor Danny crying like that, the look of anguish on his face that he had to let Lea go, my heart broke for him a little. I understood.

But with Dave Gahan going on about grabbing hands grabbing all they can, I wasn't sure what to do with my feelings. So I started making a bed for Danny on the in-flatable mattress with an extra set of sheets. But as soon as I set them down I felt so tired all of a sudden, and when I realized how cool and smooth the clean sheets were I decided I wanted them for myself. Danny could have my bed and if he didn't want it, *tough*. I sat down and curled up under the sheets and found myself face-to-face with the huge purple jeweled crucifix our Argentinean roommate insisted on putting in the common room even though the common room was also *my* room. I tried to look away from it and found I couldn't.

At that moment, I wanted more than anything for us to get away from the room, away from my roommates, away from the drugs. I wanted to go for a walk and show Danny the real New York, my New York, which was soooo far away from Rhode Island and soooo my home now. I wanted to call Lea and make things right between them. I started to think about how to suggest the idea, but my head was too distracted by Danny's hands, which had somehow ended up on my hips, to let my mouth in on the idea. Though part of me knew this was wrong, way wrong, the coke was calling dopamine to the front lines, convincing me that this was also a defining moment in the history of the universe. Have fun, our bodies belong to no one, ride whatever thought comes into your head because it was the right one and so you unbutton his shirt and are amazed to see how much bigger his chest is now than it had been just a few years before. His body is just the way you like it, in fact, a six-pack with a belly gone slightly soft, just slightly. You don't even bother with a condom because you're on the pill and he's a good boy and it's not just his chest that's bigger and you nearly come from the feeling of him alone. You look him in the eye and he looks back and you know he too is amazed at how good this feels and what a perfect fit you are and why did you never realize this before and you want to keep staring into his eyes but then he puts his hands on your hips again and flips you over and though a little something disappears and why don't guys get that? this is just fine too, at least it is until he starts fucking you harder which let's be honest would have also been just fine, except as he's doing it he puts his hand over your mouth and you realize it's not just to keep you quiet now but to keep you quiet forever and you know how wrong this is now but there's no going back and though you nearly came the second you felt him inside you something happened the coke the hand over your mouth and it's become painfully clear that you're not going to come at all tonight even though you love him you love her he loves her she loves him and it doesn't matter that neither love you not really because what you're doing is love and how can love be wrong?

In my fucked-up head, fucking Danny seemed the only way to bring balance to a world where everybody died, where everybody took what they wanted and threw away what they didn't, where all love was unrequited. It was the only way to help him, to understand him, and in so doing help and understand Lea too. It was only afterward that I began to have the nagging suspicion that perhaps Lea wouldn't see my action as quite the pure gesture I'd intended it to be.

The next morning, I pretended to be asleep when Ben came in, shook Danny awake, and said, Dude, let's get out of here before she wakes up, and I might have opened my eyes if Danny had done anything other than grunt, lumber over to the bathroom, piss loudly with the door open, then start packing up his stuff. But I just stayed there, motionless, praying that he'd at least wake me up to say good-bye. But he didn't.

As soon as they shut the door quietly behind them—I'd never seen either of them do anything that quiet—I opened my eyes. All of a sudden my apartment felt so much bigger than it had before, even though I didn't even have a real room, just a couch and a pile of clothes. It's just—they'd taken up so much space. Big boys, football-playing boys, boys I'd known all my life. I noticed my crazy roommate's crazy purple cross was now laying on the floor—it must have fallen while we were . . . And I stared at it for a few seconds before deciding I was not fucking hanging it back up. I realized I had nothing to do but the rest of the coke from the night before and nothing to think about but the fallout from what I'd done.

Like how at this very moment Danny was probably telling Ben what had happened and Ben was making a stupid comment about my ass. *Line.*

And how Lea was probably feeling terrible now that her mom was dead and her boyfriend was gone. *Line.* And how Danny was probably feeling terrible now that his girlfriend was gone and he'd gone and fucked me. *Line.* And how I was feeling terrible now that they both were gone and neither of them was thinking of me, at least not in a good way anyway.

Line, line, line, line, line.

I didn't talk to either one of them—Danny or Lea—until months later when I got a call from Lea asking me to be a bridesmaid. I didn't know what to say. Did she know and had she forgiven me? After her outburst at me today, I knew the answer. She didn't know and Danny was never going to tell her, and so neither was I.

After I tell Shawn all this, I close my eyes and think of nothing but how good it feels that he's here for me, how good it's always been to have him here, and I'm about to propose that heterosexuality does have its advantages when he sighs and tells me that I remind him of Holly Golightly and I open my eyes and see that Audrey Hepburn is on TV and I say I don't look a thing like her and he says, No, you're even more beautiful, and I hug him and then he adds, And sluttier, and I laugh and close my eyes and before I know it, I'm no longer at the Windham or my dorm room or at Holly Golightly's party, I'm laying down on the couch in the basement of the house I grew up in, wrapped up in my mother's chakra-balancing blanket. And instead of Shawn or Danny or Paul Varjak at my side, Jason's there with me, only I don't remember if we ever even did that in real life.

He died almost a decade ago but I miss him still and I wonder if he's looking at me and Danny—I mean, me and Shawn—and if he's mad at me for not dying when he did because really we should have died together. It's what we always talked about doing before he went and did it himself without even having the courtesy to tell me first.

I don't know if he expected me to join him but even after all our talk of how fake the world was and how much we wanted to escape and meet up on the other side where there was no bullshit, I couldn't get up the nerve to do it. Maybe it was because I was afraid that I wouldn't be able to find him on the other side or that time would move differently there and one hundred years would have passed since the day Ben found him in the woods with his mother's pills and a bottle of vodka and some Robitussin. And I never told anybody, not even Shawn, that Jason and I always talked about going out like Romeo and Juliet, at first because I thought Shawn would have been jealous, but later, when I thought about it more, because I know he would have blamed me, even if he didn't want to.

Everyone was so surprised when it happened. Everyone except me because I knew he wanted to do it. But I had to act surprised too, and in a small way I guess I was, because I always thought it was our thing and now I realize it was only ever Jason's thing. And maybe he always knew that. I mean, maybe he didn't and maybe he was waiting for me to join him but I don't think that's true. I think he did it himself to stop me from getting there first.

I wonder what it's like. On good days I think it's like a big wide-open mountainous field, like in *The Sound of Music*, only without the clothes made out of drapes and the Baroness threatening to marry the Captain for his money.

On days like this I think it looks like the mental hospital in the documentary. A place with no windows or light and mean nurses and broken glasses and straitjackets. I try not to think of it like that but sometimes when I'm alone in the dark with someone like Shawn who's passed out now or Danny who passed out after we fucked and then left without saying a word to me, I can't help but think it's like being locked up in a place where nothing works, and no one listens, and no one remembers you're real.

bonus
TRACKS

SHAWN

It's well into morning before I start drifting to sleep, but I can't really call it sleep. The TV's still on and my mind is racing, pulling bits of low-volume lyrics and commercial chatter and the flashes of light on the other side of my eyelids into my mind and whipping them around like a film reel gone madly out of control. It's like my life is flashing before my eyes, only not in the cool walk-into-the-white-light kind of way, more like a music video montage celebrating the anniversary of MTV, complete with the dystopian insanity of *Æon Flux* and all that other weird Liquid Television stuff, all the fights from *The Real World*, and Madonna icily dismissing an attention-starved Courtney Love. My eyelids are fluttering rapidly, filling with tears, blurring my hallucinations, and I am filled with a wave of regret that I never learned to paint or draw or animate, that the things in my mind will be known only to me and lost forever afterward. I have my guitar with me but I don't have the energy to transform these visions into 4/4 time, so as soon as I see them, they are gone.

I cannot sleep, not in this state, and I curse myself for not asking Alex if she'd brought a sleeping pill to help me leave the madness of the world behind, if only for seven or eight undisturbed hours.

I open my eyes to see a lone man onstage, his hair soaked with sweat, his arms rippled with muscles. A mushroom cloud behind him, his hand goes down his pants. My God, I want to fuck this man. No, fuck that, I want to *be* this man. Before him, a crowd full of people, crying the words to the song, thankful that someone understands what it is to Hurt.

The first time you listened to this album was in your room, with the lights off. It was yours and yours alone. You were terrified to listen to it too closely because it was all about the death of God. Only you were too young to understand that didn't mean the devil was talking, not by a long shot. You just figured that if a singer has jet black hair and talks about fucking and animals in the same sentence, then Satan has got to be involved, right?

That's what you thought, because you were young and Catholic and everything was the devil in disguise; your priest said the Golden Girls were the devil's handmaidens, dreamed up by sinful big-city homosexuals, and who wanted to think about grandmothers fornicating anyway? I mean, you couldn't argue with him there; grandmothers fornicating was gross, but the Golden Girls were a trip, man, there was nothing evil about Rue McClanahan outside of her hideous caftans.

Still, you weren't yet ready to hear that God was dead. Not then. Not two days after your best friend offed himself. In a way, you wanted to believe that there was no God to punish Jason. But then, in another way, you also wanted to believe that there was a God because then, at least, Jason would be somewhere, instead of nowhere. Because even if somewhere is burning, at least it's somewhere, and anyway, if God was really the kind of God you wanted him to be and not the one you read about in crusty old Jonathan Edwards's essay, then he'd know that

Jason was a good kid and shouldn't have to suffer for too long.

Still, you didn't listen too close to the lyrics for fear that God would catch you doing it and then you'd be every bit as damned as Jason. Back then, God was a boogeyman; he was hiding under your bed, in your closet, in your mind. He was ready to catch you thinking impure thoughts—especially impure thoughts that culminated in you dreaming about other guys. He was a little like Freddy Krueger that way, and there were nights you didn't go to sleep, for fear that he'd start shredding the sheets with his nine-inch nails the second your dreams got good and dirty.

And you wish you'd spent the evening after Jason's funeral praying for his soul, but instead you prayed for forgiveness for the horrible things you'd said to him before he died, and the worst part about it was, you really just said these prayers so that God would think you were a good guy, which is so fucked up because of course, God could hear you thinking that selfish stuff on top of the good stuff, which made the whole exercise pretty fucking pointless.

So you put the album away.

And only now do you realize how much you miss it. And only now do you really understand it.

They found that same album in Jason's collection after he did it, and the foolish women in your hometown made sure that every record with even the slightest hint of melancholy or rebellion got banned. You wanted to speak up and tell them they were fucking crazy—that the music had nothing to do with it—that kids don't kill themselves because of music, that sometimes music is the only thing that keeps us here. But you were too scared. So you shut yourself in your room and listened to it by yourself until the tape tangled itself up into a spiderweb. You couldn't buy another one because the ladies won and you were only sixteen so you started playing the guitar again. You got good.

Or something like that. Like I said, it's all kinds of fuzzy here with the fly buzzing around my eyelid like that.

I look over at Alex. She looks almost peaceful, or at least she does until a violent twitch overcomes her entire body and she lets out a strangled sound like a scream caught in her throat. Truth be told, she's kind of freaking me out.

I've got to get the fuck away from her.

BEN

–And remember when, I say, remember when we smoked that chronic and were driving the backroads, and the deer, that fucking deer, just jumped right out in front of us, and you stopped, you stopped just in time, but that fucking deer just stared at you, like, like, he knew we were all lit up . . .

–Yeah, Dan says, that was crazy.

–And how bout the time . . .

I launch into another historic tale of the plights of Dan and Ben but my heart's not in it. I can see that everyone has left the bridal suite except the two people it belongs to . . . and yours truly.

But it just doesn't seem right to cap the night off so early; tonight's big event, I'll remind you, had all the ingredients in place to establish itself as *la fiesta del año*—though, as I might as well admit, it's not as if it had a lot of competition to contend with, now that everyone's working and the gang only gets together during holiday breaks and even then, there are family trips, long-standing commitments, there are only so many *días en el año*.

Lea stretches her arms in the air and lets out a yawn—she's too polite, God bless her, to kick me out outright—and Daniel follows suit by standing up, smoothing his hands over his pants, and loosening his tie.

I must, I realize, bring my tale to a close so I skip over a few climactic embellishments that we all know too well and jump right to the punch line:

–So then Lou says, Well if you don't like piss in your mouth . . .

and Danny finishes off the now infamous line,

–Then why are you sucking my cock?

We all chuckle, except perhaps Lea who, as I recall, was friends with the person who did not, as it would come to pass, like piss in her mouth. And I stand, take a little bow, first to bride, then to groom, throw my coat over my shoulder, drain the Bud can in my hand dry, crinkle it in my mighty paw, and take my leave.

ALEX

The first thought I have after waking up is thank the Goddess all the terrible things that just happened in my dream—a scrambled mess of memory and anxiety, people giving me pills and powders, me taking them or not taking them—weren't real. The second thought I have, and it doesn't come too soon after the first, is a desire to go back to sleep anyway because at least there I don't have to do anything.

I roll over, expecting to find Shawn there but he's, like, totally gone. He probably just up and walked home since his mom only lives a few blocks away. I wish he would have told me.

I don't like to be alone.

Except, no, wait, there's his suit right there. What the fuck? He went somewhere without me? Where could he have gone without me? Why wouldn't he have woken me up? How could he do this to me?

Well, there's no way I'm going to be able to fall back asleep now. The pot might have bored the coke into submission long enough for me to doze off, but Bob Marley has clearly skipped town leaving me alone with Robert Downey Jr.

Only Robert's gone too, the best of him, anyway, my little baggies sucked clean of their contents hours ago. He has, however, left a hammer in my head, a fountain in my nostrils, and a general state of unease in my mind about the current state of my reality. I don't want to go back to sleep, not after what I saw under my eyelids that last time

I was stupid enough to try it, but then again staying awake is no more appealing.

Maybe Cort has another painkiller. Except, shit, I'd seen her falling all over some geek we'd gone to high school with and the last thing I wanted to do was walk in on hippie sex. Like, gag me with patchouli.

I'd turn on the TV but I'm scared about what I'll find there and I'd get up to search for Shawn but I'm terrified to leave the room. For a moment, just a moment, I think of Jason. I could do it too, you know, I say softly to him, to anyone. And wouldn't there be something beautiful and tragic and romantic about ending it all here where at least there'd be no mystery about why I did it, no question about exactly whose fault it really was . . .

Except, as selfish as I am, and I think everyone would agree I am a most selfish individual, I won't leave Lea and Dan with that wedding-day memory. I smile when I realize how pathetic it is that the best I can offer this world at this moment is, when you think about it, nothing at all.

And then, and I'm not quite sure why, I walk over to the other side of the room and pick up Shawn's guitar. I only know a few chords—Shawn started teaching me once before getting all huffy and telling me that if I wasn't going to at least hold the guitar right, well, then he wasn't going to waste his time—and so I don't know why I do it but I guess it's because all of a sudden I need to make something, anything, just something better than myself.

The only chords I know are minor ones but it's okay because I've always found them the most beautiful. I start playing my favorite song, you know the one, and humming it softly too and before I know it the tears are streaming down my face and . . .

I don't know, it's probably just the drugs listening or whatever, but I swear I've never heard anything so beautiful in my entire life.

SHAWN

As I open the door and step outside, I don't know where I'm headed exactly, as long as it's out of the room. It's too early to expect anyone would be enjoying the complimentary continental breakfast in the lobby, but I figure I'll head in that direction anyway. Only . . . as soon as I walk out into the hallway, I see a large body lumbering up the steps to the second-floor rooms. I squint to make out who it is.

Shit. Ben. I put my key back in the door, in the hopes that it will seem like I'm just getting to my room, but Ben is too drunk to notice the difference. Hey, Riley. How's it hanging?

–Um . . . *well*? How are you?

–I'm drunk, but not enough. Everybody else pussied out on me, he says. Hey, do you want to get a drink or something?

–Um, isn't it like six in the morning or something?

–Aren't you, like, Irish or something? Come on, my treat.

–I just mean, we're in Galestown. Nothing's open.

–The cash bar in my room is open.

–You have a cash bar? We don't.

–I've got a suite—you know, being best man and everything. And, hey, who's "we"? Ben walks closer to the room and peeks in. Oh, *shit*! You got Alex in there? Lucky dog. Um . . . I mean, well I guess it doesn't matter much because, um, well, you know . . .

–Because Alex and I are such good *friends*?

–Yeah, Ben sighs, relieved, as if the mere mention of my sexual preference might force him to think long and hard about his love of *Monday Night Football*.

I look at him there, shuffling from one foot to the other, and find that I almost feel bad for him.

–Okay, sure, I say. I'd love a drink. Anything to help me sleep.

I walk back to his hotel room which, as I suspected, is littered with crushed beer cans and smells like a pub frequented by donkeys. Still, I'm slightly amazed. When did he find the time to wreak such havoc? I sit down on a five-inch space on the bed that isn't covered by wet towels, boxer shorts, or tube socks. Ben is kneeling in front of the bar for what seems like an eternity—I realize he seems to have forgotten what he was looking for, when he smacks himself in the head and pulls out the green bottle and two shot glasses.

After five minutes and two shots of Jäger each, it becomes clear that Ben and I have nothing to talk about except for the one thing that neither of us has the guts to bring up. Well, make that two things. I decide that him killing me is better than this boredom.

–Listen, I know how fucked up it must have been to have found Jason like that.

Ben's eyes widen, as if he can't believe I brought it up, and he smiles sadly, in acceptance of my olive branch.

–Yeah, he says. That shit doesn't go away, especially with the state I was in.

–Um, that's the thing, Ben. About that.

He waves this away with his hand. Don't bother. I know

it was Jason who drugged me. I just don't know why he hated me so much.

Huh? Jason? What is he talking about?

–I mean, *everybody* made fun of his stupid ears. . . .

–Wait, wait, I say. Shit, Ben. That wasn't Jason who did that.

–You don't need to cover for him, dude. What's past is past.

–No, I mean it. It really wasn't Jason. . . . It was . . . it was me.

I shrug my head into my shoulders, bracing myself for the blow I'm a hundred percent sure is coming. But when a few seconds pass with no punches thrown I open my eyes and Ben finally breaks the silence.

–That's okay.

–It's okay? No, it's not. It's not okay at all. It was totally fucked up.

–You're right, it was but, well, I kind of deserved it.

–You didn't deserve it.

–I know. I said I *kind of* deserved it.

–Okay, you *kind of* deserved it. But you didn't deserve what happened after.

–Yeah, maybe. But none of us deserve anything that happens. I didn't deserve to find a dead guy, you didn't deserve getting your ass kicked by those dudes back in the woods. Life isn't about getting what you deserve. It's about how you deal with it.

–I guess, I say.

And then I laugh.

–Actually, Ben, I did deserve getting my ass kicked by those dudes.

–Why?

–I, kind of, you know, pissed in their Gatorade.

Ben laughs, Fuck, man. What's up with you and Gatorade?

–You'd be amazed at what secrets Gatorade can conceal.

–Apparently. He pours another shot for us both. Anyway, I should be honest. Other than, you know, the Jason thing, that day was pretty fucking awesome. . . . I mean, I don't mean to . . . you know . . . be disrespectful, though. I know he was your friend and everything. And, shit, man, I mean . . . there was a time . . . you know . . . he was, sort of, my friend too. I'm just . . . I'm sooo sorry about what happened.

–I know, I know. I am too.

We just sat there, and I felt that everything was a little bit better. Not great, you know, but better. And then I say, I wish I could have told Jason I was sorry.

–What do you mean? You guys were boys. What did you do to him?

–Let's just say the last things I said to Jason were not good things. I mean, I know that I shouldn't blame myself for what happened and I don't anymore, not really, but . . . you know.

I go on, not exactly knowing where all this is headed. I've never talked about this before with anyone.

I was just so pissed about him and Alex. It used to be

the three of us and then it wasn't. And that does something to you, you know. It's one thing to be against the world when you have two people to help support your opposition. It's another thing altogether when you have to do it on your own.

I mean, it's not impossible to do things on your own, but it is, like, a journey or something. Like, remember that movie *Labyrinth*? The one with Jennifer Connelly and all those creepy Muppets? And David Bowie plays the evil Goblin King named Jareth but because he's also David Bowie he's not really content with ordering creepy Muppets around. He, you know, sees that Connelly's a piece of ass, even if she's not legal yet. Anyway, the way the labyrinth works is that nothing's as it seems and every time you open a door, you're falling down some dusty pit and sometimes it ends up being the place you're supposed to be, but most of the time it's really lonely and cold and dirty and hopeless.

That's about how I was feeling when Jason called me up this one time to see if I wanted to hang out, just the two of us, no Alex, like it used to be. I would have been, like, whatever, except, like I said, I was at the bottom of the dusty pit and when you're there, any friend is welcome, even if it's a hairy monster, a goblin king, or a dude who dissed you for a chick.

I told Jay I'd go to his house, but he wanted to come to mine. My mom's always hanging around, you know, but your mom is, like, never home.

So I said, sure, whatever, and then did my best to clean

up the place which was tough when you've got as many fucking cats running around as Bowie had Muppets.

Only the thing is, he never came. When he called me later that night, he explained it was cause Alex came over, and get this, they had sex, like, real live sex, and I understood, didn't I, man? But I didn't understand. Not at all. I just started yelling, You're such a selfish prick. You ruined everything. We'd have both been better off without you, I said, which is kind of what I thought, but it wasn't everything I thought, because part of me was thinking that Jason and I would have been better off if Alex had never come along, but I couldn't say this to Jason because he wouldn't know what I meant and then he said,

–You know what, Shawn? You're absolutely right.

And then he hung up.

And then . . .

–Dude, Ben interrupts me. Stop.

–What?

–Stop. *Stop*. You gotta stop thinking of the story like that.

–Thinking of the story like what?

–Like that's where it just starts and stops, with you yelling at Jason and him killing himself. That's not how it happened. That's not how anything happens.

–But . . .

–No buts, man. No buts. It's the truth. Take it from me. I know these things. He takes a swig straight from the bottle and hands it to me. I'm the Best Man.

I laugh, accept the bottle, then take my own swig.

–I never thought I'd be saying this, but I think you're right, Ben.

–You bet I'm right, Ben says. While we're at it, do you want to know the real reason I didn't help you when you were getting your ass kicked? And believe me, you do, because it's fucking hysterical.

And you know what? He was right. It fucking was.

CORT

We've been driving for nearly five minutes and still Jared hasn't turned on the radio and he doesn't even seem to notice it's not on and who drives without the radio on, and what was I thinking sleeping with such a person when we're so obviously completely and utterly incompatible? My head is pounding and the thought of facing such a sunny day with such a dull brain is almost too much to deal with but at least with some music on I could think straight and so I reach down and turn it on.

Breathe. Breathe in the air.

Good idea. I roll down my window and remember that when I was younger I used to flip the dials on my car radio and let whichever song turned up decide my future.

–Oh, you can change that, he says.

–It's Pink Floyd. Why would I change it?

–Oh, I don't know. I just meant you can put on whatever you like.

He looks over at me and smiles and I do my best to smile back, though I know there is no future for us. It's nice of him, after all, to give me a ride, seeing as Uncle John never showed up when he said he would.

–So where exactly is it that I'm taking you? Where's home again?

I like to be there when I can.

I turn my face away so he can't see that my eyes are welling up.

–I don't know, Jared, I say and switch the station. Keep driving.

Acknowledgments

Markus, I thank you, like, fifty times a day, so one more time won't hurt. May we disprove this book's title while still loving the song. Matt and Marissa, without you this book would not exist. Thanks for reminding me to write about music.

Jenn, Tricia, Dre, thanks for your enthusiastic early reads and for your friendship throughout the years. Vanessa, thanks for being a valedictorian cool enough to quote Ghostface Killah and for the reassuring read. Dad, thanks for everything—and sorry that my characters have such filthy mouths and dirty minds. Matt, you remind me of the babe.

Jud Laghi, thanks for your general awesomeness and for making me feel like the coolest writer in the world, and thanks to Susanna Einstein, Larry Kirshbaum, and Jenny Arch for all their support. I am proud to be an LJK client.

Carrie Thornton, thanks for turning a bunch of voices into a song, coming up with a killer name for that song, and selling the hell out of it. Brett Valley, thanks for your support and belief in this book and for shepherding it through to the end. Maria Elias and Greg Kulick thanks for the bad-ass design. Thanks to the production editor, Rachelle Mandik, for all her hard work; thanks to Melanie DeNardo for her energy and impressive organizational skills, and to Jay Sones for his ideas and support from beginning to end. Thanks also to Anjali, Ben, Amber, Anna, and Liz for liking the book and for offering valuable feedback in the early stages.

Thanks to all my friends in Syracuse, New York, and Cranston, especially Jules, Shannon, Jess, Bri, Beth, Greg, Vanna, Randy, Hannah, Courtney, Mat, Brian, Julien, Liz, Claudia, Ali, Lara, John, and Mark.

Thanks to all the teachers in my life, especially Bill Glavin, Melissa Chessher, David Miller, John Souza, Marsha Oaken, Lynn Davis, Jane Antos, June McKeon, Bonnie Sorgle, Lorraine Minto, Paula Akers, Monique Jacob, and so many good friends at Central Falls.

Thanks to Roger Scholl, Hollis Heimbouch, Barbara Verrocchi, Kristin Leigh, and Ian Donnis, for being such supportive, inspiring employers. Thanks to my friends in publishing, especially at Doubleday Broadway and Collins, for their support and advice.

Thanks to my family—the O'Connors, Rainones, Pontarellis, DiPietros, and beyond—the Floating Keg, the Distro, the Belligerents, the members of Box Set, my fellow UCB classmates and Student Voice alums, and to Mikyum Kim, Deborah Grody, Rebecca Tuffey, Judy Gee, Mary Chan, Stuart Yeh and Mike Zazzalli, Don and Jennifer Hanson, and Marina Marino, for their guidance, help, and wisdom.

Thanks to all the musicians for inspiring me and giving me something to write about. And thanks to Cranston, Rhode Island, because unlike one of my characters, I believe Ghostface had it right when he said "I remember them good ol' days because, see, that's the child I was what made me the man I am today."

about the AUTHOR

Sarah Rainone is an editor and writer living in Brooklyn, New York. She grew up in Cranston, Rhode Island, and went to Syracuse University.